THE CAPTIVES

THE
CAPTIVES

A NOVEL

DEBRA JO
IMMERGUT

ecco

An Imprint of HarperCollinsPublishers

HarperCollins books may be purchased for educational, business, or sales promotional use. For information, please e-mail the Special Markets Department at SPsales@harpercollins.com.

FIRST EDITION

Designed by Renata De Oliveira

Library of Congress Cataloging-in-Publication Data

Names: Immergut, Debra Jo, author.
Title: The captives : a novel / Debra Jo Immergut.
Description: First edition. | New York : Ecco, [2018]
Identifiers: LCCN 2017042689 (print) | LCCN 2017056643 (ebook) | ISBN 9780062747563 (ebook) | ISBN 9780062747549 (hardcover)
Subjects: LCSH: Prison psychologists—Fiction. | Family secrets—Fiction. | Psychological fiction. | Suspense fiction. gsafd | BISAC: FICTION / Literary. | FICTION / Psychological. | GSAFD: Mystery fiction.
Classification: LCC PS3559.M5 (ebook) | LCC PS3559.M5 C37 2018 (print) | DDC 813/.54—dc23
LC record available at https://lccn.loc.gov/2017042689

18 19 20 21 22 LSC 10 9 8 7 6 5 4 3 2 1

all this time,
for John

THE CAPTIVES

CHANCE

1

REFRAIN FROM TAKING ON A PROFESSIONAL ROLE WHEN OBJECTIVITY COULD BE IMPAIRED

(American Psychological Association Ethical Principles and Codes of Conduct, Standard 3.06)

What happened to me is universal. And I can prove it.

Think back on the people you knew in high school. Now zero in on that one person, the one who starred in your daydreams. The one who, when you glimpsed him or her down the corridor, set off that pre–Homo sapiens sensation, that brainstem jolt of pure adrenaline. The crush, in other words.

See that person walk toward you now. Approaching along the noisy crowded hallway, toward you, toward you, and by you. The hair, the stride, the smile.

Your pulse has just heightened a bit. Right?

That shows you the power. You're picturing a kid, this is years later and you're picturing some gawky school-bound kid, and yet the image of this kid in your mind's eye can still vibrate your cerebral cortex, disturb your breathing pattern.

So you see. There's something involuntary at work in these situations.

NOW IMAGINE THIS: YOU'RE A THIRTY-TWO-YEAR-OLD MAN, AND you're a psychologist. You're sitting in your basement office in the counseling center of a New York State correctional institution. A women's prison. And you've come late to work on a Monday morning and haven't had time to review your case files or even glance at your schedule. In walks the first inmate of the day, dressed in a state-issued yellow uniform.

And it's that person.

Looking shockingly unchanged from the kid approaching down the hallway lined with slamming locker doors. The hair, the stride.

Would that not throw you for a bit of a loop?

Be honest. There's no telling what you would do.

I RECOGNIZED HER INSTANTLY. WHO WOULDN'T? SHE'S NOT THE KIND you forget all that easily. At least, not the kind I forget. Especially not the face. I might compare it to the variety of flowers my mother used to tend in beds alongside our house, pretty in an unsurprising, backyard-grown way, but giving glimpses of inner complexities, if you looked carefully enough. This face had lingered around the fringes of my memory for almost fifteen years. Every so often something—a tune of the correct vintage, the sight of a female runner with long reddish hair—would summon her to the forefront. If I were the kind of guy who attended reunions—I'm not—I would have sprung for a ticket and pinned on a name tag just to get news of her, to see if she turned up. To see what had become of her.

Now I saw. She sat in the aqua vinyl chair across from me with NYS DOCS stamped in blurry black ink across her heart.

She didn't remember me. This was clear. I couldn't see a flicker or a flare of recall.

So I didn't address it. What could I say? Crow out her name, how the hell are you, what brings you here? No. While trying to process this situation—her? here?—I propelled myself to the file cabinet in the corner, where I kept the makings for tea: a small red hotpot, boxes of oolong and Earl Grey, cardboard cups, plastic spoons. My brief tea ritual injected a mild coziness that put my clients slightly more at ease, and so I performed it at almost every session. As I shakily prepared two cups, I spewed out my usual opener, which is welcome, thanks for coming, let's establish some ground rules, what you reveal here doesn't leave this room. A speech that, after six months on the job, I could reel off without thinking. I offered her a steam-crowned drink, and she accepted, with a smile that stabbed me a bit. I returned to my seat, let my hands steady around the warm cup. A note clipped to her file folder stated that she'd just been released from segregation. So I asked her about this. But I didn't hear her answer. I couldn't help but sink back into that memory. A memory that had looped through my mind countless times over the years, like one of those sticky school-era radio hooks. Thinking about it with her sitting there in the flesh made me want to squirm, though I managed to uphold my professional demeanor and not squirm.

I remembered her naked back, a sweep of whiteness like a flag, and then the flash of a breast as she twisted to grab a towel from the bench. Her hair—that red with brown undertones—swished down over this breast and matched the nipple perfectly. Jason DeMarea and Anthony Li were snickering. But I was silent, clinging to the wall outside the girl's locker room, my fingertips aching against the concrete windowsill, toes of my sneakers jammed hard against the brick. This had been my idea. I'd seen the windows cracked open to catch the breezes blowing on this sunny, only slightly chilly November day, and I had seen this member of the girls' freshman track team heading in all alone after her race. I'd been covering the meet for the Lincoln Clarion. My beat was JV girls' sports, and Anthony was the JV girls' sports photographer, which gives you an idea of our status on the Clarion staff and at Lincoln High in general. Jason DeMarea just tagged along for lack of anything better to do on a Tuesday after school. They snickered and elbowed each other and after she had finished dressing (baby blue cords, shirt emblazoned with sparkly flowers), they dropped off the ledge. But I continued to cling there, watching. She sat on the bench, tying up the laces of her ankle boots. Then she grabbed her bundled track uniform and wiped at her eyes with it. I could only see a small slice of her face and one dainty ear—the ear with the intriguing double piercing, with the silver wire hoop, and, just above, the minuscule silver Pegasus that I'd secretly studied sitting behind her in trig class, wondering if it were a signifier for horse love, or drugginess, or for some other shading of hers that I would never decode. With her wadded uniform, she wiped her eyes and really looked extremely teary, she did. Her eyelids were all puffy. And then she turned her gaze up, up to her open locker. She tossed her track clothes in and reached toward the open door. Some kind of sticker was plastered there. I couldn't read it from my perch. With a certain forcefulness, she yanked that thing, tore it right down. Then she slammed the locker shut and flung her hand out to toss the crumpled decal away. But it stuck to her palm. She stared at this obstinate clump of paper for an instant and she began to really cry now. Then she reopened her locker and carefully set the balled-up thing on the floor inside. She closed the door, held her hands to her eyes. After a while, she walked out of the room, and disappeared from my view.

I HAD OPENED HER FILE FOLDER. MY EYES SKATED OVER THE WORDS without seeing them. I asked a bit about her recent stint in segregation, launched into the usual personality diagnostics. I spooled out a few sequences by rote, she responded, and I began to regain my focus then. I listened and I didn't say anything about

Lincoln High or her naked breast or the yanked decal or the fact that I was that guy from the last row of her trigonometry class. I didn't say that I'd been in the stands every race she ran, that one season she ran track, and that I knew she'd won only once, that very day, that sunny November day. I didn't say that I knew her father had been a one-term congressman, and I didn't say that I'd adored her from afar through every long and confounding day of my high school career. She clearly did not remember me. Did this bother me? In a very slight, subsumed way, maybe. Not with any conscious awareness. In any case, I didn't speak up.

We finished the diagnostic segment, and then she told me she had trouble sleeping. The noise, the shouting on her unit at night. She folded and unfolded her hands in her lap and asked hesitantly if there might be some pill that could help her. "I just need to fade out for a few hours," she said.

I couldn't help noticing that the tomato-colored polish on her nails was chipped. If there was one thing all my clients had, it was impeccable and usually jaw-droppingly intricate manicures— rainbows and coconut palms and boyfriends' names, glittered stripes and stars and hearts. Those women didn't pick at or chew their nails. They flashed them. But her nails were short. Ravaged.

I found myself scrawling on a blue slip, recommending Zoloft. Rising from my chair, I walked around the desk and held it out to her. She stood, a head shorter than me. Her downcast eyes, her long lashes. A scatter of faint freckles. I dragged my gaze away, pulled my shoulders back, summoning every inch of my height. "Just show this to Dr. Polkinghorne's aide two doors down."

She read it and thanked me softly. We both stood there for a minute. I debated about whether to say what I knew I should say. "Um, you know what?" I started. Then I said something else instead. "I'd like to add you to my list of standing appointments. I think we can pursue some solutions for you."

She bent her lips into this tiny, melancholy smile. "Wonderful," she said, then turned to leave. Her ponytail swayed gently to and fro as she walked away and out the door.

Letting her leave then, without revealing what I knew, was an ethical violation, the first in a string of them that I've committed since that moment. The American Psychological Association guidelines on preexisting relationships are very clear. They should be acknowledged, and if such a relationship might in any way impair objectivity, therapy must not go forward. It's all pretty straightforward in the guidelines.

That must have been when I stopped following guidelines. Up to that point, I was more or less your average, law-abiding, guideline-following man.

She changed all that, though she didn't mean to at all, this person in the state-issued yellows, with the backyard-flower face. She who I remembered so clearly as a girl. She who you wouldn't forget.

I can't refer to her here by name. Let's call her M, and move on.

2

MAY 1999

Miranda Greene was born in Pittsburgh, PA. She was born in Pittsburgh, PA, she lived out the larger portion of her childhood in the suburbs of Washington, D.C., and in May of her thirty-second year, 1999, one of the loveliest Mays in memory on the Eastern Seaboard, she was making plans to die in New York. In Milford Basin, New York. More specifically, in the women's correctional facility that occupied 154 shaven acres in the maple-and-scrub woods outside the town of Milford Basin.

A Rockefeller or a Roosevelt or someone rich had owned a spread in Milford Basin during the 1920s, real estate agents told prospective buyers. Unfortunately—for real estate reasons—this rich person had a zeal for the reform of wayward girls. What had been a hunting lodge was turned into a reformatory, and now, seventy or so years down the line, it had become a full-blown state prison, minimum to medium security. Women weren't regarded as wayward anymore. They were perpetrators, criminals, and in need of fourteen-foot heavy-gauge perimeter mesh, festoons of razor ribbon, and armed guards.

The prison was up and over the crest of two hills from the semiquaint downtown center of Milford Basin. Up and over those two hills was a sprawling fenced complex, and inside this complex was Miranda, formulating her plans. The method would be an overdose of pills. Pills were abundant in the system; more than half the ladies of Milford Basin were being state medicated: Xanax, Lithium, Librium, and Prozac were dosed out daily by the medical staff. Certain shadowy characters offered them for sale, too—of course, the pharmaceuticals could be purchased, so many substances could be. But often, it was easier to get a prescription from the Counseling Center, a diagnosis of depression or violent associability or even mere social anxiety. Meds were dispensed liberally, since meds worked well, all around.

Miranda wished to die because, having been incarcerated for nearly twenty-two months, she saw no point in hanging around for the remaining portion of her sentence. The sentence stretched for such an obscene number of years that she shied away from thinking about its precise length in numerical terms, preferring to think of the time as a road vanishing into a fog. She had no chance of parole, and if she were ever free again, she would be much, much older than she was now. Somehow, the promise of a taste of liberty in time to enjoy the infirmities of advanced age did not seem reason enough to cling to her mortal coil. She wanted to shrug it.

This is why Miranda visited the Counseling Center. She did not like the idea of going to a shrink. Her mother had booked her an appointment once, during that turbulent stretch of her teenhood after Amy died. She'd refused to get in the car. Simply put, she had never been the introspective type. She took after her father that way. But at Milford Basin, where empty time was dished up in yawning craterfuls, she could hardly avoid contemplating her lot in life. What else was there to do? And two weeks in the Segregated Housing Unit had crystallized her thinking.

The more deeply she searched within herself, the more certain she became. She would not wait for fate to make its move—hadn't fate already had its way with her, slapped her down hard? No, now she would take her destiny into her own small, insignificant, incarcerated hands.

ON A MONDAY MORNING AT 9:30 A.M., MIRANDA STROLLED THE ASphalt walkway connecting Building 2A&B to the long low admin building, home to visits and counseling. She passed an old lady named Onida, who was working out her frustrations in the garden plot she'd been granted by administration. Onida was not allowed garden tools—sharp-edged metal implements were not smiled upon—so she clawed at the wormy spring dirt with her hands and a spade fashioned out of a square of cardboard, humming to herself. Flats of petunias donated by the local ladies' garden club rested nearby. She looked up as Miranda passed. "God is good, he sure is," she said.

"You think?" replied Miranda. She walked on. She heard Onida muttering behind her. The sky above stretched painfully blue. The smell of shorn grass, the meek breeze warming her skin. She still couldn't get used to the idea. Walking outside, with only the dome of the universe above her. No heavy cement, no locked-down souls. She had been out of segregation just three days. Two weeks in the SHU—the shoe, the ladies called it—had flattened out her perceptions somehow, as if she'd been pressed and dried, an exotic cutting. Could she be soaked and reconstituted? "Doubtful," she whispered to herself.

DID SHE KNOW HIM FROM SOMEWHERE? AT FIRST GLANCE, HE SEEMED to shimmer with a faint familiarity, the face—perhaps she had seen it before, or maybe he just looked like someone she'd known. Gray-blue eyes, hair thick, blond, in slight disarray. Beneath pale stubble, his jaw was strong. Not a bad-looking man, in a subdued way. You had to look twice to see it. Frank Lundquist, she thought to herself, to test his name in her mind.

He was the first man out of CO uniform she'd talked to in almost a year, not counting family members and legal counsel. That could account for the strangeness.

"Welcome," he said, shifting papers on his desk with a distracted air. "Thanks for coming to see me today." He spoke with a halting, deep voice. He rose abruptly and he was quite tall, she realized. A little electric kettle murmured atop a file cabinet in the corner, misting. His back to her, he fiddled with cups for a longish moment, reciting something about ground rules. "What you say here won't leave this room." The tea was lovely, though. Worth the trip alone, perhaps. He sat and found a folder, stared down at it. Miranda let the tea vapors warm her nose and studied the forelock of hair that slipped over his brow, smooth as a bird's wing. She tried to figure out how she would broach the subject of medication.

At last he looked up from his file folder and spoke. "Says here you've just been released from segregation. Can you tell me what happened to put you there?"

Surprised. "That's not in your file?"

"I'd like to hear your side of things." He leaned back in his chair. His eyes kept darting back and forth, to her face, then away, to her face, then away.

That could get on my nerves, she thought.

"My side of things." She let slip the barest smile. "I didn't know I still had a side of things."

He nodded. "I hear you." Rubbed his jaw. A sandpapery noise. "Take a moment. Take your time."

SHE WAS WATCHING FRAYED WISPS OF WHITE, THE SUGGESTION OF clouds, trailing past a thin slice of window eight feet over her head. She lay there in a corner of her cell in the shoe, trying to see out a window designed to reveal nothing. And slowly, as she watched the wisps, she grew aware of a rhythmic rumbling. A low repeated note that reminded her, in some primal part of her being, of early childhood. She couldn't imagine what it might be.

She moved up toward the door and peeked out its little porthole, a piece of reinforced glass about the size of a kitchen sponge. All she could see was the cell door across the hall: beyond it was Patti, who'd murdered a surgeon in a dispute involving Blue Cross/Blue Shield payments.

She pressed her ear to the little metal flap that popped open three times daily, when meals were delivered. Through the thin steel, the rumbling continued.

She lowered herself to the floor, slicked with lumpy gray paint and eternally chilly, and pressed her mouth to the inch-high gap beneath the door. "Patti."

No answer. She tried again. Then, suddenly, she pegged the rumbling sound. Patti was snoring, deep and snuffly. She snored just like Miranda's dad had, nights when she'd woken from dreams as a little girl. Patti was asleep. Patrizia Melvoin, transgender HIV-positive swindler from Morrisania, the Bronx, snored in precisely the same key and rhythm as Edward Greene, onetime congressman from Pennsylvania's Twenty-Eighth District.

Miranda sat back on the floor and giggled. She giggled and the noise of her giggle was alien to her ears and snapped her back into silence. The snoring pressed on.

It was her final day in the lock, and it had stretched for eons already. She squinted up at the patch of sky. It was certainly after noon.

Usually the COs released prisoners from the shoe in the morning. Why the delay? She thought about her photos, her clothes, her Cup-a-Soup waiting for her in a locked storage bin back on the unit. She unbelted her flannel wrap, which was dull yellow and reminded her of the bathrobes she and Amy used to get at Christmastime from Grandma Rosalie—always to their great dismay. They would have much rather received those dolls whose hair and makeup you could style, or drum majorette batons, or pet rabbits. The wrap had been issued to her when they took her standard yellows away as she'd been admitted into the lock. She shrugged it off and slipped off her state-mandated briefs. In the shoe, you weren't allowed your own clothes, so it was NYS DOCS even across your ass.

She contemplated the steel toilet, lidless, seatless, a gawping frozen gullet. She sat. And began to bounce up and down. Fast.

Fourteen days ago, Miranda couldn't do this. When Patti had told her about this peculiar pastime, she'd said, "I'll never be that starved for entertainment."

Patti had chuckled. "No cable TV in here. No Reader's Digest to read."

But the first few days had been okay—she'd suitcased four sleeping pills that Lu had pressed on her when it was clear that Miranda was doomed to the shoe, tucking two tiny pills in each nostril—she'd been sure her mouth breathing would give her away, but it didn't. The pills kept her nicely conked. But they ran out and she was left staring at the patch of sky and wisps of Lewis Patterson began to drift across it, and Duncan, and worse, and soon she was in an agony of replays and desperate for anything to occupy her mind, to fill it and extinguish all thought.

And so she perched on the toilet and she bobbed. She bounced. Skeptically, at first. She even laughed. How ridiculous. She laughed, but she continued, as if riding English saddle, as she did at Camp Piney Top in the Allegheny front range, age nine. And then she heard a reverberating gulp, and sure enough, her bouncing had created a plunger effect, and the water had suctioned back down into the pipes, leaving them clear. She knelt beside the toilet, squeezed shut her eyes, plugged tight her nose, and lowered her head into the bowl.

She heard voices.

DARK CUSTOM SUITS, BRIGHT ITALIAN TIES SPUN WITH THICK SILK and tied in swollen knots. Plus matching pocket squares. One day peacock blue, the next day deep crimson with gold fleur-de-lis. Miranda sometimes wondered if that's why she'd ended up with the mind-fogging sentence. Her lawyer exuded money. The members of the jury—the line cook at a pizza parlor, the snowplow driver—imagined they were shooting down a princess perched on a lofty mountain of cash. They didn't know that the inherited capital talked up in the newspapers, the Greenes of Pittsburgh fortune built upon decades of drop-leaf dining tables and convertible settees and barrel-back patio chairs, had long since been depleted, the bulk of it bled out in advertising fees incurred during her father's final, losing campaign. Alan Bloomfield, connoisseur of exciting Italian ties and pocket squares, was an old family friend, a frat brother of her dad's, and in love with her mother, and providing his service at a steep discount.

Bethanne Bloomfield, Alan's daughter, had been the same age as Miranda's sister, Amy. They'd been best friends for a time; they'd go to Twin Oaks Mall, the movies, they'd lock themselves away in Amy's room. A pair of fourteen-year-old adventuresses. Miranda remembered standing at the door to the room once, the teens primping for a junior-high dance. Blow-dryers, curling irons—the place sounded and smelled like a small factory. The adults weren't around. The primpers decided to raid Barbara Greene's vanity table, with its chunky flasks of perfume. They lingered over the dark interesting names, Opium and Skin Musk. Then Bethanne opened Edward Greene's dresser and discovered a box of Trojans in the bottom drawer. She shrieked. "They use rubbers?"

Amy snatched the box. She studied it, then said with a frown, "I think my mom has an IUD." Bethanne grabbed the package back from her, took out one of the little envelopes, and pocketed it. Then Amy took one, too, before shoving the box back into its hiding place.

Miranda didn't know what an IUD was, and when she asked Amy about it later, she wouldn't tell.

Miranda could pass hours like this, chasing down moments from her earliest years, scenes from a safe sliver of the distant past. But somehow the memories would meander to dangerous places. Bethanne was a lawyer herself now, and married to a lawyer, and they were leasing in a townhouse complex in Bethesda. From Bethanne, her mind would skip back to Alan Bloomfield, sitting stiffly to her left, gently thumping his pencil on his legal pad, watching their case fall apart.

From there, again, though she tried to stop it, to the woman on the stand, her commanding yet tremulous voice, her mounded body, a dignitary of nerves and grief. "My brother was a lifelong bachelor. An army clerk in Saigon. Captain in the volunteer hook and ladder. My brother was a fine man." The woman would explode into tears. The woman would never look Miranda's way.

THE STATE KNEW HER AS 0068-N-97, BECAUSE SHE WAS THE SIXTY-eighth prisoner admitted to NYS DOCS Facility N, a.k.a. Milford Basin Correctional Facility, that year. She lived in C Unit 109 in cell number 34, the last cell on the south side of East.

There, CO Beryl Carmona was her Old Testament God, stern but often loving, all-powerful and terrifyingly unpredictable. Lu had sidled up to Miranda her very first day on the unit, eased an arm around her shoulder, and murmured to her about the lead guard. "Carmona is a very smart kind of stupid," warned Lu. "Watch her."

Ludmilla Chermayev, late of Moscow and Sheepshead Bay, was right about this, as she would be about almost everything at Milford Basin, Miranda found. In her first month on the unit, Carmona had ticketed Miranda twelve times.

Barb Greene couldn't fathom how her daughter had accumulated enough discipline violations to be one ticket away from being tossed into the shoe. "In school, all I heard was how well behaved you were. Best comportment in your fourth-grade class," she'd sniffled, hunched in the din of the visiting room, shredding a paper napkin. Miranda's mother had struggled not to weep that time, but once again she did. Copious tissues, dislodged contact lenses. "Can't you just follow the rules, sweetheart?" Barb had pleaded. "Can't you just try?"

But Miranda did follow the rules, she did try. Stay sane and stay out of trouble's way, just minding her own business and doing the time: this was the pact she'd made her very first week. She'd even written this vow in April Nicholson's paperback copy of the abridged Bible, as April, who commanded the cell across from Miranda's in reception, had insisted. "You're just like me," she'd said, that first awful night, a deadly solemn expression on her round face, the polished-bronze cheeks and lovely dark eyes and red-plum mouth that provided a bit of comfort, of beauty, across the dim corridor. "I am not street and I have never been and I never will be street," April had said, in that voice Miranda grew to rely upon, low tones swirled with vague southern softnesses. "You just do the same as me, and you won't have a problem here."

And Miranda was not the problem. The problem was Beryl Carmona. That very first night she'd moved out of reception, dragging her prison-issue garb in a black plastic bag, April following with her books and stationery, Carmona had been waiting for her in 109C. "You're looking at the head CO on this unit," she said, pointing to her badge. Curly brown hair framed a long jaw, and when she walked, her handcuffs and flashlight flopped around her wide hips, the front pockets of her khakis popped open like little ears. She glanced at the pile in April's arms, then turned to Miranda with a grin. "You read? I do, too. That's great. We can have discussions. But don't let me see you wearing those foot thongs." She gestured at Miranda's blue rubber flip-flops.

"They were issued by the storemaster."

"They're for the shower. I don't like to look at toes."

Several women were standing around, watching with good-natured curiosity. All of them were wearing flip-flops on their feet. The unit was hot and airless, after all.

Carmona followed her gaze, then heaved an exaggerated sigh. "Please don't look on these ladies as inspiration. They're sorry, without a doubt, but born sorry. You, I'm holding to a higher standard." Winked and hoisted her giant knot of keys. "I just like the idea of you. I do. Now let me show you to your room."

Carmona often called her Missy May. Other COs called her Miss Lady. The ladies usually called her Miss Prell or Lady Prell. "She has got Prell hair," observed Chica in the unit kitchen one day during Miranda's first week, looking up from the beans she was stirring and waving her wooden spoon in the direction of Miranda's thick, glossy, russet hair. It had grown long, past her shoulder blades at that point. "Like my brother," said Chica. "Shiny Prell hair. He shampoos twice a day. Always Prell. Always."

"She Prells her hair, you can tell," added another.

The ladies talked about each other in front of one another like that. Miranda knew her input wasn't required or desired. She'd just shooed a fly from her grape-jelly sandwich and continued to read about Tess of the D'Urbervilles. She hadn't minded being dubbed Lady Prell, not at all. She'd always been, admittedly, just a touch vain about her hair and was kind of glad it still shone. She hadn't conditioned it in weeks. Those instructions—apply generously, comb through, wait five minutes, rinse—don't really float in a prison hygiene room.

Chica was the lady with the bath mat, in fact, the thing resulted in the thirteenth ticket, the one that landed Miranda in the lock. Powder pink, and shaggy, and just a bit dirtied up around the edges. Miranda had coveted this bath mat from the moment she first saw it, because it evoked for her the Hotel Flora in Rome. Age twelve, with her father speaking at some conference. All expenses paid. Dad, Mom, Amy, and Miranda, put up for free in a hotel with floors of dark green marble, and white molded babies winging across the ceiling. Every evening a maid came in and turned back the beds and laid a thick pink towel on the cool floor by her nightstand. "For your feet," said her mother. "So the last thing at night and the first thing in the morning is gentleness on your soles." When Miranda saw that bath mat, she knew that if she could just feel gentleness on her soles, she might have a chance of retaining her sanity at least partway.

She broached the subject at lunch one day. As usual, the Dominicanas were gathered around the microwave, with the woman they all called Mami, a withered lady who'd run a safe house in Inwood, serving up a meal of canned tomatoes and instant rice. Most of the unit's Latinas did not eat in the Zoo, except for a few of the Marcy crew. Miranda was more or less welcome in the kitchen circle; she was grateful for that, the food was decent, and she only wished she'd studied Spanish rather than French and German in high school, so she could follow all the conversation.

Anyway, on this day she'd gathered that Chica's appeal had gone through, and she was to be out in a week's time. Before Miranda knew it, she'd piped up. "Could I have that bath mat, Chica?" The ladies tittered.

"Lady Prell wants your mat, Chica," one of them said.

Chica smiled at her, a very kind, gap-punctured grin. "Come by my room on my day. I think yes."

The ladies and even the COs called the cells "rooms," as if they were all in the Hotel Flora.

On Chica's day of release a particular tension permeated the place, because during the night a woman in D unit had been found convulsing from a fermentation of torn toast, sugar cubes, the skins of Red Delicious apples, and a splash of peach-scented body spray. Everyone had been locked in and subjected to cell searches all morning. Four ladies had been found with the hooch and sent to segregation. A bruised anger pulsated along the corridors into the afternoon, when Miranda walked to the far end of the block, to find Chica packing up her things. Across the hallway, a woman called Dorcas, lanky and powerful with a face as hard and burnished as a chestnut, provided commentary: "Judge turned down my appeal. Give Chica a go. But COs wouldn't have shit to do if Dorcas got a go."

"Yeah, yeah, Dorcas," came a voice from behind her. Her sidekick, a doughy girl named Cassie, was lolling on Dorcas's bed, doodling on her pasty foot with a ballpoint pen. "Only reason you're here is to give COs shit to do."

"Chica," said Miranda. "Remember what we talked about the other day?"

"Look at that girl's arms. She has got the skinniest arms," said Dorcas, regarding her distastefully.

"She thinks she's something," said Cassie.

Chica picked up the bath mat, almost sadly. "I even washed it for you, lady. My sister gave this to me. A nice thing to have." She stroked the pink fuzzy rug as if it were a pet and then handed it to Miranda.

"I am so happy you're leaving, Chica," muttered Dorcas. "You don't know."

Chica scowled and, with an annoyed tug, covered her doorway, a sheet of scratched clear vinyl—a privacy curtain, they called these flaps, which were designed to be transparent, though the ladies always had their ways of clouding the view. She reached around the back of her bed and pulled out a tiny razor blade. "It gets fuzzy sometimes. I used this blade to trim." She pressed it into Miranda's hand. "Keep that very hidden," she whispered.

Miranda put the razor into her pocket, then rolled up the bath mat and headed back to her cell. She hid the blade in the crack between the wall and the sink. Then she laid the mat out on the floor next to her bed, kicked off her sneakers, and put the soles of her feet to its warm gentleness. She lay back, her legs hanging over the edge, and passed two hours this way, thinking of the Hotel Flora and trying to recall every detail about that trip to Rome, the strange way the windows opened, the way she'd envied the Roman girls on the backs of their boyfriends' scooters. Her mother would read to them from a guidebook in the Forum, the insane brilliant flowers everywhere, and orange trees. Amy all blond curls and tight jeans, drawing stares from men in the streetcars, her dad puzzling over the bills in restaurants. Twelve years old. Family together, intact.

Just before the evening count Carmona appeared at her door, shadowed by Dorcas and Cassie.

"What'd I tell you," said Cassie. "There it is."

"Well, Missy May." The CO strode over to her as she sat up on the bed. "I'm let down. Stealing a bath mat from this sorry-ass."

"That's bullshit."

"You want me to charge you for profanity?"

"I think you should charge that girl for profanity."

Carmona turned to Dorcas. "Shut the fuck up."

She faced Miranda again. "I will charge you for profanity if you don't give me that mat. It doesn't belong to you."

Miranda sat down on the mat. "Chica gave it to me."

Cassie piped up petulantly. "Chica gave it to me, she always said she would and she did."

"I am trying so hard to actually believe this is happening. I am fighting over a bath mat."

"Not in the White House anymore," observed Dorcas with satisfaction.

"I am ticketing you for theft. You will be called to a hearing. Now give me that goddamn thing." The CO shuffled toward Miranda, who clutched the mat with both hands as she sat on it.

"I won't."

Carmona grabbed for it, and Miranda dodged her. Shoulder swiveled, smacked into the guard's flailing arm. By this time, a small crowd had gathered at the door to the cell. They shrieked in excitement, for they all knew what was coming next.

"That's assault!" cried Carmona triumphantly as she straightened and stepped back. "You are so fucked, Missy May."

The ladies were in a tizzy, onlookers at the scene of a thrillingly gruesome accident. Carmona pulled her ticket book out of her back pocket even as she began waving them all away from the door.

"What about my bath mat?" wailed Cassie.

"You'll be getting it soon enough," said Carmona. As the crowd dispersed, the CO strode back to the bubble, waving her mighty sheaf of tickets, taking a pen out of her pocket and pulling off its pointy cap with her teeth.

MIRANDA SQUEEZED HER EYELIDS EVEN TIGHTER AND MOVED HER ear closer to the outflow. You will never occupy this particular spot ever again, she promised herself.

"My mama loves John Wayne." Miranda recognized this voice as belonging to Viv, the woman in the first slot, the one with the view of the desk. She cut in, asked Viv to check for any sign of an escort CO.

Hoots flooded through the tubes. "Hang on. I'll just look," said Viv.

Silence fell over the pipes, but for a low angry murmur: "That one gets out."

Viv returned. "That guard is here now, hon. Paperwork, seems like. You're out any minute."

Miranda settled down on the floor next to the toilet, leaned her head back against the cool wall. Then Carmona's wide rosy face appeared in the window, cut off at the brows. She smiled as the triple locks turned. The door swung open. "Come home, Missy May," she said with what sounded like true affection. "All is forgiven."

Miranda couldn't tell if she knew what had happened just before the SHU guard had come for her, two astoundingly long weeks ago. Dorcas ambled by her cell, pausing in the doorway. "Cassie says keep the fucking mat. I told her it was wrong. I stole what wasn't mine but I never said something was mine that wasn't mine. Understand?"

Miranda did understand, funny thing. Prison logic was beginning to make sense to her.

SHE TOLD FRANK LUNDQUIST ALL THIS. THEN LAPSED INTO SILENCE, sipping her cooling tea. Finally he raised his eyes from his notes, gave her a small nod. A murky expression seemed to pass over his face, or was it a change in the light? She glanced up at the window behind his head. Luminous blue sky, a leggy shrub, seen from this basement vantage. It must have been wind in the branches, shifting the shadows in the room.

"I'd like to do some diagnostics with you," he said. "Lay a baseline."

"Sure," nodded Miranda.

"Please answer true or false to the following statements. 'I daydream very little.'"

"True. Are these from the MMPI? I've already been through a slew of tests."

"Humor me. I know it seems ridiculous."

"Sure, go ahead." As long as I leave here with that medication remand, she thought. And she felt sure now that she would. Something too open about him, for a corrections staffer. Too human.

"'My mother often made me obey even when I thought it was unreasonable.'"

"True. She was a good mom, though."

"I'm sure. Please just answer true or false."

He said this gently, not as a reprimand. Two COs passed in the hallway, voices booming, something about overtime pay.

"'At times my thoughts have raced ahead faster than I could speak them.'" He leaned back in his swivel chair, a clipboard resting on his knee. He looks, thought Miranda, as if he's confused by me. And why wouldn't he be? I am confused by me. Deeply. "True."

"'I have used alcohol excessively.'"

"False."

"'Sometimes when I was young I stole things.'"

"False." There was that time with her mother's rings. Did that count? she wondered.

"'I have no enemies who really wish to harm me.'"

"True."

He jotted on the clipboard. His forehead was traced by worry lines, though they were visible only when he raised his brows, which he did each time he began to write. She found this faintly likable. She asked herself again: Did she know him? He looked to be approximately her age, or a few years older. She could have met him anywhere, wedged together in an airplane row, on a buffet line at a friend's wedding. Miranda checked. No ring.

He looked up at her again. "'I have never done anything dangerous just for the thrill of it,'" he said.

"What?" she said. "I didn't hear."

"'I've never done anything dangerous just for the thrill of it.'"

Were those tears stinging her eyes? How did they come so fast? She blinked hard. She forced herself to meet his gray-blue gaze. "False," she said.

3

DO NOT ENGAGE IN SUBTERFUGE OR
INTENTIONAL MISREPRESENTATION
(Principle C)

I have to admit: I was curious.

Curiosity is an unacceptable emotion for a mental-health professional—or any kind of health-care provider, in fact. Satisfying a curiosity is tantamount to fulfilling a desire, and a mental-health counselor has no business fulfilling his desires (or hers), even mulling over those desires, when working with a client.

But how could I not be curious about M, this girl-turned-woman who'd float across my memories bracketed by bright sparks, who'd always seemed a key player in my story, though we'd hardly ever exchanged a word? After she left my office, I sat for a long time paging through that file folder. And it became clear that her crime was serious. This wasn't embezzlement, it wasn't a case of substance abuse careening out of bounds. M was in for murder.

I passed my ten-minute note-taking break launching my

small foam basketball into the hoop on the back of my office door. I sometimes offered the ball to fidgety clients who might need more than a cup of tea—for some, movement was more soothing. Lately I'd been using the ball more myself. It calmed me, too, the well-aimed bank shot. At home, for the same reason, I'd take to the playground courts in Riverside Park. I had height, and I'd occasionally sink a respectable layup. Neighborhood teens sometimes nodded approval. This could be satisfying, for someone who'd been pretty clumsy as a kid. And it passed a few hours on those warm weekends, when the city could seem lonesome.

On this afternoon, though, my aim was off.

I had to assume she was guilty. White, well connected, well off. She didn't fit the profile of the unjustly imprisoned. To have slid so far, spiraling down into the grim bowels of NYS DOCS, she'd taken some devastating missteps. Why? How?

Yes, I was curious, and that was wrong. But there was much more to my decision than that—my decision to keep quiet on our shared history.

I feared that if I did speak up, she'd bolt.

And I just figured I should help her in any way I could.

You didn't need shared history, test results, or a degree—you didn't need to know anything about her to see that her emotional state was dire. And this was my job, correct? Dispersing emotional shitstorms. Long-term therapy wasn't in the budget at Milford Basin, nor would the taxpayers have stood for it. But crisis intervention, that was the idea.

Here was a crisis, someone needed to intervene, and she and I, we had navigated the same school hallways, we were schoolmates, after all. So I was convinced: for intervention, she needed me—specifically me.

I missed eighteen shots until finally I sank it.

THE REMAINDER OF THE MORNING, I POWERED THROUGH SEVERAL admissions evaluations, then did a session with a regular, a half-blind seventy-year-old Brazilian in for smuggling coke in her cane. At lunch, I ate the chef's salad in the staff mess down beneath the inmates' gym, with the clamor of nonstop stomping and dribbling above. The four of us in the Counseling Center always sat together, set apart, in the corner nearest the door. The guards, looking in their cocoa-colored uniforms like a herd of broad-backed cattle, dominated the rear of the room, by the window wells that let in the only natural light and air to the stewy-smelling mess hall. They didn't trust us. The guards felt somehow that in the Milford Basin's endless version of summer-camp color war, we sided with the yellow—the inmates—and not with the brown. Which, in my case, was pretty unfair; though sessions with clients were often dominated by the women's venting against the COs, I still had a whole lot of sympathy for the guard staff. Talk about your difficult jobs! No wonder they almost all had weight problems. I'd guess that compensatory eating disorders were widespread among them—in fact, one look at their lunch trays confirmed that.

In any case, I know that Suze Feeney had a bad attitude toward the COs. She called them "swine" under her breath. "That one—Villanovo—that one is a little Hitler," she'd hiss as a guard swaggered past carrying a phone-book-sized portion of lasagna. Suze had a white buzz cut, wore fringed shawls and swirling skirts and cowboy boots, specialized in substance abusers, and was a founding editor of The Person-Centered Review. She had a rapport with the inmates that I could never match.

"So, Frank," said Suze. "What did you think of the case I sent you?"

"A complex profile," I stammered. Next to me, Corinne Masterson, bent over a bowl of four-bean chili, giggled quietly.

A delicately composed woman, her regal head topped with an intricate map of cornrows, she was attending med school part-time and gunning for Charlie's job. She put down her spoon. "She was assigned to me, Frank, but we thought you'd enjoy her so we sent her your way." She cocked an eyebrow at me. "A better therapeutic match, we suspected. More like your Central Park West crowd."

Corinne chuckled, and Suze joined in. They exchanged a bemused glance. Those two always had some private joke going.

Charlie Polkinghorne, our boss, Counseling's sole M.D., looked up from his soup. "Who's this?"

"She was the 50 milligrams Zoloft I sent over this morning," I said.

"Right. Right." Charlie nodded his head authoritatively. I knew he was allowing his admin assistant to sign his name on the med orders again. He'd never even seen the remand slip I sent. But still I regarded him with empathy. The diplomas on his office cinder blocks were the very best, I mean blue chip all the way, and if he hadn't been a dedicated alcoholic, he probably would have been heading up a leafy inpatient clinic in the Berkshires and kayaking in rivers of cash. But mistakes had landed him here, where mistakes are paid for. He had long since settled into the life of institutional doctor, the shrink as civil servant. He lived in a ramshackle apartment in the toniest part of the county, with a balcony drifting above the shuddering tracks of the Metro North, and there he drank himself catatonic, with his alcoholic wife, Sheila, alongside.

Looking back, I think Charlie only vaguely sensed that he'd entered his sunset era at the Department of Corrections. I had a soft spot for him; he had hired me when no one else would. But Corinne didn't have a soft spot for Charlie. Neither did Suze. And with reason. He had never aspired to work in women's corrections. Suze and Corrine had. Charlie settled. So, undeniably, had I, the newest member of the team. But while I aimed for an air of humility around these colleagues—and I sometimes sensed that they appreciated my efforts—Charlie was perilously clueless.

"What the hell's her charge again?" Charlie asked.

"Second-degree murder. Stiff sentence, too," I said. "Fifty-two years. No parole."

"That's a white girl with a bad lawyer," said Suze.

"Or a judge up for reelection," said Corinne.

"That's a shame." Charlie fished for the final pea in his minestrone.

"And her father was a U.S. congressman, stranger yet," said Corinne.

"Only one term," I said. "Never won another election." Maybe I said this with a bit too much familiarity. Suze looked up at me quickly. "That's what I gather," I added with a shrug.

They didn't know about the connection M and I had, of course. They didn't know where I went to high school or even where I grew up. They didn't know much of anything about me, in fact, except that I'd been in a cushy practice in Manhattan and was tossed out amid some kind of litigation mess. Mistakes were made, and now I was here, where mistakes are paid for. In the half year I'd been working at Milford Basin, I didn't talk about myself very often. Which is typical, I suppose. I'm not in the habit of talking about myself much. I'm more of a listener. It's my job.

THAT EVENING, I ARRIVED HOME TO TRUFFLE THE CAT—HE HAD BE-longed to my ex-wife, Winnie; I'd somehow inherited him, and we lived together as incompatible roommates—and a ringing telephone. My baby brother, Clyde. He explained that someone named Grigori had promised to maim him if he didn't come up with three hundred dollars by midnight. "I'm out here right now doing business, Frank. Just give me two, I'll make the rest."

I sighed and I rooted around the living room for my car keys. At the tawdry corner of Amsterdam and 108th Street, I idled with a chunk of twenties fresh from the money machine clutched in my shift hand. Posted at an overturned Whirlpool dryer box topped with a turquoise plastic tarp, my brother smiled at passersby and lovingly indicated his wares, like the proud fromager I'd once seen selling disks of goat cheese at a street market in Paris. Urbanites, with faces mostly weary or worried, rushed around in the evening haze. Watching them pass Clyde and his offerings without a glance, well, it rubbed my heart the wrong way.

My brother peddled tube socks on consignment. He worked for a man I will call Jimmy, who marshaled armies of sellers of tube socks, windup plush toys, hats and hair ornaments, and balloons. They ceded him 85 percent of the proceeds in return for a cot in one of several rodent-riddled row houses Jimmy owned in Sunset Park, transportation to and from Manhattan, and a half a gram of heroin a day.

"It's a version of life," Clyde used to say.

That night he was far from his best self: his brown hair hung in lank strands around his face, cold sores flowered violently on his lower lip. Clyde had been a junkie for going on a year now, and so calamitous and steep had been his decline, I worried that someday soon I'd never remember him any other way. He was just nineteen, my junior by many years. He'd shrugged off higher education; unlike me—always the uneasy underachiever, neglecting homework then asking for extra credit assignments— he'd been a placid D student in school. He dreamed of being a pastry chef in a swank New York eatery, but obviously, other things happened instead.

He spotted my car and sidled to the curb, slightly bent, an unsettling combo of anorexic teen and decrepit old man. But his eyes were achingly clear and he greeted me so thankfully, throwing his arms open to hug me as I climbed from the car. Sporting a grubby Princeton sweatshirt, he looked like a demented frat boy who'd been starved and beaten for a week.

"You could use a shower, pal," I said, hugging him gingerly.

"You're telling me, my friend. But thank you God, at least I've haven't got the louses." He was starting to talk like Jimmy, who was Macedonian. He eased the cash from my hand and stuffed it into the pocket of his pants, which were filthy green, embroidered with minuscule mallards, someone's old golfing trousers.

A woman towing a sobbing toddler paused to look over Clyde's showroom. "These are dynamite socks," Clyde said to her. She started off down the sidewalk again, dragging the child behind her.

The smelly smoke of frying fat from a churros stand on the opposite corner wafted around us, a greasy fog. "I'm dog-tired from work and I don't understand who Grigori is," I said.

"Short version," said Clyde. "Last week some kids stole my socks. I had to borrow money to repay Jimmy for the lost inventory. Grigori is Russian, the Russians are the bank, and you don't stiff the bank."

"Stole your socks?"

He looked down. "Sleeping on the job."

Sleeping, I understood, meant nodding, meant he was high, propped against some piss-covered wall, slumped in some doorway. That queasy despair again, the guilt, rising again, upending my gut. How could I let this happen to this boy. My blood, my sole sibling, my dead mother's late-to-the-party joy.

"Grigori has one of those crooked Russian crosses tattooed on his shaved head." He grimaced. "Even Jimmy seems a little spooked by those Sheepshead Bay guys."

"What about readmission to Llewellyn? I've been asking around, I think I can get you a spot—"

"When I'm ready, Frank. Just not ready yet." He slipped

the money from his pocket again. Rubbed the corner of each bill between thumb and forefinger, as if ensuring the ink was smudge proof, or testing the paper's weft. "I promise."

I had given him five hundred. "Buy yourself some food," I pleaded. "You're so goddamn thin."

"And yet the girls are all over me."

Heat of tears building behind my eyeballs, I returned to my car. I powered down the passenger-side window. "When will you be ready, if you please?"

"I'll be ready when I'm ready." He was counting the bills again.

I rounded the block and headed for home, the sun lowering now, spilling gold all over the river as it fell. The timing of Clyde's arrival in the city a year earlier couldn't have been worse. My career had cracked up a few months before, and, when he turned up at our apartment, establishing residence on our sofa, Winnie and I were already crouched in a kind of ongoing sniper exchange, striking each other with startling frequency and precision. After a few days in the free-fire zone, Clyde decided to evacuate. He fell in with a girl he'd met in Washington Square. Flor was her name. She was a junkie. As I skittered into a tailspin, out of a job and out of my marriage, he was sucked into something much more dire.

A year later, I found myself still reeling through the days. Shell-shocked by his implosion. And mine.

And yet Clyde claimed to enjoy his unfettered new life. "It's like I'm dangling on the very edge of everything and it's actually not a bad place to be."

Bumping down into the garage beneath my building, a neogothic hulk on Riverside Drive, I wondered why so many people were tossed by fate to the outer edges.

Take M. Here was a person teetering on a precipice.

Climbing the echoing stairwell from the garage, I realized that, maybe, I was very slightly dismayed that she didn't remember me. Because we surely had talked a few times—trig handout, fire drill. As far as I could remember. And I think I did remember every word I shared with her during those school years. She laughed, once or twice.

Back in my apartment, I paused at the long mirror Winnie had fixed by the bedroom closet. In many respects, I felt profoundly unchanged from that wobbly ninth-grader, easily flustered, needled by self-doubt, and not able, in any consistent manner, to abide by the standards for morality and honesty by which I judged those around me. A difficult truth, for a licensed professional who is tasked with helping others evolve. But, at that moment, in that dingy airshaft-view room, with the cat blinking atop my ex-wife's pillow, it seemed clear to me: if I were slightly more string-bean shaped, and still driving my grandmother's boatlike Buick Ventura, I would have been the same guy. The same boy who been fired from Burger Palace for deep-frying his buddy's hat, who had called girls' houses—including M's, a few times—only to slam the receiver down when someone said, "Hello." The same eager-to-please cutup, the same chronic striver, never quite attaining the pinnacles that had been predicted for him by certain achievement tests. Tests administered by one Erskine Lundquist. Yes, that Erskine Lundquist, of the Lundquist Curve. That's my father. Clyde's father, too. Clyde hadn't tested as well as I had. Dad was left badly shaken by his scores.

But no. No revisiting all that now. And I was not still that cringeworthy freshman. I scooped old Truffle into my lap and lightly scratched behind his molting ears. He tolerated this as I contemplated my reflection across the room, lifting and lowering my chin. I wasn't unhandsome, perhaps, at age thirty-two. Women double-glanced on the street sometimes. I saw them, and I walked on by.

4

The lime-green linoleum of the game room floor glimmered like a lake of antifreeze fluid. Someone had managed to set fire to a Scrabble board and the smoke had triggered the overhead sprinklers. Miranda and Lu swabbed up, pausing every now and then to rake wooden tiles out of the sopped string mop heads. They piled a wet alphabet on the windowsill.

"I found the zed," said Lu.

Miranda looked up, startled by the sound of her voice. She'd been watching the strands of the mop slop around the puddled floor, wrinkling the water. She had been submerged in her end-of-life planning again. What would it be like to drown? Delightfully quiet, she imagined. What an appealing notion— after the ceaseless din of Unit 109C, Building 2A&B, to be suspended eternally in a cool, clear gelatin of silence. Problem was, the prison didn't offer a wide selection of places to drown. You could try the toilet—clog it, fill it, dunk your head in—but she still had some pride. How about standing under the shower head with your mouth open, like a goose in the rain? Just let your innards fill up with the powdery-tasting shower water and then you'd topple over, dead?

She longed to be finished with the feelings. Such tired rubbed-raw feelings, grief and shame and regret. And the noise, the noise. An eternal silence brought on by water—yes, that would be an attractive way.

Miranda straightened up and leaned against the wall, let her mop rest against her collarbone. "Do you think you could drown yourself in the shower?" she said.

"First you must stop the drain. Then someone could hit your head," said Lu. She paused in her work, adjusting her state yellows, which she'd altered with a contraband needle and tailoring skills bred in her Russian bones to fit neatly over her long and slender torso. "Someone could knock you down. Then you might drown like a baby in a little bit of water." She pursed her carefully drawn red mouth ("put on leepstick, don't be sad mouse," she often scolded Miranda). Bent over her mop again and said firmly, "Alone this could not be done. You would need help. And who would you ask? Not me, because I wouldn't do it."

"April."

"April would not do it. No way." She wrung the mop into a blue plastic bucket with her pale, strong hands. She shook her head, letting out a sarcastic little guffaw. "April hit you over the head? Come on, Mimi."

No one had ever called Miranda Mimi, but Lu did. She claimed that in Russian, Mimi means "little crow." "And when you sit on your bed and look sad, with your shoulders all pinched, you look like one, too," said Lu.

Jerrold Liverwell, the head CO of the second shift, appeared at the door. "Welcome, Officer," Lu said.

"Hello, ladies. Better get moving, count is in ten." He glowered at a line of plastic chairs, each molded seat cupping water, like a row of birdbaths. "I'd just love to know who did this shit." He ran a hand across his close-shaven head, a handsome man, with a small paunch and dark, mottled skin like silver left to tarnish.

"Officer, how are we doing?" asked Lu, peering at him through her yellow bangs as she wrung the mop again. Miranda saw the guard glance her way.

"Not bad," he said. "Ask me later."

Ladies started yelling down the hall, and Liverwell cursed and disappeared in the direction of the row. Miranda and Lu worked without speaking for a while. Lu had a way of vanishing into herself, shifting to an impenetrable mode, an antigravity force that repelled all who approached. When Ludmilla sank into this state, Miranda grew a little panicky. Without her, without April, Miranda doubted if she could function. She never had been so dependent on anyone in her life. Not one of her boyfriends had been more essential to her well-being.

Perhaps Duncan McCray. Certainly none of the others.

But then she had never been a person who felt at ease by herself. This is why her time in the shoe had been such a special agony. When too much alone, her mind would drift toward trouble. Solitude had never been her strong suit.

Miranda could trace this way back. One day when she was about eleven, she dawdled home from school only to find the front door of the house open. The place was deserted. Her father was in Pittsburgh, campaigning for reelection. They all tagged along sometimes, when her sister and her mother and Miranda herself had to be onstage with him, but this day he went alone. He was in a bad mood. November was coming, his polls were way down, she had heard him screaming into the phone. Amy was maybe at a friend's house, but where had her mother run to, leaving her purse? Her car was gone. (She didn't find out until years later that Karsten Brunner, her mother's lover, had a cardiac arrest that day.) She found a sink full of dishes in sudsy water, and her mother's engagement ring with its big emerald-cut diamond and the wedding band etched with twirling vines were set in the little blue saucer on the sill, their customary place while dishes were being washed. Miranda climbed up on a footstool and stared at the rings. She put them on her hand—fourth finger, left hand, that was the place—and took a tour of the rooms of the house, the big brick house with its smell of old wood, so much bigger than their little one-story place in Pittsburgh. That house, you could hear everyone talking—the walls, Dad had said, were made of spit and Kleenex. This house all you heard were whispery creaks and echoes, like ghosts passing by your room.

Miranda heard those creaks as she climbed upstairs. Stopped at her parents' flowery bedroom. Smells of shaving cream and those dark interesting perfumes, adult smells, heavy and almost sickening. The cluttered vanity table, the vast ruffled bed. The closet where, if you knew how to clamber up the shelves of sweaters, you could find The Joy of Sex under some old ski pants. Easily reached, if you were a good clamberer like Miranda. But she didn't stop to see those drawings now, the ladies with the hairy armpits and the bearded men joined in various ways, wearing nothing but gentle smiles. She returned to the hall and continued along to Amy's messy den, heaps of albums and secret notebooks in which she wrote poems that Miranda read on the sly and thought were really good. She brushed her hair, looking into Amy's mirror, its glass half covered with "Greene for Congress" stickers.

Finally, to her own room, the best room with a view of the backyard and the fluffy blue carpet she had picked out herself. She stood at the window, staring out at the yard. Fall was definitely coming, a lot of the leaves were yellow and some were already down. Beyond the woods she could see the dull gray of the parkway, and beyond that the river.

Was that when she began to have a taste for the forbidden? She had never even thought of going to the river alone. The floor of the woods was moist and mulchy, fallen leaves gone black and sticky in the damp. She slid down the culvert to the concrete pipe that ran under the parkway, tall enough for her to walk through without bowing her head. Here were mangled tin cans, scraps of tires, and clumps of dead branches tangled with all kinds of trash you didn't want to look too closely at. It could be that a serial killer had left someone's fingers there, or there might be a dead bird. The cars rumbled overhead, a deep frightening roar that echoed through the pipe and penetrated her head like someone yelling in her ear. The concrete vibrated all around her as she hurried through.

She shot out the other side into an eerie quiet. One bird, calling over and over again, receiving no answer. A lonely sound. The woods here were bigger and cleaner. She followed a muddy path—there were other footprints there, whose?—down to a sandy lip where she had been once before with her father and Amy, one Sunday not long after they'd arrived in Washington and moved into the house. Dad had let Amy and Miranda bring the fishing poles they used to use at the lake place in Pennsylvania, and they sat there, dropping their lines in and reeling them back out, while Dad smoked a cigarette and stared off down the river. He had just started smoking again and Miranda was mad at him for it. He said to give him some slack. He said he was under stress, because being a representative was a tough balancing act. They didn't catch any fish, and after a while, they got hungry for lunch and left.

Now Miranda sat on a small rock where her father had sat that time. There were cigarette butts littered on the sand there, and she wondered if one of them might be his. She bent down and picked up one with the name of Winston, which was his brand. But she decided no—it had been almost two years since that day they'd gone fishing. She dropped it in the river and watched it float, spinning swiftly away.

About thirty feet out in the water was a huge split rock with a tree growing from its broken center. Miranda thought the rock looked like a giant cracked egg with a fuzzy chick's head sticking out. The rock was covered with spray-painted messages in red, orange, white, and silver—left there by teenagers, she supposed. They had written names and hearts, and she saw the word fuck a lot, which was definitely the worst of all bad words, and Miranda could understand why they'd want to write it there, where their parents would probably not see it.

Sitting on this small rock on the riverbank, digging the toe of her sneaker into the sand, she wondered what would become of her if no one ever came home. How long would she be able to stay in her house, doing the cooking and the cleaning up, taking in the mail? Could she get the lawn mower started on her own? That would be key, because uncut grass was the giveaway—that's how the neighborhood had found out that Mr. Semsker down the street had kicked the bucket. He lay in there, dead, until his grass grew long enough for someone to take notice. If she couldn't pull that cord hard enough and get the mower going, surely she would be taken to an orphanage. And she knew from her reading—Daddy-Long-Legs, just for starters—that orphanages were dreadful.

Miranda noticed that a tall tree had fallen into the river, extending its branches nearly to the split rock. She went and investigated it, and she could see that its trunk was wide enough to walk on, and that you could shuffle out far enough to make a jump to the rock. Amy would have bossed her, told her to stop, but Amy wasn't around, so Miranda clambered up onto the tree trunk, and holding the branches that stuck up on either side, moved out over the water. It was easy, actually. She got to the place where the tree dipped under the water and stopped. From here, it was just a giant step over to the rock, and she could see how to grab onto the slim trunk of the little tree growing in the crack and pull herself up to the ledge. She took a deep breath, held it, and jumped.

The rock was more slippery than it looked, but she did catch hold of the tree, and she was able to pull herself up. She sat there, her heart pounding, and felt a hot glow of self-satisfaction. Clearly, it was no accident that she was also the only girl in her grade able to do penny drops from the monkey bars. Clearly, she was talented.

In the heart of the broken rock, there was a little round plateau of sandy dirt, and here was where the tree had planted itself. Resting at its base were two empty bottles, Jack Daniel's bottles with the familiar label she recognized from a T-shirt that Benjamin LeHargue had worn almost every day to school at the start of the year until Mrs. Yee told him it was inappropriate and asked him not to wear it anymore.

Many more names and messages were scrawled on the inner walls of the rock. Miranda leaned against them and dug into the pocket of her jacket. She pulled out the piece of chalk she always kept on her, in case of an impromptu hopscotch match. She squatted down and found a clean bit of rockface, close to the edge of the crack. She wrote her name. If she was taken to an orphanage, at least there would be some proof that she had once lived here, had a home, and a family.

She rose again and went to the other side of the little plateau, the one that looked out onto the wide river. The sound of the traffic on the parkway behind her was softer than the sound of the river before her. The water was black in some places, brown in others, and gave off a smell of rotting wood and moss. It was a dank and dirty odor, like the smell of the science classroom's cloudy fish tank magnified by a thousand. But the wind that blew down the river was fresh, thought Miranda. You could tell that it had come down from the mountains, as the river itself had, if her father was to be believed. He had said the river bubbled up from a hole in the ground in the mountains of West Virginia.

Miranda briefly considered spending the night on the rock—wouldn't that worry them and make them spoil her for a week and make them sorry that they had left her alone. But when she truly considered being out here in the dark, she grew scared. She scampered back over to the shore side, and, in a bit of a panic, leaped back to the big tree. She landed just fine on the trunk, and for an instant, she was congratulating herself again. Then her sneaker sole, worn thin from blacktop scraping, slid on the slick bark. She fell backward. Into the water.

And it was deeper than you would have thought. She sank all the way under, and still she didn't hit the bottom. She bobbed back up to the surface, gasping with shock. The frigid cold of the water hit her all at once. She floundered wildly for a moment, her brain in a kind of wild freakout, her heart pounding so hard it made her gag. She grabbed hold of a branch that stretched out from the trunk and tried to pull herself back up onto the thick body of the tree, but she couldn't—her arms were too weak. She just dangled there, kicking and whimpering, tasting the rotten water in her mouth, until the branch broke and she plunged back down into the darkness again.

When she surfaced this time, though, she was calm. She began dog-paddling to the shore, which was really only about ten yards away, though she had to get there slantwise, because of the stubborn current. When she was halfway there and her arms were getting very tired and heavy, she stretched her feet beneath her, and touched the mucky floor of the riverbed. She waded then, shivering, picking her way among boulders back to the banks.

When she got to the house, she could see immediately that it was just how she'd left it—empty, no lights on. She peeked into the window of the den—only the TV stared back at her, blank and gray. Hiding her wet shoes and socks in the milkbox, she slipped in the side door and up to her room. She was already in the shower, her soaked clothes shoved under her bed, when she remembered her mother's rings. They were gone.

She thought about going back to look for them, but when she went to the window, she saw that it was nearly dark. She couldn't make herself go back into those woods. She thought about the cigarette butt whirling away on the current and figured that those rings might be heading out to sea by now. There was no getting them back.

Heavy with the knowledge of her own impending doom, she slowly dressed and dragged herself downstairs. She was ravenous, and surely when somebody came home she would be sent to bed without dinner, so she took a pop-top can of chocolate pudding out of the refrigerator and walked like a condemned man down the three steps to the den. She turned the TV on to Channel 20 and sat down to eat her pudding while watching what would undoubtedly be her last episode of Scooby-Doo for months. Because what could be the penalty for drowning your mother's diamonds in the river? A long exile from TV land, certainly, and other punishments that might even be worse.

Sometime later, she woke with a start. The den was dark, the television off. She rubbed her eyes, feeling cranky, and heard her father's voice. She only remembered the rings when she stumbled into the bright kitchen to see his body on the checkerboard floor. His head was stuck in the cabinet under the sink. Amy was kneeling by his legs, bent over the open toolbox.

"Those are the pliers, Amy. I need the wrench."

"What's going on?"

"Mom lost her rings down the drain," said Amy. "Isn't that so tragic?"

"Where is Mom?"

"Upstairs."

Her father's voice sounded from beneath the sink. "Don't bother her, Miranda."

"She's upset," whispered Amy dramatically.

The disposal was emptied, a terrifying green-black goo that plopped into a bucket. The pipes were examined. No jewels were found. Her dad frowned and shook his head. "Must've washed straight down the main."

The three of them ate TV dinners around the kitchen table. "How much did those rings cost, Dad?" asked Amy.

Their father grimly cut his turkey slab. "A fuck of a lot," he said. Amy and she exchanged wide-eyed stares. It was the first time they'd heard him use "fuck," though it would be far from the last.

After they ate, Dad retreated to his study to talk on the phone, Amy to the TV room. Miranda sat at the kitchen table, staring at the sink, trying to figure things out. While she was sitting there, her mother came into the room, her eyes red-rimmed, in her robe and slippers. She went to the high cabinet and took a bottle of aspirin down, and she poured herself a glass of beer. She looked at Miranda. "When did you get home?" she said.

"I don't know," she said, shrugging. Her mother gazed at her a moment, then turned and walked back out, carrying the aspirin and the beer. Miranda listened to her footsteps trudging up the stairs, and she was flooded with understanding. Her mother thought the rings had been stolen from the house, left with its door gaping open. Her mother didn't want her father to know that she'd left the house with its doors swinging wide like an invitation for every masked burglar who happened by. Her mother didn't want to get in trouble, so she'd told a lie. That was something Miranda could begin to understand.

Nothing was ever said about the jewelry again. Two months later, her father lost the election and his seat in the House. Three years later, Amy was dead, and two years after that, her parents' marriage was legally dissolved. Miranda knew when their troubles began. It was the day she let her mother's diamonds go drifting away.

"WOULDN'T YOU SAY THAT'S A LITTLE EGOCENTRIC? TO ASSUME THAT you were the cause of everyone else's misfortunes?"

Frank Lundquist could be such a pain in the ass.

Still, she found herself liking him. He had some strangely adolescent moves. For example, the way he flicked his head when his hair slid too far over his eyes. Tearing small notches in the rim of his empty tea cup. He was eager to help at all times, so unlike the rest of the somnolent, grudging staff at Milford Basin. It was touching, kind of. Also, sadly irrelevant. The man was merely a medium for getting the medication she needed. Still, in the weeks she'd been seeing him, she'd often found herself moved to reflection in his presence. Something about his manner—the fillip of concern in his questioning—lit up certain dusty corridors of memory, in a way she'd never expected.

The problem was, she didn't want to start reliving her life right now. Now that she was ready to end it.

"We probably all walk the path we deserve," she ventured.

"Come on." He leaned his forearms on the desk, his eyes intent. She could tell he thought they were making strides. "You were a kid. A kid doesn't deserve that."

She shrugged. "What about original sin?"

"Are you a Catholic?"

"I've always been intrigued by the idea of going to confession."

He sat back, his chair let out a groan. "Is there something you want to confess?" he said quietly. "It won't leave this room."

She didn't like the way her heart revved at his question. She stood. "I just did that, remember? My mother's rings. I was the culprit."

"I think we're moving forward," he said.

"I think our time's up," she said.

THEN SHE LEARNED THAT ZOLOFT MIGHT BE TOO WEAK A DRUG TO do the job. Standing in line at the meds window waiting for her daily dose, she had met Delina, a pharma authority with three attention-grabbing gold teeth. "I know you're cheeking the stuff," Delina chuckled one day as they returned to the unit. Spears of summer sunlight pierced the long hallway through its slivered windows and flashed on her dental work as they walked and talked. "You're looking to OD, I bet. I would, if I was you. Couldn't handle that kind of time."

Her hair was worked into tight knots across her head, rows of tiny dark cabbages. "You need Elavil or some such strong stuff, fifty, sixty caps' worth. You come up with the cash up front, I might be able to help you out."

They had reached the unit. Miranda nodded but said nothing as they filed through the door. "You let me know," said Delina as she glittered on her way.

April, waiting for Miranda in the common area, witnessed this exchange with a scowl. "That is the worst news in this place. What could she want with you?"

Though five feet flat, April frequently stepped up to defend Miranda, and the ladies took note; they knew she was a veteran. The army had granted her a height waiver due to her lofty IQ and flawless marksmanship. "I was a sharp girl with a sharp eye," she'd told Miranda soon after they met, as they fitness-walked the weedy, hard-dirt track that traced the perimeter fence. "In the service, I was the complete package."

Now, Miranda put a hand on April's shoulder, steered her into a quiet corner. "Delina said she could get me some pills, maybe." April glared, disapproving. "Just for sleeping," lied Miranda.

No, she hadn't told April that she was leaving prison the easy way. Of course not. Miranda understood that she was the only person April had left on the planet. April's father, a chief petty officer at a naval air base in Pensacola, had cut her off when she'd been convicted and forbade her mother to visit or even write to her. "Before I fucked up," she told Miranda, "I was his girl." Once she'd shown Miranda a gold bracelet he'd given her when she'd made staff sergeant, delicate gold links with a heart-shaped charm dangling below. She had never taken it off until she got to prison, where she kept it hidden at the bottom of a baby-powder bottle. Showing it to Miranda, she'd emptied the bottle onto a sheet of paper, fishing out the chain, rubbing the powder away with her fingertips to make the gold gleam. Her father had bought it in the jewelry district of Manila, she said. He had the heart engraved, To A from Dad. "That just touches me," she had whispered as she showed Miranda these words. "Every time I read it, I feel like God loves me or something."

Now her parents didn't even send a card at Christmas. "He says I brought shame to their door. They don't want to know me," April told her. She still wept about it at least weekly, often daily.

Now she said, "You don't want to trust the stuff that gets passed around in here. It's half poison. Girls cook it up with Ajax and who knows what, Mimi."

April had picked up the nickname from Lu. But from her North Florida lilt, it sounded sweeter. "You need sleeping pills, get it from the doctor."

Miranda could only hope that she could continue compiling her stock of Zoloft until she had enough to do the job. She'd need at least six weeks' worth, or eight, perhaps. Could she stand Frank Lundquist's perturbing presence that long? His unwelcome attempts to dislodge carefully stowed chunks of her past. And what if, in the end, his meds didn't work? The last thing she wanted to do was kill herself only to wake up alive.

As for April, Miranda tried not to think about what such a death would mean to her. Another abandonment.

A WEEK INCHED INTERMINABLY PAST, AND IT WAS TIME TO SEE HIM again. She navigated the barren corridors that smelled of chalky stone, like still-hardening concrete, though these passages had been built years ago. The final corridor led to a black steel door with a wire-reinforced window. Beyond it, rain streamed from the eaves, a glassy wall. The guard stationed at the security point, an older man Miranda didn't recognize, looked over her pass. "You've got a few minutes yet. Stand here and see if the rain'll ease up." She was taken aback by his kindness. She searched her mind for an appropriate comeback. "Thank you," she finally said. The guard returned to his Daily Racing Form, and she stood at the door, staring out through the scratched glass at the drops slamming down into the mud of Onida's garden, flicking the begonias' heads from side to side, making the yellowing tulip stalks, stripped of their blossoms, bob and weave. She tried to think about what she might say to Frank Lundquist.

She kind of wanted to tell him everything.

"You oughta get going, rain or no," said the guard, nodding at the clock.

The buzzer sounded explosively, right next to her ear. She leaned into the door, and it opened, dumping her into the cold rain. She walked quickly, raising her face to its pelting.

She decided: she would not tell him everything. Instead, nothing.

In fact, she would tell him that she had no need to see him anymore.

Delina's message stuck: Zoloft wasn't the right exit strategy, the foolproof one she craved. She'd go back to this golden-toothed pill genius, or find some other way to get what she required. She had generally accomplished whatever she'd set her mind to, and she was going to free herself. End this misadventure, also known as her life. Talk about wasting time: Frank Lundquist was just wasting the little time she had left.

5

END THERAPY WHEN A CLIENT IS NOT LIKELY TO BENEFIT FROM CONTINUED SERVICE
(Standard 10.10.a)

"That's some downpour," I said. Strands of her hair had slipped free from their restraints and were stuck to her cheeks. "A little chilly?" I took my jacket from the coatrack by the door and offered it to her. She declined.

"Fill me in. How are you? Besides wet, I mean."

She squinted at the floor, as if absorbing some meaning from its pattern of scratch marks and rainy-day mud spots, then raised her eyes to me. "I don't really think these visits are helping. This isn't the right thing for me now."

Current literature on therapist self-care warns us not to panic at a premature termination. A client's decision to terminate therapy may very well be rooted in the client's resistance, and not in anything we have or haven't done, say the experts, and it's most important that one should never experience a termination as a personal rejection.

But nevertheless. A dark surge. Flash flood of dismay. I sat back in my chair, stared at her composed face, her lowered eyes. I realized: I simply could not let her go. Way too much at stake. Hers was the case that would lead me out of the wasteland, banish the depression that had been hounding me for the last year, since the Zach Fehler matter, since Clyde's slide. Her progress would deliver mine.

"Listen," I said. "It would be a big mistake for you to stop coming here."

Her eyes, suddenly guarded, met mine. "Why?"

"You're resisting something. I believe we're going somewhere."

"I'm not going anywhere," she snapped. "I'm never going anywhere. What can you do about that? How can you possibly help me with that?" She gazed at me in the most penetrating way. Against the small window, the rain fell heavier. A barrage of white noise.

I walked around the desk. I leaned back on it, facing her, within an arm's reach. I took a calculated risk. "We are actually very much alike," I said. "I understand a lot more about you than you think."

She bowed her head, hiding her face in her hands. Her shoulders trembled. I looked down at the place where her hair parted. It was pale like a part of someone that you don't regularly see. The space between the toes or under the arm. It seemed too private a part to stare at. I turned away, grabbed a few tissues from the box on my desk.

How I wanted to say, I know where your locker was, just outside the typing room. For years when I heard a manual typewriter I thought of you. I really care about what happens to you. Helping you suffuses my life with meaning. You have become my best reason to get out of bed.

But I couldn't say that. Not now. The timing seemed all wrong. "Kleenex?" I offered.

I decided to use a judicious bit of self-disclosure, instead. Anna Freud believed that the therapist-client relationship could often benefit from the acknowledgment of a common humanity. "You know, I used to be in private practice," I said. "I didn't always do this prison job. I screwed up, and I ended up here. Kind of like you."

She looked at me tearfully. "You couldn't possibly understand what I'm going through here."

"Hey, why don't you try me."

Shaking her head, she bent her face to her hands again. I squatted in front of her chair, offering the tissues. She took one, wiping her eyes. I rose and leaned against the desk.

"Do you have a life?" She looked up at me. "I mean, are you married, kids, all that?"

"I'm just finalizing a divorce," I said, reluctantly. "No kids."

"But you have your work," she said.

"Yes, true. Though this is not where I imagined I'd be, at this point in my career."

"Is it a pretty deadly job?" She sniffled. "I bet it is. A lot of stupid people, a lot of complaining."

I shrugged. "Pays the bills."

She held the wad of tissues over her eyes. "When I think about what I've thrown away."

"What have you thrown away?" I said softly.

"Everything," she whispered. She began to weep again. "A life. Possibilities. Children." She wiped her nose. "I think I should go. I don't feel like talking anymore."

As she stood, crumpled tissues tumbled from her lap to the floor. I watched from above, feeling a strange sense of disembodied flight, as she crouched beneath me to gather them one by one. She straightened, tossed them in the trash, turned toward the door. I reached out then and grasped her wrist. "M," I said. "Give me a chance."

It wasn't my touch, I think, so much as the way I said her name that made her stop, turn to face me. Suddenly, she seemed quite clear-eyed. Maybe she saw something right then. Some hint in my expression. Some hairline crack.

"Stick with this," I said. "Have some faith."

"Then get me a stronger prescription." she said. "I want Elavil."

CERTAIN CLIENTS RIPPLE YOUR PSYCHIC POND. ZACHARY FEHLER DID that, with his furious shiny little chocolate-drop eyes and the frown lines between his brows, the terribly selfish and incompetent parents. I couldn't stop thinking about the kid while treating him. He had me pacing my living room floor late into the night. Winnie complained. The downstairs neighbors complained.

When I was still in training, I was assigned to a cancer-riddled Presbyterian minister, who was terrified of dying because he was sure he'd be sent to hell for beating his kids. He'd imagined what the underworld would be like down to the smallest detail, telling me about how the devil would flay the skin from the soles of his feet and make him dance on floors of glowing-hot metal.

I had nightmares for years after this man was dead and gone, the kind of nightmares that have you waking up shrieking and tearing at the bedsheets.

But my clients never knew how indelibly they marked me. This is why therapists burn out. Certain stories get incised in the mind. You hear Zach's tale and you want to gather him in your arms and press his anguished little face to your shirtfront and take him for ice cream with sprinkles and sing him to sleep with soothing songs, but you can't. You sit there trying to talk to him for forty-five minutes, twice a week. You do your play therapy, you ask leading questions. The time is up, and he is sent to the wolves again.

But this case, the case with M, would be different: I was determined. For her, I would orchestrate some unmistakably positive outcome, some significant change in her life for the better. Zach Fehler's parents, in their lawsuit, had claimed that I'd done just the opposite with their child. That I—and my methods, the damned role-playing, the damned puppets, and yes, that one breach, those irretrievable seconds when I let myself slip. That blip. That somehow this, my swerve away from therapeutic detachment, had ignited his fury, turned it deadly. That his crack-up, the whole horror, was somehow my fault. I have always been 90 percent sure that this wasn't true—but the doubt, the doubt enveloped by that last 10 percent, destroyed my practice, my marriage. It precision-bombed my self-confidence, naturally. One would expect that.

All would be set right with M though. Now that I had treated her for some weeks, I saw that this person, this memorable classmate, had reentered my life as a gift, an opportunity to do something true and truly good.

That's how I found myself in the lofty reading room of the public library's main branch, where, at rows of dark wood tables, the underemployed discreetly napped or basked in dusty slabs of sunlight. A staffer ushered me to a microfilm reader, and soon back issues of the New York papers whizzed before my eyes. I stopped when I reached June three years previous: EX-CONGRESSMAN'S DAUGHTER ARRESTED.

Charged with second-degree murder in a botched robbery attempt in Candora, a town in upstate New York. . . .

Police said the suspect had admitted to having disposed of a firearm in the Oshandaga River. . . .

. . . two men with fatal gunshot wounds, one identified as the captain of the Candora volunteer fire squad. . . .

. . . the other fatality, whom police have tentatively identified as the accused's accomplice, was the co-owner of two New York City bars, one shuttered last year for drug violations. . . .

. . . the suspect's father served one term in Congress, representing the Twenty-Eighth District of Pennsylvania from 1976 to 1978, and was later named in an influence-peddling investigation. Charges were never brought.

FRIENDS, FAMILY MYSTIFIED BY A PROMISING LIFE GONE AWRY. A longer piece.

Her boss at the marketing firm where M had worked: "She was a dream employee. We were grooming her. Our minds are boggled by this whole thing."

M's cousin: "If she was involved in this awful episode, it was not of her own free will."

M's close friend since college: "I worried about her relationships sometimes. She suffered a lot. But she's an incredibly loyal person, she doesn't give up on people."

The state's attorney in Utica: "We intend to prove that she knowingly participated in this crime."

M's attorney: "My client is innocent of the charges. This was self-defense, against a man she thought she knew. She had no idea what she had gotten herself into."

A DAZED BUS RIDE HOME TO THE APARTMENT, WHICH, UNIMPRESSED by the summery glare outside, received me with its usual gloom and dark. I dug into the stacked boxes of albums in the coat closet and found my mother's favorite Leonard Cohen. I hadn't even thought of it in years, but now for some reason, fragments of its songs were rattling around in my mind. I lay on the scratchy sofa, an olive-green barge. I listened now to these not-my-taste but richly familiar tunes, and I wondered: What had I gotten myself into?

Throughout my career, I'd always tried to avoid a fusion of roles. I tried to build a high wall between my personal life and my professional one. But, to be honest, I often failed. It's a major myth, that in a counseling capacity a person can listen with scrupulous detachment. Psychologists—even psychiatrists—are just humans, after all. Like everyone else, we carry our whole lives with us to the office, and we bring what we witness in the office home again at night.

I'd arrived at Milford Basin with my life in shreds. Practice lost, Winnie and I already talking to lawyers. So let's say I had demons during my stint there. I wrestled them as I drove to work each morning, and too many days they refused to stay in my car, parked outside the electrified mesh. Instead, they followed me in and bedeviled me while I worked. If Lana started talking about how her mother always thought she'd take over her Aunt Fay's hair salon, but she didn't because she got hooked on the pipe, my devils would prick up their heads and start swinging around me, cackling like zoo chimps at feeding time. If Pet sobbed about her sweet baby who she left to die in a park one rainy night, my demons struck up a conga line and pranced jubilantly through my brain.

And now, M's case was chasing me home at night, keeping me awake, driving me to the library on a summer Saturday when I should have been sweating through my T-shirt launching free throws with my teenage neighbors in the park. But this woman. I knew her, or I had known her. This client evoked the past perfect tense, came bundled with a history. This client changed everything. I couldn't simply play the games I might've been playing on a summer weekend unclouded by the knowledge that she was sitting in a cement box, locked in, alone, in need of my help. I couldn't simply compartmentalize her plight.

Perhaps the best I can do is paraphrase Bugental, that brilliant shrink to the shrinks, because in this point he hits the nail on the head: the whole idea of "therapeutic detachment," he says, is an oxymoron, a fib one makes to one's self. The notion that a therapist can remain detached from his client is, he writes—this is so true—"a seduction for the fainthearted."

Well, I thought, I may be wrongheaded, but I'm not fainthearted.

I lay my head back on the couch and listened to the singer croak about his famous raincoat. I thought about my mother, Colleen, thought about her fanning a deck of paint chips, pregnant with Clyde, wearing a flowery cotton blouse and a headband in her hair. The starburst of color between us on the guest room bed. She said she thought the new nursery should be Honeydew or Buttercup, but she just couldn't decide. "How about stripes," I suggested. "That way you could use both. I could paint them myself," I added in an offhand way, thirteen, not wanting to seem overenthusiastic.

"Would you?" She smiled at me. Her loose brown curls, the slight gap between her very front teeth. "I think it's a wonderful idea."

Colleen often pointed out those stripes when visitors trundled through to see the new baby, once he arrived. "Frank did such a good deed," she'd say. Of course, she wanted the world to see the best of me, she was my mother. But still, as the visitors gushed over my paint job, I felt grateful to Colleen. She never mentioned how I'd used the leftover Buttercup. How I'd discovered a nest of mice in the corner of the nursery closet. How she picked up the roller pan and saw the stiff yellow-dunked bodies arrayed neatly in a row, embedded, smothered, in the hardening paint. How she dropped the pan right there on the new rug, how she vomited violently and repeatedly, falling to her hands and knees with her pregnant belly bowing out beneath her. This image of her, back arching and sinking as she retched, will never leave me. I'm still grateful that she never breathed a word, to Dad or Clyde or anyone.

I didn't think there should be vermin in the baby's room.

She had been gone almost three years now. Acute stroke: it snatched her straight from the living room, with my father and brother on the sofa, a pizza on the coffee table, and 60 Minutes on the TV. I still couldn't quite grasp that I'd never talk to her again. I still imagined I might bump into her in a crowd in Times Square, where she'd come up to see the shows, or on an airplane, maybe I'd find her in a window seat, le Carré paperback open on her lap. I could confide in her. Tell her about Clyde's decline. About the Fehler lawsuit, those unendurable days of wrangling over the roots of childhood psychosis and malpractice awards and the dollar equivalent of a toddler's life. I could tell her about my divorce—given her instincts about Winnie, she wouldn't be surprised—or about meeting up with M again, which was the kind of story she would appreciate. "Now there's a fine twist of fate," she'd say, approvingly.

I was lucky to have had such a foundational figure, I coached myself. Both parents were paragons, in fact. M had gone years without talking to her father, she'd told me in our last session.

"Why?"

"He did something I considered unforgivable," she'd said.

"To you?"

"No, not to me."

"You want to elaborate?"

"Not at the moment."

"But you're speaking to him now?"

"Yes."

"Did you forgive him?"

"Not really."

"So when did you start speaking to him again?"

"When I did something unforgivable."

Leonard was singing about a bird on a wire and a drunk in a midnight choir when I fell into a dreamless sleep.

ON SUNDAY, I SOUGHT CLYDE. ON WEEKENDS, HE OFTEN WORKED THE tourist trade at Battery Park, so I headed for this southern locale. The day was overcast, blankets of clouds tossed over the city, smoothing out the shadows. The park was jammed by some kind of Rastafarian gathering, and the shaved ice sellers were out in force, pushing their big glassy blocks and tinkling bottles of syrup back and forth. An out-of-tune reggae band sent music booming through the park, and everywhere, people shuffled to their stuttering rhythm. I found Clyde near the Vietnam Veterans Memorial, lounging on a bench behind his big pile of socks, immersed in conversation with a bearded man, who sat in a wheelchair beside him, clutching a bunch of glinting zeppelin-shaped balloons. The balloons swayed above their heads like psychedelic thoughts they were having.

Clyde smiled as he saw me walk up. "Look who's here. Jackson," he said, turning to his companion. "This here is my brother, Frank."

"Hey," said Jackson congenially. "You the shrink?"

"Yeah," I said.

"I keep having this dream, man. I'm riding a motherfucking whale. I never even seen a whale, but in this motherfucking dream I'm sitting on a whale. What do you think, Frank?"

"Well, you know, dream interpretation is a tough nut. There are no easy answers . . ." I shrugged.

"Tough nut. No easy answers. That's the whole fucking problem. I saw a shrink in Bellevue one time. Said the same goddamn thing. No easy answers." Jackson grinned at me and shook his head. "Hand it to you, Frank. You got a good fucking game." He turned his wheelchair suddenly, his balloons bobbling above him in agitation. "No easy answers," he muttered, smiling. "Yes yes." He looked at Clyde. "I'm heading on to the Seaport, man. I did supreme business there last week. You ought to blow this mess off and check out the Seaport."

"Jimmy's picking me up here. I'm sticking."

"Later, then." Jackson looked me up and down again as he started to wheel himself away. "You got yourself some handsome shoes, Frank." He laughed. "No easy answers. Yes yes."

Suddenly he stopped and turned toward us again. "How about a balloon for your kids, Frank?" he said.

"Don't have any kids," I said apologetically.

"You got a lady, though?" asked Jackson. He rolled a few feet back to me. "Come on, buy one for your lady. She deserves it, right?"

"Gee, I . . ." I looked at Clyde. He nodded and gave me a look that said, Just go ahead. "All right." I handed Jackson a ten. He presented me with a pair of pink Hindenburgs.

"She is gonna love you good when she sees, man. You will thank me." He gave a little bow from his waist and grinned and rolled away chortling.

"You did a good thing," said Clyde. "Balloons are a hard sell these days, he was telling me. Everyone's buying those windup pigs instead."

I tied the airships to Clyde's bench and sat. Kids squirted each other with high-powered water pistols, yowling and yelping like roughhousing predator cubs. I watched them for a while. Knew I had to spill.

Clyde, in his junkie phase, had been serving as sort of a confidant for me. Those of us in the counseling profession often suffer from secret overload: you are the keeper of everyone else's secrets, and therefore you have no room for your own. I'll admit it: I'd begun to use my baby brother as an outlet. Talking to him was like talking down a well.

"One of my clients went to Lincoln High," I said.

He looked at me wide-eyed. "No way."

"I remember her perfectly."

"Someone from Lincoln's in jail?"

"Prison. She doesn't remember me. I haven't told her."

"What's she in for?"

"And I should have told her right off, probably. Second-degree murder, armed robbery gone bad. Not unserious. Long sentence."

"What the hell?"

"It wasn't premeditated, far as I can tell. A boyfriend involved, of course. Something went very, very wrong."

"No shit."

I sighed. "She dated this kid Brian Fuller in school, who was such an ass. Always bragging about how he had to wax his hairy chest for swim team."

Clyde scrutinized me for a moment. "And she doesn't recognize you?" he said.

"Nah." I stood and looked out over the railing, at the bay marbled with froth. Staten Island huddled in on itself, skulking, a dog expecting to be kicked. "I should have said something right off. I guess I was curious, I felt sorry for her, I thought I might embarrass or upset her. She's clearly been through a hell of a lot."

"And you wanted to keep seeing her."

"For treatment. She's thoughtful, you know? I feel like I can really help her."

"Sure," he said. "She good looking?"

I turned to him and rolled my eyes. "Grow up."

He grinned. "She is."

"I actually have been helping her," I said. "I think. She's in a lot of pain."

"Committing murder might just do that," he said with a skeptical little chuckle.

"Hey," I snapped, "everybody fucks up, right, pal?"

He frowned at me. "Too true," he said. He turned to restocking the rows of socks laid out on his Whirlpool box, pulling fresh pairs from a ratty woven bag.

"Let me take you to dinner," I said. "Katz's. Pastrami."

He told me Jimmy would be by in a half hour, no way, he had to be there waiting.

"Come sleep at my place," I pleaded.

"Nah," Clyde said. "I'd just steal your wallet again."

I leaned my head back, seeking a little simplicity in the summer sky, but it got all carved up above this corner, so many wires and buildings and airplane contrails, a crosshatched scribble above our heads.

I couldn't really imagine why she did it. How she arrived at that place. "She's not a cold-blooded killer," I said.

"Whatever." He shrugged.

"I'm just trying to make a small difference in someone's life. I'm struggling against futility here, Clyde."

"I hear you." He was thoughtfully arranging his socks in alternating rows, red stripes then blue stripes then red stripes again. "Futility sucks."

6

JULY 1999

The COs shattered her jar of Nivea. They upended her box of Georgia O'Keeffe floral postcards, littering them all over the floor. They broke the spines of her blank-faced prison-library hardbacks—One Hundred Years of Solitude, Go Tell It on the Mountain, Little Dorrit—and shook them so hard that clouds of musty paper dust changed the smell of the air.

A lady (known to them only as Bean) had turned up dead from a crack overdose. A ball of plastic wrap holding four more rocks had been exhumed from a tub of margarine in a refrigerator in D Unit. Banished to the passageway, Miranda listened to the COs toss the rooms all along the passageway and noticed how the plastic grids on the fluorescent fixtures overhead—baffles they were called maybe?—resembled the gridded trays in her grandfather's old tackle box, each square filled with a cherry bobber or a rubber minnow or a knot of small barbed hooks. She knew they wouldn't find the two dozen Elavils. Delina had shown her how perfectly the pills slid into the hollow-tube arms of a state-issued plastic clothes hanger.

When the search party moved on, Miranda began to clean up. She wiped up the spill from her plastic water jug. Letters she'd received were scattered, soaked, handwriting and jet-ink smeared. Her Life cereal had been dumped. Her Cup-a-Soup, happily, had been spared.

Beryl Carmona stuck her head into the room. "I don't make the rules, I just enforce them," she said.

THE BODY BAG WAS GURNEYED PAST WHILE MIRANDA SAT IN THE kitchen with April, waiting for noodle water to boil. The wheels squeaked savagely; they reminded her that Bean had been six foot three and sturdy. April's gold-brown eyes glossed over. She rubbed them with the heels of her palms, making Miranda think of early childhood, of Amy, of their stormy girlish games and the way one sister would go solemn while the other had her cry. "I am so afraid of that shit, Miranda. I am so afraid," said April. Miranda understood. She had heard the difficult history, no, she had absorbed it into her being like a course of radiation, the retellings and rehashings, until it had changed her at a cellular level—just as April had absorbed Miranda's.

After the First Gulf War, April had reenlisted, landing in Berlin during the drawdown. She headed up a guard detail at U.S. Forces headquarters and fell in love for the first time in her life, scorchingly in love, with a logistics specialist named Kar-lee. Karlee worked on dismantling the base, shipping out deli slicers from the PX, pinball machines from the rec center, data servers from the secret listening post where intel operators had eavesdropped on the Soviets. Karlee dismantled April's heart as well. One day she told April she'd taken up with a German postal worker she'd met on the job. "Martina. She was beautiful, a lot more beautiful than me. But I thought Karlee was the one. I was out on that limb." She'd just been home on a leave, a week before it happened, and had broken the news of her love, of herself, to her parents. "Daddy knocked me straight across the kitchen. Boom." She'd punctuate this by swatting the air with the back of a hand.

April accepted separation pay and an honorable discharge and moved to New York to work for the Apple Bank. "They have terrible rates there, don't you ever bank there," she told Miranda.

One day she had walked out of her job with $14,000 in her pocket. "I was on the pipe, Miranda. Pray I never see the stuff again." She would shake her neatly shaped head, tufted with soft whorls. "I'm not going back down that way."

"Of course not," Miranda would always say.

"You're my sister," April would always say. Depending on Miranda's mood, this could please her deeply or make her hands tremble.

The worst thing that happened during this particular cell toss was that the COs had drenched the handbag Miranda had crocheted for her mother, and on the very day she was supposed to present it to her. It was a sad thing to begin with, goldenrod-yellow yarn, about the size of a slice of sandwich bread, with a long strap and a floppy tassel. Sopping wet, it looked like something you might use to scrub a bathtub. But Miranda was proud of it. A Colombian prison elder named Maria Juana had taught her to crochet. No woman in the Greene family had ever known how to do that, at least not since Great-Grandma Schmidt, on her mother's side, had come over from Graz.

"HOW SWEET! IT'S SWEET," MURMURED BARB GREENE, SLINGING THE strap over her shoulder. She didn't say anything about the purse's mildew smell, and anyhow, the general aroma of the visiting room may have overpowered it—the place reeked of Cheetos from the vending machine, Cheetos and microwave pizza and the dirty diapers of babies trundled in by sisters and grandmothers for a visit with the women who bore them. It was a weekday afternoon, and so Miranda and her mother were both able to get seats at one of the scarred tables—on the weekends they often had to stand.

"Are you sleeping?"

"Some."

"Alan wants to see you, Miranda. He really does."

"That's not happening, Mom. Sorry."

Miranda's mother took her hand away and stared at the grime-spattered floor. Always, during these visits she was on the verge of tears. She clutched a tissue in her hands and had back-ups, Miranda knew, stuffed in the pocket of her camel-hair blazer.

When Miranda was arrested, her father had persuaded Alan Bloomfield to handle her case. Miranda hadn't had too much say in the matter—she was locked up in the Oneanta County Jail at the time, acquainting herself with the realities of her new life. After she'd been held for twenty-two hours, Alan showed up with a change of clothes from her mother and a mini gift basket of expensive soaps and shampoos from her dad, along with a note: "Miranda—They said they'll let us see you after the arraignment—can't wait. Thinking of you. Love Edward."

Miranda stared at the basket with its outburst of cellophane. "Where does he think I am, the Hilton?"

Alan chuckled briefly, a thick-waisted man, with a thin shingle of gray hair and a fleshy brow that seemed to droop under the weight of thoughts undisclosed. "Sweetheart, all things considered, your folks are managing well. Last thing they expected, to be slammed with something like this."

"Are you going to get me out of here?" asked Miranda.

"Whatever it takes. You'll be out of here ASAP." He studied her with his sharp dark eyes. "He must have been some lay, this McCray. I hope it was fucking amazing, hon."

Miranda should have tried harder to get her parents to hire a new lawyer. She never trusted Alan Bloomfield. But consider what she had been involved in. Things that a month ago—a week ago—would have been unimaginable, to each and every one of them, Miranda included. She knew that she deserved what she got.

And Bloomfield was right—she was out on bail the next day, thanks to Grandma Rosalie Greene's life savings, which her father had inherited just a few months before, Grandma having finally gained eternal release from her Alzheimer's, a week after Christmas the previous year.

Alan Bloomfield had not been blamed by any of them for the guilty verdict. He had advised her skillfully, and he'd convinced the prosecution to drop the armed robbery count and to downgrade the murder charge to second-degree. The long sentence? Oneanta County justice, everyone said. Hard country up there. After Miranda was classified to a minimum III custodial level and assigned to Milford Basin, Barb moved from Washington to a high-rise in Riverdale, to be nearby. She joined a small travel-agency group in New Rochelle. She was alone, except for Alan Bloomfield, who lived in the city. He was divorced, she was divorced. "Alan collects Chinese jade, Alan likes my chicken Marbella, Alan gets house seats on Broadway because he litigated for the Shuberts," she'd said. "Alan and I have history together."

Miranda didn't blame Bloomfield, but she didn't like him, either. Still, he represented an upgrade from Karsten Brunner. "Your father drove me to him," Barb had told her once, when Miranda had asked what she'd seen in that unsmiling functionary of the Austrian embassy. He'd approached Barb at the Safeway's meat department, package of beef in hand, asking her, "Please, my dear, what is 'flank'?" Later Barb always shuddered at his memory. "His idea of a good time was to sit on the floor and listen to avant-garde jazz. No talking, just listening." She sighed. "But your father was so unavailable. All that time on the road, the campaigns."

Miranda had her doubts about Alan Bloomfield, but at least her mother wasn't bereft. Alan had driven her to the cemetery on Amy's birthday, Barb said, dabbing at her eyes again with her tissue. "He brought a reblooming rosebush and he planted it himself."

A pudgy toddler in a red tracksuit flailed and bellowed in his mother's arms at the next table. "He does not know me," the woman was saying indignantly. "Does not know who I am." Barb watched this for a moment, then turned back to Miranda.

"Lynn Sherrill had a baby," she said.

"That's nice."

"A boy. Named Justin, which is a name I have never liked."

Miranda gazed at the wriggling child. "I wish I could have gone with you on Amy's birthday," she said after a while.

Her mother took her hand. "Me, too."

"Mom," she said. "I'm sorry."

"You don't need to say that every time I come."

"I'm so, so sorry." She didn't know what else to say.

Barb passed her a piece of paper with a typed list scrolling down it. "I wrote up this list of what's in the box. Make sure they give you everything this time." Last month, COs on mail duty had pilfered her package and stolen Havarti cheese, boysenberry jam, a copy of People magazine, and a pair of knee-high socks. "I typed it up on my new computer," Barb said. "Did I tell you Alan gave me a computer?"

"No," said Miranda, glumly.

"You look pale. Are they letting you out for fresh air? You do thrive in the outdoors, Miranda. You used to like to camp out in the yard, remember?"

Miranda checked the clock, set far off down the long row of tables with their loose clusters of weepers and squirmers, infants in car seats displayed like centerpieces, a few vague old folks wheeled up alongside. Visiting hour was drawing to a close.

"Look, Mom, please don't make me remember anything right now. I'm keeping my mind in the moment."

"I'm worried about you." She blew her nose with as much politesse as possible.

"I'm going through a rough patch. Soon everything will be fine."

Miranda had tried to imagine how her mother would react to the news of her death. In the short term, severe grief. There could be nothing more devastating for her. But in the long term, she'd be better off. Closure. No long years of visits to this chaotic room, where she looked like some kind of karmic joke in her tailored blazers and her gold-knot earrings. It was clearly a shock to her system to be there, and she aged more every time she came. This is exacting a more vicious toll than any death could. Miranda was convinced.

SHE HAD BECOME FRANK LUNDQUIST'S PET PROJECT. THIS WAS CLEAR from the way he'd spring from his seat each week as she entered his office—she was a little afraid he'd barrel right into her and knock her flat. He wore an encouraging smile and a neatly pressed shirt.

If she could have, she would have told him the truth. It's not as if she enjoyed deceiving him. You're way too late, she'd tell him. I'm already a goner, and you are simply speeding me on my way.

Each week she banked another dose of Elavil, laid down another layer of chemical sediment, a powdery white stash of potential.

But she didn't tell him this truth. She told him about her memories, her dreams, her regrets, and he gave her the pills. It was a kind of exchange, to her way of thinking. And like all exchanges involving the unveiling of private parts, it felt a bit sordid.

One day after a session with him, Miranda, unsettled, went to ask Lu about this. She had just finished hot-waxing her legs in the unit microwave. The thick piney scent lingered.

"Would you sell your soul if you had to?" she asked.

Lu ran her hands over her gleaming shins. "I have sold my body one time. To Visha. He wanted me, and I said, yes, you can have me but in return you give me Long Island house, European car, American Express charge card, and also boots and coat, my choice, from Barneys. And he said okay. And he did get me . . ." She counted with slight bobs of her head. "Four of the five things. Also, time in jail, not in the bargain but that's life, as you say."

"But you love Visha."

"Yes. I wouldn't sell my body to a man I did not love, Mimi. Or my soul. That I would not do."

Miranda felt deflated.

But still, sequestered with Frank Lundquist, lulled by infusions of hot tea and his sympathetic gaze, she found herself compelled to lay a few things bare. She was using him pretty ruthlessly, it seemed to her, and she didn't feel right about it. In fact, she felt fairly terrible about it, and that led her to reveal more in their sessions than she generally planned to. Which is how she found herself telling him about the blue car.

It was a 1969 Pontiac LeMans, and it had a snout, a long insinuating snout that ended in two nostril-like headlights. The windshield raked backward, like a greased pompadour, and the convertible top opened at the push of a button, making a celebratory wail as it reared up slowly and then folded itself into a slot tucked behind the back seats. The paint was ice-blue. The seats were cream-colored vinyl.

Miranda first saw this car when Neil Potocki, her father's biggest financial backer, parked in front of their house in Pittsburgh in the weeks just after Edward Greene won his congressional seat, when the moving boxes started filling up the hallways and corners. The men would powwow around the kitchen table and her mother would shoo Miranda and Amy out. And there was this convertible in the driveway. Miranda pretended to steer, Amy preened in the mirror on the flip side of the visor. Miranda was nine, Amy twelve.

Neil Potocki was softer around the middle then. He owned the television station in Pittsburgh that showed blurry broadcasts of city council meetings and the Channel 23 kiddie club. Brown suits, brown ties, brown mustache, small brown eyes, smoking skinny brown cigarettes. And the blue car.

He must have really adored that car. Years went by, and in 1981, when Miranda was thirteen, Neil Potocki turned up again, this time in Washington, on Super Bowl Sunday. The convertible was the only thing about him that hadn't changed. He lived in northern Virginia now, on a hilly estate way out in what her parents, with a hushed thrill in their voices, called "hunt country." At the top of a rise, overlooking a neighboring farm where blanket-wrapped steeplechase horses grazed from carts of hay, the house was sprawled. "It's not a house, it's a mansion," her mother had said, as they steered up through the snowy slopes along a serpent-curved driveway. It looked old, all white wood and brick and stone railings, but it smelled new. Neil Potocki no longer was dressed primarily in brown. Instead, a deep red sweater and khaki pants, his hair salt-and-pepper gray, mustache gone. He looked thinner and smoked menthol cigarettes and sometimes a pipe. The blue car was parked out front, next to a clean white Mercedes-Benz. Miranda's mother told her he had sold the Pittsburgh station, made a killing, invested in cable television, made another killing, and bought a great deal of real estate all over the East Coast.

"Is he a millionaire?" she asked her mother.

"Oh, yes," she said.

"And he gave Dad money?"

"He gave the campaign money, sweetie, not Daddy. Both campaigns."

"So was he mad when Dad lost?"

"I don't know," said her mother. "And whatever you do, don't ask him."

The Super Bowl played on the biggest TV any of them had ever seen—so big it had its own projector that sat across the room and beamed the picture onto the enormous curved screen. On low couches, men in boating shoes and women in wool pants and gold jewelry drank Bloody Marys and ate little crackers smeared with salmon spread. The drinks must have been strong, because they were all talking very loudly and most paid no attention to the game or to the gaggle of younger children who were slapping each other and arguing over Parcheesi in the next room. Miranda sat on the arm of a sofa next to her dad, listening to him talk about a big lobbying deal for a lumber company. She thought she might pass out from sheer boredom. Her skirt, a plaid kilt kind of thing, itched. Scratching under the waistband, she watched the man who sat next to her father, his thin sandy hair and big bland eyes. He nodded at everything her father said, but he kept sneaking these glimpses toward the game on the TV. She watched his eyes shifting back and forth. Adults are so endlessly fake, she thought. She vowed to herself she wouldn't wear this awful skirt again.

Finally, she wandered off to search for Amy, passing through a number of rooms, each with a slightly different arrangement of perfectly puffed-up sofas and chairs and polished wood tables. On a bookcase, there was a framed picture of Mr. Potocki shaking hands with the president. The president grinned; Mr. Potocki was caught talking, his mouth open. He looked like a toad trying to trap a fly.

She found Amy in the vast kitchen, speaking Spanish with

the hired bartender. Amy was in third-year Spanish and was trying to talk her parents into letting her spend next summer in South America. She sat on the butcher-block counter, her long legs in white wool tights and loafers dangling.

"Miranda, this is Joaquin." Amy gestured toward a short stocky man in a burgundy vest and bow tie, who was busily slicing lemons and limes. "Joaquin, mi hermana," she said to the man.

"Yes, pardon," said Joaquin with a little bow. "Now I must find Mr. P. I need more tonic." He looked relieved to have found an excuse to leave the room.

"You want to drive me home?" Miranda asked when he was gone. "I'm bored out of my mind."

Amy slid off the counter and absentmindedly began practicing some steps from a pom-pom routine. "I don't know—you think Dad would let me?" She had gotten her license three weeks before, on the second try ("I really don't get why blinkers are that important," she'd said with a shrug).

Miranda flopped down in a chair by the oversize kitchen table, which was covered with trays of food waiting to be served, rare roast beef slices rolling in pink waves, the potato salad piled into chunky yellow hills. Amy, still moving her feet to an unheard beat, plucked a pickle from a bowl.

The swinging door flew open and in walked Mr. Potocki.

"Goddamn it, Rosie, we need tonic and—"

He stopped short when he saw Miranda and Amy. "I'm looking for my housekeeper."

"Rosie has dolor de cabeza," said Amy. "She had to go lie down for a minute."

"Shit." He frowned and stared at the floor. Then he looked up, as if remembering they were there. "You didn't hear that, ladies." He winked. He still had a little potbelly and his neck was thick, but otherwise he might be considered debonair, as Miranda's mom would have said.

Turning to Amy, Mr. Potocki said, "Can you drive, sweetheart?"

"Sure." Amy smiled.

"She only just got her license," said Miranda.

"So you're completely legal then," said Mr. Potocki. "You'd probably benefit from a little more practice." He tugged a heavy key chain from his pants pocket, a dozen keys clustered with a thick letter P sculpted in brassy metal. "I can't leave my guests. Why don't you take the Mercedes, go get me a case of tonic? There's a C-Mart just down the road a ways."

"I don't know," said Amy, as if seeing the big key chain had given her second thoughts.

"Tell you what." He put the big clump of keys back in his pocket and, from a narrow drawer beneath the telephone, pulled out a ring with a single key dangling from it. "How'd you like to drive a vintage convertible? It's a very sporty car."

"The blue one?" said Miranda.

"That's right."

Amy reached for the key. "Okay."

He regarded her appraisingly. "Willing to make a deal. Your dad's girl." He winked. "You could even put the top down, cupcake, it still works."

Amy nodded, looking a little dazed.

"It's freezing out!" said Miranda.

Mr. Potocki scoffed. "The sun is shining. Convertible weather."

"Should I go tell my dad?" Amy said.

"I'll tell him," he said, picking at the roast beef platter.

"I don't think she should drive," said Miranda.

"Shut up!" snapped Amy.

"Little ladies," said Potocki. "Play nice." He folded a slice of beef into his mouth, then reached into his back pocket, pulled out a black leather wallet, and plucked out a fifty. He handed the bill to Amy, giving her hand a little squeeze. "Thanks. And get diet tonic, please. A half dozen diet."

"Wait till I'm gone before you tell them," whispered Amy to Miranda.

Miranda agreed. In the end, she almost always did whatever Amy said.

She watched from a big bay window in the breakfast nook. It took Amy a while to get the car started and the top down. She wore the gloves Grandma Rosalie had bought at Garfinckel's. Cashmere, cream colored. She gripped the wheel tightly as she backed out of the parking area. Then the car slipped out the twisting driveway and disappeared amid the violet snowy hills. Above the hills, the winter sun dangled, a worn silver locket against the pale skin of the sky.

The car hadn't been driven for a year, and its brake lines had begun to rot. And then a patch of black ice, or maybe a deer, though no animal tracks were ever found. Instead, just the swerving path of tires, the car with steaming blue snout buried in snow, and a girl of sixteen, far away in the drifts.

THE PETITE WIRY WOMAN WHO LIVED IN THE CELL FACING MIRANDA'S had worked the streets of Syracuse's Tenderloin District for more than twenty years. Gossip in the unit had it that she slashed the throat of a john who tried to skip without paying and had only missed the electric chair because the man had been an escaped con and African American on top of that. Her name was Weavy Moore. All day every day she sat at the little desk she'd fashioned for herself from a sheet of thick cardboard and stacks of boxes, scrawling a missive to the world across the smooth flip sides of sandpaper squares, swiped from her job in the chair caning shop.

On this morning, Weavy looked up as Miranda left her room, heading for the kitchen. "You talk all night," she said.

Miranda stopped. This sinuous deep voice. Weavy had

never spoken to her before. She hesitated by the cell's open door. Beside Weavy's desk rose a knee-high stack of sandpaper. The walls were bare but for a torn magazine page taped above the desk, a photo of a young, handsome Jesse Jackson.

Weavy didn't lift her eyes from her writing. She sat very straight in her chair, clenching her fat marker. A black-and-white scarf covered her head, wrapping around it neatly and tightly, as if her mind were a wound that needed dressing.

"You talk in your sleep. You say nonsense things."

"I didn't know."

"It disturbs me."

"I'm sorry, but I don't know what I can do about it. I didn't even know I was doing that."

"Well, it disturbs me. You disturb me."

"Don't worry," said Miranda. "I'll be gone very soon."

Weavy looked up then, turning her broad wrinkled face slowly toward the door, and regarded her with a profound indifference, a void Miranda felt she might fall into forever.

"Gone. Yes," Weavy said. "You will be gone directly to hell."

Miranda backed away. Backed all the way into her room. Without volition, a toy figure reeled backward by a string. Shut the door, leaned into its steeliness, her forehead pressed against the chill.

Forehead pressed against the chill.

She saw a girl in flight. A new driver.

Now the girl was flying over snow, straight across the center of sight, just behind her shut-tight eyes.

And behind the girl in flight, another tableaux: a moving picture, aglow in red and blue. She pressed her forehead against the chill, thirteen years old, accepting the cold of the glass window, as she watched the dots race around in the night, red and blue, red and blue, in the darkness just outside the breakfast nook of the new-smelling, old-looking hunt-country mansion.

Small blurry dots of red and blue skimming speedily over the dark driveway. Circles of light, rafts of radiant beings, chasing one another in the night. Her forehead against the chill.

Behind her, in the room, a tangle of sounds. Gasping, gulping, strangled cries from her mother, as if someone were dunking her over and over into deep water. "She was a new driver," she yelped. Male voices, her father's mixed in. Muttered talk. Then the jangling of bracelets, loud, coming close to Miranda's ear. Strange hands landing on her shoulders, perfume smell falling over her in a choking mist, the bump of a kiss on the top of her head. "Poor dear." A voice she doesn't even know. "Poor little dear."

Far behind, the burble of the football game, still playing, somewhere people on TV cheering, somewhere music trilling. "She flew thirty yards from the road," a voice said.

She considered this. She tumbled this idea in her mind. It tumbled there still.

What must it feel like to soar over snow?

She leaned her forehead into the steel of the cell door, a coolant to the skin outside her brain.

So fast you'd sail, so light. So free.

7

TAKE STEPS TO MINIMIZE HARM WHEN IT IS FORESEEABLE
(Standard 3.04.a)

Elavil—its generic name is amitriptyline hydrochloride—is a tricyclic antidepressant. And not a particularly heavy-duty one. Some doctors use Elavil to treat bulimia, to ease chronic pain, to prevent migraine, or to tamp down a pathological weeping and laughing syndrome associated with multiple sclerosis. The standard dosage of Elavil is 75 milligrams per day. It is not considered a dangerous drug, but an overdose of Elavil can be fatal.

I had no reason to think she would overdose.

In fact, I believed she was improving. I felt she was unfurling. The story about her sister seemed like a breakthrough. It clarified, too, the origins of that moody, clouded quality that had set her apart, back when we were at Lincoln. Not that she'd seemed always troubled. In fact, she'd been popular, often surrounded by the more insistently blow-dried girls and the more cocksure boys. But you could sense a hard-earned soul wisdom in her. I could anyhow. In my adolescent eyes, this set her apart from the clamoring masses of our Lincoln peers. Something about the expression on her face when she passed me in the hall-way, both of us walking alone. I would always notice. I would even, sometimes, turn and trail her, after she passed. I thought she looked deep, astoundingly deep; even the tilt of her head from behind, her walk, spoke of soulfulness. Of course, I be-lieved that I, too, was deep, had hidden dimensions that no one had plumbed, disguised as they were beneath the forgettable ex-terior of a late-blooming boy.

One winter day, feeling especially bold or bored or bad, I trailed her all the way down two flights of stairs to an under-ground passage leading to the ceramics studio, a remote basement realm veiled in obscurity and pulverized clay, tucked away near the custodial caverns. A mumble of gas flames from the school's furnace filled the air. I followed her until suddenly she stopped short, just outside the studio door. She hesitated there, appeared to study a sign-up sheet for kiln firings. I froze, trying to blend into a thicket of handles protruding from a row of mop carts.

Did she glance my way? Did she see I was there with her?

Perhaps. I couldn't tell. I still don't know.

Down in that sublevel of earth dust and fire, I was fifteen and felt sure that the years ahead tracked up toward some sat-isfying outcome. Maybe I didn't see greatness in my future—I didn't really hope for the heights my father had attained—but I assumed, at least, that my actions would have some impact. That I would bump the course of a life or two, and in a good direc-tion. And so maybe it's reasonable—maybe—to ponder: in that hushed moment down beneath the chaos of high school, hav-ing wandered closer to the furnace's flames, to the planet's core, maybe I sensed that somehow my fate would be linked with M's? Maybe she sensed it, too?

Maybe. I still don't know.

She vanished into the pottery room. I was marked tardy for chemistry class.

AFTER WE'D UNCOVERED THE STORY OF HER SISTER, I THOUGHT OUR therapeutic relationship had finally hit its stride. But the next week she turned up in my office downbeat and remote. I knew when I saw her that we'd taken a step backward. Which is not uncommon: after a clinical breakthrough, one often observes a retreat.

What I didn't know then was that she was planning to be dead before week's end.

"So how're we doing?" I asked.

"Oh, fine," she said.

"What we talked about last week. Amy's passing." I hesitated a moment. "How terrible, for you, and your parents. I just wanted to say again how sorry I am. A seriously traumatic event—and you at thirteen, a very vulnerable age."

"I appreciate your condolences," she said flatly.

"Recovering from something like that is a lifetime project."

She gazed at me, her face somber. "Do you have a well-calibrated moral compass?" she said. "I'm curious."

"We're not here to talk about me," I reminded.

"Because mine seems to have been knocked out of whack at some point. And that bothers me."

"I see."

"But I think people who really do understand the distinctions between right and wrong, not just understand but live by them, are more rare than we realize. Do you think that's true?"

"Possibly."

She frowned at this noncommittal answer. This cop-out. "I'm just raising this issue because you seem like a person who trusts others a bit too much. And I like you, so . . ." She trailed off.

"Well, thank you," I said evenly. "I like you, too. But I suppose I do believe in the innate morality of the average person."

She shrugged. "That's certainly your right."

"What makes you think you've . . . lost your compass, as you say."

"Well, come on," she said with a little impatient laugh. "I wound up in this place. I've done a lot of stupid things. I obviously veered off track pretty early on."

"Okay, so when?" I sat forward, my pulse quickening a bit. Maybe I could draw her back into the therapeutic stream again. "When did you begin to lose your way?"

"Who knows?" She sighed. "At some point after Amy. When Neil Potocki started saying that she'd stolen the keys from his kitchen."

"But you were there—"

"His word against mine." She brushed her hands along the tops of her thighs, as if trying to clear away crumbs of nervous energy.

"That's a lot for a kid to handle."

"My father said as long as we knew in our hearts that Amy didn't take the keys, that was what was important. And I believed him, I guess. Until a couple of years later, anyway."

"And then? What happened?"

She fell silent for a long moment, her eyes resting on mine. Finally, she said something that nearly toppled me from my chair.

"You look familiar."

I felt my chest tighten. "What do you mean?"

"I just wonder if our paths didn't cross. We both lived in New York at the same time, I bet. You've lived there for a while, right?"

I nodded. Uncomfortable. Rested my chin in one hand.

She squinted at me. "Did you used to jog around the reservoir?"

"Never, bad knees." This was true.

She sighed. "I used to love to run there. I thought maybe I saw you."

Suddenly, suddenly a turbulent impulse reared up within me. I wanted to dash around the desk, grab her by the shoulders, and tell her. Everything. Not just that I knew her, followed her around the high school. No, everything about me. About my string of failed romances, my broken career. About Winnie. About Zachary Fehler. Listen! I know something about pain, about loss, about mistakes. If we could talk over coffee—I think we could connect—

Stop! I told myself. Wrong. Entirely inappropriate.

I needed to derail this line of thinking—and do it immediately. Did I have a moral compass? Absolutely. Yes.

"I think I want you to see one of my colleagues," I said, willing my vocal cords to not quaver. "I can't say we're still making the kind of progress you need; I can't see the wisdom of continuing—"

"I've gotten a lot out of our meetings," she interrupted. "Believe me."

She stood. She pinned me in my chair with her gaze. In those eyes, slowly beginning to brim with tears, flickered many hues of autumn leaves, a forest full of deep colors. I did not want to forgo those eyes. But I would, to be good.

Several plump drops escaped and raced down one cheek. "You're right," she said, brushing them away. "I will stop coming here."

"Why don't we call it a breather." Gathering myself again, I stood, too, my heart restarting. And then I sensed just a slight uplift in my spirit—I really was doing the right thing here. The moral thing. "Take a little time to reassess. If you decide you want to continue, I'll gladly send you on to another staffer. Dr. Masterson, maybe."

"No," she said, barely audible. "I've gotten where I wanted to go." She walked to the door, tossed me a heartbreaker of a smile. "Truly," she said, "I'm done."

THAT WEEKEND MY FATHER FLEW INTO TOWN TO BE INDOCTRINATED into the APA's Legion of Honor. The association had booked him into the Warfield, a squat brick pile near Columbus Circle. I staked out a spot on the hotel steps, waited for him to arrive. It was Friday afternoon, mid-July, Broadway. Touring Japanese ladies shaded themselves with golf umbrellas, and excited kiddies clustered around shaved ice sellers. Women went braless in the heat.

A white stretch limo rolled to the curb, and Dad climbed out, abashed. "Ludicrous car. I'm going to talk to the budget committee about this," he mumbled as I hugged him. He squeezed me tightly for just a second, then released me. I scanned his face. His eyes were rimmed with red. "You've been crying?"

"No," he scowled. "Where's my bags? Has the bellhop taken my bags?"

"Dad. What's wrong."

"Your mother would love that. The white leather. The TV. She would get a rise out of it."

"Yeah." We both stared at the car. Colleen's wide smile seemed to flash there, where sun careened off the window glass.

If heroin was Clyde's vice, and mine was—well, whatever it was—then denial was Dad's. Colleen had been dead three years, and he still spoke of her in the present tense most of the time.

"But, hey, be happy," I said, snapping out of it. "Here you are, getting an award."

"It's a lot of hogwash, and the only reason I came is the free flight. Did you track down that brother of yours? How is he, Son?"

Truth was, Clyde had temporarily disappeared. I had

trekked out to Jimmy's, but no one had answered the door, though I knew that many people occupied this row house, slumped beneath the blackened undercarriage of the Gowanus Parkway. Stained bedspreads and sheets of plastic covered the windows, rain-gutter rust oozed down the siding like sores. I rang the bell, which sounded in a many-toned chime, I think it was a bit of Beethoven's "Ode to Joy." The highway arched overhead, its superstructure looking from here like the rib cage of a vast dead beast. A roasting wind funneling through it. Minutes passed. I leaned again on the bell, then rattled the curlicued iron gate that overlay the front door. At last, someone yelled out the window, "You ain't got a warrant, you ain't getting in."

"I'm not a cop. I'm Clyde's brother. I'm looking for Clyde."

"I don't know Clyde. Nobody here knows Clyde."

The previous time I had come here looking for my brother, I had heard the very same line. This was how Jimmy ran his business. When outsiders approach, deny everything. Black-hole yourself. The whole venture was based on the concept of the black hole.

I knew that Clyde sometimes simply slipped off to what he called "unpaid leave." This involved finding a woman with cash and a stash of her own, and burrowing down into some rodent-stinking apartment in an abandoned precinct until both resources dried up and the relationship lost its inner glow. Girls easily fell for Clyde's sleepy, sweet blue eyes. He'd inherited Colleen's good looks.

My father insisted that Clyde's addiction was simply a passage, an extended adolescence, a refusal to enter adulthood. "I still could send him to that farm school in Vermont," he said, sighing. "He'd just make the age cutoff, I believe." He imagined country living might set him straight.

This was denial, Dad's specialty. I think he still pictured his youngest—his beloved, indulged later-in-life child—ensconced in some latter-day version of his teen-era bedroom, sprawled on a fake-fur beanbag chair, smoking joints and watching MTV. "I tried to leave a message for him at the place he's been living," I said. "I tried to let him know that you're in town."

He plucked a toothpick from his pocket and began to gnaw on it, furrowing his woolly gray brows, rumpled yet dapper in his seersucker blazer and sagging khaki pants and slightly crushed straw fedora. "If he needs money, he'll show, I bet."

"I'm afraid for him, Dad."

He winced. "A phase, it's a phase. It's developmental, you'll see."

WE RODE THE HOTEL'S ELEVATOR TO A SUITE ON THE TOP FLOOR, over-air-conditioned and smelling of wood polish, overlooking a landscape of tar roofs and treetops, droopy leaved in the heat. Dad disappeared into the bathroom to check on his catheter. A fruit basket the size of a German shepherd sat on the bureau. I peeked at the attached note, which said, "Congratulations, Dr. Lundquist, on 30 years of testing excellence."

I think I mentioned that my father is famous in his field. If you work in early education or child psych, you will have heard of Erskine Lundquist. He is the author of the most widely administered success predictor test in the USA. Whole generations have been pegged by his ingenious combo of play exercises and simple cognitive games.

And, yes, I was his first testing subject, at the tender age of five months. In fact, you might say that the test is me and I am the test. It goes by my name—his name, too. He modeled me as the quintessential child, the high end of the bell curve. Every other tot in America, just about, is judged by how they stack up to me. Will they succeed and live a life of productivity and prosperity? Or will they fail? It depends how they compare to me.

You see the problem, though. The quintessential kid did

not, it seems, grow up to be a quintessential man. Not to be too harsh on myself. I am a good-enough psychologist. Yes, over the years, I may have gradually lost footing, slipped down onto the shady slope of the curve.

But accept thyself. Love thyself. Forgive thyself.

I stretched out on a gold-striped chaise lounge by the window. Contemplated the room's walls, riotous in emerald-and-red flowery paper, charming or lurid, I couldn't quite decide. A towering canopied bed tickled the pink ceiling.

I thought about M. Uneasy about the way that last session had gone. Terminating our work that way—moral decisiveness was good, but difficult. I wondered what she might be doing at that moment. I hoped she was feeling positive.

Turned to gaze down through the haze at the packed sidewalk tables of an Italian restaurant across Broadway. M had mentioned eating there when she lived in New York. I'd been to the place, too, many times. Maybe she was right, maybe our paths did cross in the city. I wondered if she and I had dined there on the same evening ever, eaten the same chef's ravioli, drunk from the same bar bottle of wine.

Dad came out of the bathroom then. "Let's get a hot dog," he said, zipping up his trousers with a delicate wiggle. "I like the Big Apple dogs."

MY TUXEDO, THOUGH PROFESSIONALLY CLEANED AND VACUUM packed at the rear of my hall closet, still smelled of my wedding day. I ripped away its shroud of plastic, and a cloud arose from its folds, a complex burst of cigar smoke, Prosecco, and beneath it all, a rimy whiff of flop sweat. Where had it been dry-cleaned? I wondered, lifting a sleeve to my nose. Not a shop to patronize again.

I showered and shaved. I tried to bend my mind toward the speech. I'd been asked to toast Dad at the banquet. At this particular moment in my career—following the last session with M, clearly a rupture—and coming just a year after the whole Zach Fehler debacle—I didn't relish addressing the top minds in psychology today.

The cat eyed me from atop the television as I slipped on the various components of the tux. I faced him and raised an imaginary stem of champagne.

"Here's to Erskine Lundquist, whom I may outlive but I'll never outshine."

That didn't sound right.

"Here's to Erskine Lundquist, who has been everything a father should be and more. I am honored that you chose me to be your first test case, and I'm sorry I didn't bear out your theories in a more convincing way."

"Crap," I whispered. I let my hand drop to my side.

How could I possibly toast my father. The love and admiration I felt for him melded too closely with my own disappointments. Scion of one of clinical psychology's greats, and what did I have to show? I'd been banished, literally and figuratively, to the sublevel of the field, to the purgatory of a prison counseling center. And there, I'd allowed an ethically dicey situation to linger far too long. And with a client whom I valued more than any I'd ever treated.

But there was nothing to be done. Not now, anyhow. Except fasten up the cummerbund and hunt down the cuff links. This night is about Erskine. Tomorrow you can think again about her.

FIFTEEN MASSIVE CHANDELIERS HOVERED LIKE ALIEN CRAFT ABOVE the crowd in the banquet hall. Piano music tumbled from a balcony; the air-conditioning system was weak and everyone sweated, so many faces gleaming, so many damp palms and upper lips. People air-kissed reluctantly, afraid of sticking. People slurped chilled white wine as if it were Gatorade.

The crowd was studded with big names, a tribute to my father's standing, but also because shrinks love to party. Harvey Privett was there, the guru of the self-dynamization movement, wearing a salmon-pink bow tie and waistcoat, surrounded by acolytes who laughed at his jokes in silvery peals. Bella Olivera Azevedo, the great Brazilian theorist, held court at a table dead center, her thick hair coiled on her head, a dark crown of her own devising. Half the editorial committee of the DSM-V clustered around the hors d'oeuvre buffet with toothpicks in their hands, spearing cubes of Jarlsberg, fishing for the peeled shrimp that bobbed in a pool of melted ice.

I felt, as I'd suspected I would, extremely uncomfortable. I tried to look busy at the margins of the room, studying the paintings mounted in the entryway—views of the Hudson, actually, not far from Milford Basin—lingering at the bar, making small talk with the bartender who'd had to amuse a million wallflowers like me at banquets in this room. He told me, in a bored voice, that he had panic attacks and should probably see a shrink himself but that his HMO didn't cover it and he couldn't see shelling out bucks just to talk to some guy about his problems. "No offense," he said. "I do a lot of psychologizing in my job, anyhow. Tending bar. So I guess I can just talk to myself."

"That is probably the wisest course of action."

A hand landed heavily on my back. I turned, first saw only mustache, brush thick and graying. Looming up behind it was the face of Gary Grover. "You never called me for burgers," he said, his hand still on my back, rubbing it vigorously. "We were supposed to have burgers."

"I'm a vegetarian now," I lied.

"So? Tofu burgers. Such things exist, I think." He stepped back and looked me over. "You must be eating healthy. I think you've dropped a few."

I shifted uneasily under his scrutiny. My mouth went dry.

I tried a quick internal dialogue, as I often advised clients to do: What have I really got to lose in this situation?

The answer, as concerned Gary Grover, was clear. My ex-partner had been witness and accomplice to my professional downfall. He was romancing my ex-wife. Nothing left to lose. "I think you've gained a few," I said. My tongue still gummy. "So how's Winnie?"

"She's in Peru, encephalitis breakout in some Amazon village. You know Winnie. Very dedicated to her work. An inspiration, really."

"She certainly is."

"And how are things at the prison," he said, his voice dropping. "I hear you're doing just splendid work there."

"Fascinating. Fascinating client base. I'm loving it."

"Women's prison, isn't it? Yes, I can imagine you'd get some doozy dissociatives. Fun stuff, eh? A nice change?"

"It's a different crowd."

"I bet." He sipped beer from a bottle, leaned one elbow on the bar, and surveyed the crowd. "Park West doesn't get that variety, no. But the practice has really bounced back. Mostly the same old urban angst crowd, no thrills." He chuckled. "And that's just fine by us."

"Good, good, glad to hear it," I managed.

"I do have a case now that made me think of your Fehler kid." He cut his eyes toward me.

I didn't flinch, though. "Yeah?"

"The parents are class-A pains. I've got the kid doped up, but he's still banging himself around, roughing up the nanny. And he's a screamer. Jesus, my eardrums get raw. But you know about that."

He was studying me. "Mmm." I nodded, plucking a glass of wine from a passing waiter's tray.

"We learned from history, though. We've got Mom and Dad signing releases from here to kingdom come." He shook his head. "Our malpractice tab is still through the roof. Even though we parted ways with you." He added quickly, "We did exactly what those goddamn insurers demanded, and they still screw us on the bills. We sure miss you, bud."

I kept my cool. "How old is he, the kid?"

"Seven. Same age as the Fehler boy when he . . . crashed."

I badly wanted a peek at my watch. Wasn't the cocktail hour finished yet? Just then, I saw my father standing nearby, surrounded by a fawning crowd. "You never met my old man, did you, Gary?"

"No," he said. "I'd be honored."

I steered him over to the cluster of people surrounding Dad and made the introduction. "We loved practicing with Frank. We miss him, we really miss him, Doc," I could hear Grover saying as I moved away. "Goddamn insurance crooks," he was saying. "Goddamn lawyers."

I FOUND MYSELF A WING CHAIR OUT IN THE LOBBY, WHERE I'D GONE just to regroup, just to get some air. I watched the tour groups milling around, women with powdered-milk skin, bulky purses, and low pumps, waiting to be herded through Midtown to the various theaters. Their faces looked bland and kind. Many had big bosoms and hefty soft arms, and I wished they could just envelop me and pat my head and tell me that everyone makes missteps, everyone fucks up a time or two, everyone comes to the point where they know they are going to hell.

Child of fury. A term I first heard in a play-therapy training course. Mistrusting, impulsive, quick to anger. With such kids, violent, even sadistic behavior in sessions with puppets and dolls is commonplace, said the professor. "A constructive processing of rage," she said of this extreme acting-out. Play therapists must be prepared, must maintain calm amid the tempest.

At our first session, Zachary Fehler grabbed a toy drumstick and whacked the frog puppet I was manipulating, whacked it hard enough to leave a yellowish-purple contusion on my puppet hand. This is where we began.

By week two, he had cracked my office window, hurling a wooden dollhouse sofa. But we had a breakthrough dialogue. I took up the frog head (proposed, by me, as a stand-in for the adults who'd betrayed him, the mostly absent father, the barely functional alcoholic mom). Asked him to tell Frog what made him angry. "I hate you. You smell bad, you make me think of dog poop. I'm glad when you die." Constructive processing of rage, I jotted afterward in my notes.

And then, our last session. Week three. I donned the frog, asked how he was feeling that day, and he bit the puppet. Hard. Sharp little child teeth. Caught a nerve in my thumb. Pure reflex: I struck at him with the uncovered hand. Right across the crown. He fell down, gaped at me for a long, excruciating moment. A stripe where his scalp met his forehead, an awful reddening strip. Then he unleashed a piercing, terrifying wail. I was afraid his mother would knock at the door. But we recouped, I was able to stop his screaming, I put the frog puppet on the floor, let him stomp on it for a while. Tire himself. Then I apologized, explained that therapists, too, get mad, lose their tempers, just like their patients do. I make mistakes just like you, Zach. And I'm so sorry.

He said nothing. He continued to weep. He wouldn't look at me.

But his sobbing gradually faded to snuffling and he seemed to settle down. I thought perhaps it was over. Soon he was back to plucking the limbs off the multicultural family dolls. But he wouldn't look at me.

I said nothing to his mother about the stripe. She was drunk and I didn't know if she'd notice.

That very night, Zachary cracked.

And on this July evening, as the shrinks of the world gathered in New York City, little Emily Fehler would have been five and a half. Sleeping by this hour, dreaming, alive. If that play-therapy moment had played out differently.

After the news of the girl's death reached the office, I confessed the whole incident to Gary Grover. Of course, I can't blame him for severing ties. I think he tried, in his way, to make it as swift and painless as possible.

I don't know how long I'd been sitting in that wing chair when I looked up to see Grover's mustache looming over me. "Frank, they sent me to find you, for chrissakes. The speeches are starting," he said. I had an impulse to flee. As if he sensed this, Grover put his hammy hand on my arm. "This is a big moment for you, bud," he said. "Face it, how often have you had a chance to make your dad proud?"

And then, seated beside my father on the dais. Before us, a roiling sea of psychologists, a thousand faces trained to dissect the workings of personality.

"Are you okay?" Dad asked. "I didn't know where you were. Anything wrong?"

"Not a thing," I said, mopping my face. "It's just so warm in here."

"It's positively Finnish in here," said the woman seated next to me. A diminutive blonde, in a bare-shouldered dress. Her emerald stud earrings matched large green eyes. "We haven't met," she said, extending a slim, manicured hand. "I'm Lydia Buchanan. I was just elected to the board last month."

"Frank Lundquist." I clasped her hand. "Son of." I gestured toward my father.

"Of course. I know. I wrote my doctorate on the Lundquists. So you can imagine, I'm in heaven."

My father leaned over me and beamed. "I'd like to read your paper sometime."

Lydia Buchanan blushed. "That would be such an honor for me, Doctor." She looked at me. "And you are in the family business as well, I understand."

I nodded. "Out in Westchester." Way, way out. Beyond the razor-wire fences.

"I'm in New Jersey. Summit. Eating disorders, primarily." She threaded a fishbone from between her lips with finesse and said something about body dysphoria, but I barely heard. I had a bizarre sense that someone was watching me. I turned around to meet the gaze of a pair of blank eyes. On a felt-covered stand directly behind me sat the crystal head, transparent, life-size, that was the APA's Legion of Honor trophy. My father's name was inscribed on the base. Its pupil-less eyes regarded me with antipathy. I turned around again quickly, my face burning.

I deserved the antipathy. I knew this, knew it deep in my marrow, in every red blood cell sloshing around inside that marrow.

Silent, gliding waiters in burgundy dinner jackets spirited away the dinner plates. A piano that had been tinkling continually from somewhere above us suddenly ceased. The president of the APA, short, balding Jerry Stidwell, took to the podium. He spoke, I'm not sure for how long. Time twisted. He occasionally gestured toward my father. Erskine nodded and laughed a lot, dabbing at his forehead from time to time with his folded napkin.

They were lively, loving, caring people, up here on the platform, out there in the room, people who helped others better themselves and their lives. And what had I done?

I had mishandled a seven-year-old client. The client snuffed out his sister. He had twisted the girl's neck. She didn't snap back together like a multicultural doll. With poor therapeutic technique and one lost moment, one terrible lapse in clinical detachment, one betrayal of therapeutic trust, I seemed to have nudged furious little Zach over a cliff, into damnation.

And now M. Lovely M. The sweet smart smile. The melancholy autumnal eyes. My classmate. My crush. I hadn't lifted her up with those weekly chat sessions. I hadn't been helping her at all. In fact, thinking of her now, she seemed to be sliding down. I had terminated her, I had abandoned my most treasured client.

My back prickled, I could feel that clear head's gaze. But there is a way to right my wrongs, I thought. I could still better M's lot, I explained to the head. And I wasn't talking about a talking cure. Talking had nothing to do with it.

Perhaps I could free her. Free her.

Then a thousand faces turned my way, looking like dapples of sunlight on the surface of a dark pool, like pale petunias turned toward the sun. Jerry Stidwell was calling my name.

I stood. Someone shoved the trophy at me. I took it in both hands, a palm over each ear. How cold and hard it felt. How heavy.

I set it with shaking hands on the podium. It stared back at me. The crowd stared, too. I leaned over the microphone.

"I'm Frank Lundquist." My voice boomed across the room, too loud. I pulled back a bit. "I was honored to be the first taker of the Lundquist test. I was always proud to be Baby Zero. Even more than that, I was proud to be Erskine Lundquist's son."

That sightless glassy gaze. I paused, shifted the trophy around to face the room. Then, again, I bent over the microphone. "My mother worked as a secretary at NIH, and she always said she married my dad because he was the only brilliant scientist she'd ever met there who was kinder than he was smart." Perspiration stinging my eyes. "My father won the most prestigious grants and fellowships, but he'd always let my brother beat him at Monopoly. And when I got rejected from nearly every Ph.D. program, all he said was, boy did they miss out on a good thing." My voice wavered. My father looked up at me, blinking hard. I took another deep breath. "The Lundquist test predicted a successful outcome for me, Dad. But the only outcome I've ever wanted was to be a little bit more like you."

I wasn't really aware of the applause, just a tornado of sound swirling around us as we hugged. "Gol darn it, Frank," my father said. Then he was holding his crystal head and bulbs were flashing and I was slinking off the podium and out the side door, desperate for a cool swig of water and a quiet place to think.

Think about this: perhaps I'd been focused on the wrong cure for M's woes. Forget the therapeutic fixes. I needed to give her freedom. Free her.

I had just reached the water fountains when nearby the door to the ladies' lounge swung open, and out glittered Corinne Masterson, sheathed in midnight-blue sequins, almost unrecognizable as workaday Corinne of the Counseling Center and the commissary. Snapping closed a small evening bag, she looked up, spotted me, and said, "Frank!" in a startled voice. "You look terrible! Shame, this OD, on your father's big night, and all."

"What?" I said, baffled. "What OD?"

She pursed her lips, agleam with a fresh coat of paint. "I don't believe it. She's your client. They didn't call you?"

She had been found unconscious, tanked out on a combo of Zoloft and Elavil; they'd rushed her to Hudson Valley Med Center for a pump-out, and this had all happened just an hour or so ago. Her prognosis was fifty-fifty. By the time I thanked Corinne for this news, I had to shout at her. I was already jogging across acres of red paisley wall-to-wall, searching for the exit signs.

8

Soaring above snowdrifts.

A girl in flight.

Her clothes flutter like banners, feet white in tights as her shoes drift away.

Ribbons of long hair, mermaidlike, shifting and snaking into fascinating shapes.

Limbs shifting too, at times awkward—akimbo?—but sometimes with delicious grace, in water-ballet arcs and swirls.

And her face: gently smiling. Or was that too much to ask? If so, then maybe just blank, aslumber.

Winter's pillows, piled deep, are waiting to receive her. In she sinks, creating a girl-shaped cradle.

Sleeping teen with her milk skin and silken hair spread like rays or draped across her face like strands of seaweed.

Yes, some details here are borrowed from a soft-paged book of fairy tales, bought for a quarter at a Pittsburgh yard sale.

Tales to be retold a million times.

In this particular tale, the winter sky has lost its sun, its clasp broken. The snow melt has hardened on the cold bed of the road. A sharp curve, a nervous swerve, perhaps to spare the life of some creature no one but her ever glimpsed. A nervous swerve by a new driver in a muscle car, unharnessed by brakes, riding bareback on a wild steed of machine.

A heedless car from a more reckless time. No shoulder belt to bind her down. Just a simple strap at her slender hips. The girl is free to slip loose and fly.

THE AFTERLIFE HAD A SMELL, APPARENTLY. STRONG, FLOWERY SOAP powder. Rubbing alcohol. Lemon-fresh floor wax.

And it looked different than Miranda expected. Dark with flashes of yellow and cobalt that slowly revolved in front of her eyes. Sometimes a blur of whiteness, something seen through a dozen layers of window screening, shadowy shapes drifting around.

She was surprised to hear television, but she heard it constantly—game shows, soap operas, the portentous chords that announced the nightly news. And even after death she heard the squawk of walkie-talkies and the drawling of COs complaining about their bosses and their lovers. "Why I always have to be the bad guy. She got lips and a tongue, she could speak up. Why am I always the bad guy?"

And then suddenly, the mist lifted. She was awake. She was alive. She began to cry. A bony-armed CO was slouched in a chair next to her bed. "She is up," he yelled out. A face, gold hair tamed by black bobby pins, appeared at the other side of the bed. "She sure is," the face said.

Miranda fell in love with this nurse's dark brown gaze. She fell in love with the high-pitched laughter pouring in from the room next door. In fact, she was instantly in love with every iota of matter in the living universe. The air, the light seemed to wrap her in a silky benediction. I am back, I am back, I will never leave again, she heard her brain singing. So her brain was still working. Rejoice! What a wonderful thing. She had tried to kill it, but it wouldn't die. What a fine, strong brain it was. She congratulated herself on not dying. You are so cool, she said to herself. You are fucking amazing.

Tear juice was running down into her mouth, and her nose was running. She reached up to wipe away the wetness, when her arm stopped with a clank.

Had she turned to metal, rusted, like the Tin Man? She tried her other arm. It moved an inch, then froze into place. Clank. She tried both arms again. Clank. Clank.

"Don't try to move, dear," said the nurse. "You just rest easy." She had a kind, over-made-up face, with streaks of blusher that made her look like she'd just been slapped. "You want some o.j.?" She held up a plastic cup with a lid on it. Protruding from a lid was a long, curly straw. The nurse bent the straw toward her lips. Miranda raised her head to drink. As she did, she looked down at her arms. Her wrists were circled by lustrous cuffs, which were locked onto bars that ran along the sides of the bed.

"Lemme wipe your nose," said the nurse. "Lemme get you cleaned up a bit."

As the nurse dabbed at her nostrils with a tissue, Miranda waggled her legs. They, at least, seemed to be free. "Blow," said the nurse. Miranda blew.

"I got to say. You are lucky, girl." The bony CO was speaking with the most lovely Caribbean accent.

"What happened?" Her voice rasped. She realized her throat was raw. God, it sounded good, though. She liked to hear her voice. She took another sip of the sugary, watery elixir.

"There just happened to be a ten P.M. count last night," said the CO. "On account of someone sparking up matches in her room. Safety violation, so they woke everybody up for a count.

And you didn't rise up out of that bed. Another hour or two, you'd have been long gone, girl. You are lucky."

Yeah. Miranda smiled at the ceiling tiles. I am lucky.

FOR THE NEXT DAY, SHE DIPPED IN AND OUT OF CONSCIOUSNESS, IN and out of memory. At one point, Amy stood next to her, humming a Top 40 song just under her breath—If you leave me now, you take away the very heart of me—the lyrics winding through Miranda's head. As always on a Sunday, they had listened to the countdown in the car. Now Amy stood next to her in a navy blue wool coat with electric blue fake fur around the cuffs and collar. Miranda in lace tights and a red coat with big purple buttons. Her knees prickled in the November air. She looked across the parking lot at the big Sears store and wished she was inside of it, instead of shivering up on this flatbed trailer, crowded in with her sister and mom alongside the big speakers. Down at their feet the voters' breath hung in the late afternoon air like tiny personal clouds. Green signs with white letters waved back and forth above a field of fuzzy pom-pom hats and many types of hair: GREENE FOR CONGRESS, GREENE FOR CONGRESS. A cement-colored sky hardened over bare trees by the highway.

They stood on the steel flatbed, and the cold from the metal came up through the soles of Miranda's patent leather shoes. Behind them was a gas station; every now and then, a little bell dinged as a car ran over the black tubes that snaked across the pump area. The air smelled like gasoline and the hot cider being dosed out from thermoses by the Greene for Congress ladies. Miranda tucked her chin down into her coat collar and shivered, waiting for her cue: "And what will the current inflation rates mean for our children?" At this, her father would turn to her. She shouldn't be picking her nose or scratching her bottom in her itchy tights. She should straighten up with a serious and thoughtful expression on her face that said, I am nine years old and I am worried about what inflation will mean to my future.

Her father would turn to her—his head would turn to her, anyhow, though his body still stayed square to the audience. His face would crinkle into this funny, almost sad little smile, and he would just look at her for an instant. Then his voice would drop, like he was talking just to her in their living room, but it would still travel through the mike and go booming and echoing out across the Sears parking lot. "I think about a little girl named Miranda, who in the year 2000 will turn thirty-three. She wants to be a dentist." Here, she would nod solemnly, and an appreciative chuckling would ripple through the crowds. "And why shouldn't she have her American dreams? I just want to make sure she and every other kid with that kind of good character and determination has a chance to see those dreams come true. . . ."

Then her dad was off on his river of words, the same words each time, drifting away. The weak light would be bleaching the sky. The tips of her fingers hurt in the little white gloves, her toes burned when she wiggled them. She started hopping from one foot to the other, till a hand came gently, firmly down on her shoulder, urging her to be still. Her mother's hand, gone ghostly with the cold, the big diamonds looking dull beneath this dirty slush sky.

She tried to listen for Amy's part—"My older daughter, Amy, came home from school one day asking if it were true, what she had heard at school, that the Soviets could kill every American twenty times over—why would they want to do that, Daddy? she asked me"—because when he got to that part, it meant he was nearly done and she and Amy could pile back into the station wagon and Mom would take them to the make-your-own-sundae bar at that red-roofed cafeteria near the mall. Miranda clenched and unclenched her freezing hands and stared out at the smudgy red faces in the crowd, the fidgeting bodies, the people on the fringes who broke away, uninterested, and walked off toward their cars. Those uninterested breakaway people wounded her. She felt ashamed for her father when they turned their blank backs on him and walked away.

Finally the speech came to its end, a bit of applause swirled through the field of people like a stray gust of wind through long grass, and the crowd began to scatter. She and Amy jumped off the edge of the flatbed trailer and collected the green signs that lay here and there on the blacktop and tossed them into the way back of the station wagon. She could already taste the hot caramel sauce, warm and slippery as it oozed across her tongue.

She had played out her part on the flatbed stage, just like girl actresses on TV pretend to laugh or cry. She wasn't really worried about the future. She wasn't worried about inflation, whatever that was, or the Soviets killing them all twenty times over.

In fact, she was only worried about one thing, and that thing didn't happen—not then, at least, not in the freezing November of 1976, that first time he ran for office, when all the kids in her school had the green-and-white "Greene" stickers pasted onto their textbook covers made out of grocery bags, when she acted her part on the flatbed stage, when her mother still looked happy when she smiled and shook hands and waved, when she was nine and she held her dad's hand in the voting booth and their picture was on the front page the next day and the headline made Dad shake his head in wonder. She had only one worry, during all that time: she worried that her father, who had stood up in front of all those people and asked them to like him, would lose. And everyone would see him lose, including her. And that then things would never be the same.

ONCE, WHILE ASLEEP, SHE DREAMED OF FRANK LUNDQUIST BENDING over her bed. She saw an inflection of light as his shadow fell across her face. She felt a corner of his jacket brush along her arm. This seemed quite real. She thought his breathing sounded jagged. She wanted to talk with him, but couldn't pull herself out of the freeze of sleep. I'm sorry, she wanted to say. I wronged you. I know you wanted to help me. I wish you well.

Her romance with the notion of being alive did not dim as the last of the medication ebbed from her bloodstream. On the third day she was driven back to Milford Basin in a black Ford van with tinted windows and a square-headed guard resting an automatic rifle across his lap. Her hands were bound by plastic cuffs, the Caribbean CO (Officer Aaron Smythe, from the island of Nevis, she'd learned) escorted her to her seat with formal disdain. She didn't care. She thought she might swoon from pleasure when the sun's rays stroked her face as she walked the few steps from the hospital entrance to the van. The trees had gone blowsy with July along the winding roads of the Hudson Valley, and the wildflowers blossomed in a thick, intricate blanket draping the shoulders of the parkway. They crossed the Tappan Zee; the river looked to her like cold tea, the hills dark green above it. Miranda soaked up these sights with the same intense wonder she had once felt looking at a man's face during a pristine moment of bliss.

The fat coils of razor ribbon glittering atop the chain-link fences made her heart dip a bit, though, as the van rolled down the hill and stopped at the barred entrance to the prison. The square lookout tower with its reinforced glass, the low brick buildings, the ruthlessly trim grass, the strange silence. All unchanged since the day she had arrived there the first time, just over two years before. My life still presents a problem, Miranda thought. How do I live it?

The door was slid open with a harsh roar. Miranda couldn't move. "Let's go," said the flat-topped CO, and he shoved her a bit as she clambered out of the van, and with her hands bound, she stumbled before catching her balance. She felt scalding tears gather but she wouldn't let them fall. She took a deep breath and allowed herself to be led inside.

"Goddamn, you gave me a fright." Beryl Carmona was leaning against the reception desk, eating a plum. "You okay now?" She truly looked concerned. "I'm due home, but when I heard they'd be bringing you in, I stuck around to see." She tossed the pit into a trash can and wiped her hands on her trousers. "You won't want to try that again, will you?"

"I will not."

"Good. Because you really add something to this place."

Miranda had to smile at that. "I do my best."

"You'll be under observation for a while. But you'll be back in the unit before you know it. Won't get your cell back, though, Missy May. Your girlfriend Watkins got that."

Dorcas Watkins in her spot. She had the bath mat, too, most likely. Oh, well. It hardly mattered. What mattered was this: Miranda was alive. The other issues would solve themselves, eventually.

A FOREST OF VINE-SHROUDED TREES CROWDS THE FENCE AT THE northeasternmost corner of the Milford Basin grounds. Just inside the fence crouches a small gabled cottage, brick with white trim, once a groundskeeper's residence for the estate. A snug Tudor pile, something out of Beatrix Potter. It is now the Psychiatric Satellite Unit.

The evening of her return, Miranda stood at the barred rear window of the Psych Sat's ground floor, watching the forest darken. Behind her stretched a row of six beds, made up in white sheets and pilled blankets—the dormitory where she would be housed "under observation." She marveled at the play of the breeze in the trees. This was certainly the best view of any unit in the prison.

"There's dead people in that wildness," said the teenager who occupied the bed next to hers. "Don't look out there." She wore thin gold hoops and her hair fell around them in lustrous swoops. She sat on her bed nibbling a Peppermint Pattie. "I noticed a fucking dead person out there."

"Really." Miranda studied the girl's heart-shaped face, petal-like tawny skin, and huge brown eyes. "How old are you?"

"Why do you care how old I am?" the girl said, with a shrug. She couldn't disguise a small smile, though. Miranda saw that she was flattered by the attention. The girl continued to gnaw on the candy, turning the pattie around and around, taking minute bites from its edges. She stared at Miranda the entire time, as if she might try to grab her treat.

"You're called Miranda, right?"

Miranda nodded. "What's your name?"

The girl studied her. "I know how come you're here in the Sat," she said after a moment. "You tried to OD on yourself."

Miranda bent to slip off her sneakers. "When's dinner in here?"

"This motherfucker on my unit bugged out and bit me is why I'm here. And she said she gave me her AIDS and I'll die, right? And my CO, he told me I'm lying?" Her coffee-drop eyes glittered with the memory. "So I fucking freaked and set my cell on fire." She sighed exhaustedly and lay back on her bed. "They bring the food at, like, four thirty. And don't expect Pepsi. They think Sat ladies are, like, too crazy to drink Pepsi."

"I guess I can live without Pepsi," said Miranda.

The girl licked a last splinter of chocolate off her thumb. She flopped on her side, propped her head with a bent arm. "God does not allow people who OD on themselves to be with him. Did you know that?"

"I don't know. I guess I forgot."

The girl rolled her eyes and let out a bemused snort. "You

forgot?" she said. "That's the kind of shit you shouldn't forget." She rolled onto her back again and gazed up at the ceiling, arms pillowing her head. "That motherfucker on my unit was lying. Deputy super told me, she's not carrying even a single speck of AIDS."

AFTER THE FOUR O'CLOCK COUNT SHE GOT THE UNIT'S CO, A BOW-legged woman name-tagged Jessop, to take her to the phone, which hung in a narrow alcove, once a coat closet, near the cottage's original entry. The closet door had been removed; a bare bulb hung from the ceiling. Miranda called her mother collect.

After Barb Greene accepted the charges, she began to sob. Miranda felt tears accumulating in her eyes as well, that heaviness at the base of her neck and chest. A full minute of crying on the other end of the line. Miranda stared through the burning blur in her own eyes at the wall, its thick green paint scored and scratched. By claws? By the nails of women trying to paw their way out of the Sat, through the phone lines, into the world of the living again?

"I am so sorry, Mom."

Finally, her mother spoke. "Let me conference in your father," she said. "I promised him."

The line went silent for a moment. Then a clicking, and her father started right in. "Why did you do it, Miranda, I mean I can guess why but you know we've got your appeal going—"

"My attorney said I should be realistic about my chances with that."

"Christ, that asshole," said Edward Greene.

"Edward, please. Alan believes in honesty," said Barb. There was a silence. The three of them knew that, if it hadn't been for the rather dramatic and delicate circumstances of the call, Barb likely would have added a zinger here—More than I could ever say for you, or some other line honed to a sharp point over many years.

"Miranda, please don't ever endanger yourself like that again."

"Your father's right. Please, please don't give up hope, darling. You will get out of this somehow."

"I wish I could believe that." Miranda traced the claw marks with a finger.

"It would have killed us if you . . . if they hadn't found you. First your sister—"

"I know. It was wrong. I was just . . . desperate."

Her mother was sobbing again. "I need to see you. How soon can you get visits, dear?" she said.

"They told us not while you were under observation. How long is that typically, do you have a sense for that, darling?"

"I heard maybe a month. Depends, I guess."

Jessop rapped her knuckles on the door frame by Miranda's head. "Time," she said.

"I gotta go," said Miranda.

"You have to promise us . . ." Her father's voice cracked. "Please, please don't ever do anything, try anything again."

Finally, her tears began to fall. "I promise. Believe me. I promise." She said good-bye to them and hung up. She wiped her eyes, then noticed some letters scratched into the wall just above the telephone. Hope was here.

AND MIRANDA DID HOPE. SHE COULDN'T EXPLAIN IT, BUT SHE DID. SHE lay awake that night, listening to the snoring and whimpering of her Sat mates and thinking about how she could help them, about how much she had to give. She made plans. When she was sent back to population, she would volunteer for the literacy program. She would sign up to do bed watches at the hospice.

At some point in the blackest pocket of the night, she woke. Rolled onto her side, stared out at the woods, a band of shadow beyond the brightly lit geometries of the perimeter fence. Dead people in the trees.

I'm so sorry, Amy. Please forgive.

At age thirteen, on the night of Amy's flight, Miranda had been granted a gift, the gift of extra life. The life that continued after her sister's ended. But then she became so cavalier, so careless about it. When, and why? She had, at some point, begun to treat it as a hand-me-down that might be shrugged off—dropped on the street, left in a taxi, lost forever without much consequence.

Take the case of Nicky, for example. When she'd tried to break it off with him, Nicky flipped—he had his arm around her neck, he nearly killed her. She couldn't believe this was how her life would end. So cheaply, a story for local broadcast news. Finally Nicky turned her loose, grabbed his coat, slammed the door behind him. He still wrote her letters from time to time, heartfelt missives with atrocious spelling. Why had she let it go so far?

Why?

Why not?

Dominick Scorza represented the pinnacle of her years of "why not." Why not take an Argentinian tourist from the nightclub home to her bed? Why not try the drug that a giggling girl had slipped her at a party? Why not? It was a period in which she could not think of a good answer to the question. She had broken up—painfully—with her holdover college boyfriend, she was newly twenty-four, financially stable, unattached and healthy, and could not think why she shouldn't just do anything that came to mind.

Why not, after all? Why not?

The preparations for her cousin Gaby's wedding, the first in the family's younger generation. An event. A milestone. This was February 1992. Gaby and Aunt Ruth chose bridesmaid dresses of ivory satin: boat neck, cap sleeves, sweeping tea-length skirt. They ordered the gowns from a proudly venerable shop on Madison Avenue, a padded chamber of thick gray velvet, where the saleswomen were all lofty and fair, wielding pearl-handled pens with which they recorded customers' measurements in leather-bound books. Miranda came to the shop for her fitting one evening after work. The shop was mostly empty. A languid saleswoman, hair the color of white wine, took charge of her, easing Miranda's coat off her and hanging it carefully. At the back of the shop stretched a bank of angled mirrors, curving around three round raised platforms. Having slipped on the gown in a curtained alcove, Miranda was led to the center platform. A woman with pins in her mouth kneeled on a cushion at Miranda's feet and made chalk marks at the hem. The saleswoman moved around Miranda's back and gathered the loose bodice. "A bit more snug and a tad more cleavage," she murmured. "You see?"

Miranda did see. She forgave Gaby for asking her bridesmaids to shell out two hundred dollars a pop. The seamstress smiled up at Miranda's reflection. "Good color for you," she said. The salesgirl let the bodice fall loose again, and it slipped down to reveal most of her black bra. "Think about wearing your hair up," said the white-wine goddess, deftly twisting Miranda's long locks into a coil and pinning it up with a pair of hairpins she'd pulled from a pocket. Miranda noticed a man moving at the fringes of the reflection in the mirror. She tried to pull the gown's neckline up a bit. "Don't move," barked the seamstress.

The man was maybe twenty-one, twenty-two. He wore an enormous hooded Chicago Bulls jacket, red and black, a flattop cut. In the mirror, his reflection stared at Miranda's reflection with dark eyes. He moved slowly out of the mirror's range and disappeared.

"Dominick," cried out an accented woman's voice from a back room. "You are back from break?"

"Yeah, Ms. B. What you got?"

"Go down to stock. Two crates just come in from the airport. And please don't stay out so long next time, mister."

By the time the seamstress had finished her work and Miranda was dressed in her own clothes again, the street door had been locked and the lights dimmed. The saleswoman let Miranda out. "We'll deliver the dress in four to six weeks," she said.

The street had emptied, a frigid wind made her clutch her coat. She rushed for the subway entrance. Hearing the train pulling into the station, she dashed down the stairs, purse banging her hip, barreled through the turnstile and onto the car. Someone else hurried on behind her, bumping her a bit as the doors closed. A male voice said, "Sorry."

She turned, startled to see the stock boy at close range. His eyes were light brown, rimmed with green, his skin smooth. He loomed over her. She turned away, chose a seat in the nearly deserted car. He sat down across from her, rubbing a hand across a square, stubbled jaw. He gazed at her appraisingly, his long blue-jeaned legs splayed out toward the car's middle. He wore tremendous, loosely laced work boots. She tried to avoid his eyes. She wished she had a book to read; she almost always carried a paperback in her purse, but tonight, of course, she didn't have one.

"You live downtown," he said. She glanced up at him. His glossy black hair gleamed in the overbright fluorescence.

"Yes," she said.

"I bet you're Irish," he said.

"No," she said.

"No? You look Irish. Which is a good thing."

She gave a small smile, humoring him.

"My father was half-Irish, half-Italian. My ma, she's a goddamn P.R." He leaned forward, resting his elbows on his knees. "You know that means Puerto Rican, right?"

"I know," said Miranda.

He rose up from the seat with noticeable grace and leaned across the car with his hand extended. "I'm Nicky," he said. She slowly took her hand from her coat pocket and took his hand. It was warm and he enclosed her fingers with a gentle pressure.

"Hi."

He let go of her hand and sank back into his seat. "No name from you." He grinned at her, a knowing grin. "That's fine. You can be nameless for now," he said, shoving his hands into the pockets of his pillowy jacket. He tilted his head back against the scratched window, closed his eyes. "You know, Nameless," he said, his voice low but still clearly audible over the rumble of the train. "I can still see you in that dress." He fell silent for a long moment, then opened his eyes, catching Miranda staring at him, entranced. The train slid to a grinding halt at Union Square. Miranda stood abruptly, headed for the door. He was right behind her.

She turned to him. "You are not following me," she said.

"Maybe this is my stop," he said. He put his hand in the small of her back and nudged her through the open doors and onto the platform. Stepped off behind her. The train moved on, noisily abandoning them.

"This isn't your stop," said Miranda.

"Just let me walk you home." He smiled, a lazy, practiced, lady-killing smile.

Why not?

THE TEENAGER WITH THE LARGE HOOP EARRINGS WOKE UP HOWLING when the first daylight was just beginning to filter into the Sat. "Mentiroso, mentiroso," she screeched, over and over. Other women began to catcall and curse from their beds. The girl stood up, grabbed a metal water pitcher from a stand nearby, flung it against the window bars, producing a brain-rattling clang. The night CO came running from somewhere, tried to grab the girl's arms. She turned and slashed at his face with long pale pink nails. She aimed for his eyes. He screamed. She howled in triumph and began ripping the bedclothes from her mattress. Another CO appeared, calling for help on his radio. In a minute there were four guards pinning the girl facedown to the floor, where she still screamed and struggled and bit any body part that came into tooth range. "MENTIROSO!" The guards finally got her cuffed and leg-chained. She lay panting on the linoleum. The COs dabbed at each other's wounds with paper towels.

"I got HIV, you fucks," said the girl, laughing.

"You better be lying, girl," said one of the COs.

"Fuck you," she roared. She kept screaming that, her voice growing hoarse, as they dragged her away.

The other Sat ladies were titillated by the scene. Scattered jeering. "Have fun at Marcy, baby," one cried after her. "They got men there!"

"And a pool, too!" said another woman. "That's the slickest nuthouse in the USA!" The general hilarity continued until one of the COs came back and shouted for everyone to shut up and stand for the 7 A.M. count.

After the count, with its endless radioing back and forth between the guards and the COs' constant call of "No talking during count, ladies, no talking"—which never stopped the ladies from talking—the breakfast carts arrived. Miranda, tucking her blanket under the flimsy mattress, heard someone beside her saying, "Told you so."

She turned as April wheeled a metal cart piled with little boxes of Special K cereal to a stop at the foot of her bed. "I told you you wouldn't get out of here before me. You didn't really think about leaving me alone with those bitchwomen on 109C?"

Miranda wrapped her arms around April's narrow sturdy shoulders, her smell of lemony laundry soap. Another silent oath of thanks for what she hadn't left behind. She released her, gestured at the cart. "You're not kitchen crew."

April shrugged, flashed her shy smile. "I bribed Cherie to

call in sick. An entire case of Cup-a-Soup." Then, eyes serious, amber flecked, so lovely: "I just had to see my sister. Lu said you were planning something but I told her, no way. You wouldn't."

Embers suddenly, heating her from inside out. Miranda lowered herself to her bed. Rubbed her face with her hands, trying to cool it. Gazed up at April again, noticing once more the elegant lines of her close-trimmed head, the intelligence of her eyes, the compact strength of her. What a shameful move it would have been, to desert this precious human, this small savior she relied on more than anyone she'd ever known, alone in this miserable place.

"What about your family, Miranda? Didn't you think of your mother?" Her voice scolding, heartrending.

"April. I don't know what I was thinking. You know, I just . . . you know, fifty-two years."

"So what. You gotta bloom where you are planted, my girl."

This was the ladies' favorite motto and was even painted mural-size on the wall in the gym. Miranda nodded. "I'm working on it."

"Speaking of that, they set up a new girl in Watkins's old room. Nessa. We've been walking together, a bit." She smiled shyly. "Yeah, Nessa. She's smart. Squared away."

Miranda grinned. "I see." She felt inordinately pleased.

April shook her head, bashful. "Na, that's not it. She's just a good person." She handed her two boxes of Special K. "Lu sent you the bottom one. Don't know what's in it, but leave it to open till breakfast rounds are over. I could get into real shit for that."

"Thanks." Miranda clasped her hand over April's as she took the boxes and gave her a squeeze.

April gave a firm squeeze in return. "Can't wait till you're back on the unit."

"You really think they'll send me to 109 again?" Miranda said.

April smiled back over her shoulder as she started pushing the cart. "Beryl is dying to get at you again."

When all the food carts had been trundled out of the Sat and quiet had at last returned, Jessop reading the newspaper at her station, and most of the women playing poker in a far corner, Miranda pulled off a strip of tape from the second cereal box. She fished out a tissue-wrapped packet and unrolled it to find a miniature bottle of Harveys Bristol Cream and a pristine Revlon lipstick, a rich deep red called Luminesque. Also, a square of paper, tightly folded. Miranda opened it to find a note in Lu's strange block print, which maintained a few fragments of Cyrillic. BETTER LUCK NEXT TIME MIMI, it read.

9

BE AWARE OF THE POSSIBLE EFFECTS OF ONE'S OWN MENTAL HEALTH ON ONE'S PROFESSIONAL JUDGMENT
(Principle A)

I've always been an impassioned advocate of the unconventional solution. Creative problem solving, in all its forms. I've urged my clients: Think outside the usual parameters. Break down old patterns and vicious cycles. Ditch the habitual. Take a risk.

The risk of failure cannot be avoided if the possibility of success is to have any meaning. Hasenheide, my old mentor at NYU, said it, and in the wake of M's attempt to off herself, I meant to live it.

Step 1: reestablish contact with M. This was tricky. Psych Sat was Corinne Masterson's domain, and she grew very testy if she found other shrinks skulking around in there, messing with her observation cases. Still, I managed to get into the cottage late on the third day after M was bused back from the hospital. I'd tended to her in the hospital, of course, the night of the banquet, and again all the next day. She was bleared out, under heavy sedation; I don't think she was aware.

And now that she'd returned, I wasn't sure how she'd receive me. My pulse must have topped 200 as I walked past the guard desk at the Psych Sat entrance, mumbling something about Dr. Masterson out at a meeting. In fact, I knew Corinne was playing hooky from work that afternoon to catch a Broadway matinee.

I scanned the room, weighty dark-stained beams across the ceiling, cross-paned windows and neat rows of beds along both walls. A dusty, timeworn light fell from the old white-glass pendants high above. Omit the uniformed inmates and guards, and you might have been in a dorm at a shabby but genteel women's college. I glimpsed M propped on her bed, reading a book about Eleanor Roosevelt. "Good read?" I said. She lowered the book. I felt as if a ball-peen hammer had been raised in my chest and was tapping inside the base of my throat. The other women were staring with curious hostility. I was definitely not Corinne Masterson.

Her gaze flicked, toward me, then away. "She's my new role model. A do-gooder."

"Yes, a strong woman. From what I know. A strong first lady."

Just then, a woman across the dormitory started calling out, "Where's Dr. Corinne, I need my Dr. Corinne."

A CO hurried up behind me. "Doc, do you mind dealing with Lena over there first, she's throwing a fit of some kind."

"Sure, of course, be right there." The guard headed for the yowling Lena. I turned back to M, kept my voice low: "Please come see me when you can."

A tight grimace flashed across her face. She fixed her eyes on Eleanor Roosevelt. "I don't need any more counseling, I think," she said, just above a whisper.

"Just once," I said, then turned and walked away. When I had pacified Lena and worked my way back across the room, I found her gone. I asked the CO where she'd disappeared to. "Toilet, doc," he said. "Said she needed to access the can."

AFTER I HAD BOLTED FROM THE HILTON BANQUET HALL, I HEARD later, my father stepped up to the mike and delivered an acceptance speech hailed as one of the greats in APA history: brilliant, gracious, witty. I read it recently in an old copy of the association's annual that found its way to me. The speech was all those things and more.

Accomplished parents loom over your life, am I right? As you trudge your path, you remain constantly aware of the one they forged, tracking alongside yours. But at some point, you sense that they have somehow traversed more lush, more rewarding landscapes, scaled grander mountains and attained more majestic vistas, while you have been foggily dawdling and looping around in the flats. Maybe you gain satisfaction imagining them at the heights, even as you suspect, you know, really, that you will never stand alongside them. You linger this way, marking the years, sometimes pausing your daily rounds to glance up, to contemplate their position, maybe to steep for a moment in your longing for them, until, gradually, eventually, they fade from view.

Jerry Stidwell pulled Dad aside afterward and asked if I was looking for a therapist. "He seemed . . . a bit rattled, that's all." Stidwell confided that his daughter was a performance artist: she could be seen that very night on a downtown stage in a scatological exercise she titled "Feces/Fetus." He sighed and said, "I guess it is really true what they say, Erskine. The cobbler's kids have no shoes." He thumped Dad on the back. "Tell him I've got a slot opening Tuesday evenings, and I'd love to fit him in."

After hearing Corinne's news, a frantic drive up to Hudson

Valley Med Center to bid M good-bye. And when I got there, I found her alive. I sat by her sleeping form for a long night, as the skinny-limbed CO dozed in a chair nearby. At dawn, I stepped out to the parking lot for a breath of air. Leaned against my car and stared up at her third-floor window through a glaze of relief and gratitude. Said a brief prayer of thanks to God. And to be forthright: at that time I was not a religious man. I think that on that balmy dawn I may have become one. I sensed a benign presence in that suburban lot, with its security lights clicking off and its righteous chorus of wakening birds.

Later in the morning I met Charlie Polkinghorne in the hospital hallway: whenever a suicide was attempted, it created a major paperwork headache for old Charlie. He was waiting for a vending machine to spit out a cup of hazelnut. "I don't know what to say about this one," I said as I walked up. "I swear to you that I did a thorough assessment here, and I didn't detect any suicidal ideation."

"They throw us curveballs, my friend," said Charlie sympathetically. "And sometimes we whiff."

"She scored a 2 on the Hopkins Scale, really solid. Just some anxiety. She seemed an excellent candidate for Elavil."

I was unshaven, my hair wild. He put his hand on my shoulder. "Don't sweat it, Frank. We have deep faith in you." He picked up his coffee and sipped it. "This little lady will be scurrying around the yard in no time."

He followed me into M's room. I bent over her bed for just a moment—she was still pretty zonked but I thought that maybe, just maybe, she smiled at me through the mist. I straightened up, laid my hand on her wrist. "Pulse strong, skin tone nicely roseate," I said to Charlie. "I think she'll pull out of this with a new lease on life. I'll look forward to seeing her in my office again."

Charlie nodded, solemnly surveying this sleeping beauty. "Good man, Frank. Good man."

ALL THE WAY HOME, BETWEEN UTTERING OATHS OF THANKS FOR M'S
life, I tried to think about how I would face my father after
my vanishing act. He had left worried voice-mail messages. I
decided to return to the apartment, shower and shave, pick up
some black-and-white cookies at Zabar's as a two-tone gesture of
good faith, then treat him to dinner.

I exited the elevator to find Truffle curled atop the hallway
fire extinguisher, glaring at me with accusatory eyes. The door to
the apartment stood wide open. "Hello?" I called into the living
room, tentatively. No answer. No sign of life, but the television
set was gone, its cable dangling limply from the entertainment
center. "Christ," I muttered. Clearly, some local crackheads
had ripped off the tube and fled. And in their haste, they had
dropped the remote, which lay in the center of the throw rug. I
kicked it under the couch and walked back toward my bedroom.

Then, a rustling. Coming from the bathroom. Heart
thumping, I ducked across the hall into my room, glanced
around me for a weapon, seizing on a reading lamp. I unplugged
it and held it aloft. "I'm armed," I called out, backing toward the
phone by the bed. "I'm calling the cops."

I picked up the receiver and dialed 911. The rustling in
the bath became louder. I could hear the shower curtain being
pushed aside, hear someone stepping from the tub. Then a huge
crash—a twenty-seven-inch Hitachi exploding against ceramic
tile.

"911 operator. What's your location?"

"Three sixty-six West Eighty-Fourth. There's an intruder—."

The bathroom door flew open, smacking into the wall.
A tall hunched figure, long hair, the remains of my television
heaped around his feet. "Don't, bro, please don't," he whim-
pered. "I'm holding."

"Operator, never mind." I hung up the phone. I dropped
the lamp, sat down on the bed, and exhaled, trying to catch my

breath. Clyde peered unhappily from beneath the brim of his faded Yankees cap and fiddled with the laces of his begrimed hoodie. "You got a broom?" he ventured. "I'll sweep up."

"This has got to be a new low."

"I was only gonna pawn it. I would've bought it back for you soon as I could. I swear."

I sighed. Kicked aside glass, opened my arms to him. Skeletal, my baby brother felt. Like holding a bundle of sticks. But his hair, brushing my cheek, carried memories. Our mother's hair, Colleen's hair, the same fine waves, feather-light against your skin.

And then I realized that his unlawful entry could be a very good thing. I released my embrace. "You get back in that shower. Scrub yourself up. I'll handle the mess." I hurried to the closet, pulling out a blue oxford shirt and a pair of khakis for him.

"Frank, man, I'm sorry—" I turned to see him kicking aside splinters of wood-grain plastic with a shamefaced frown. I strode over and plucked the cap off his head, then turned him and gave him a firm shove.

"Get to it," I said. "Your dear old dad is waiting."

A SULTRY JULY NIGHT, THE STREETS WERE HALF EMPTY, WE LUND-quists rocketed freely around the city in the white stretch limo. Dinner on the East Side, gelato in the Village, a spin around the Battery so Dad could tip his hat to Lady Liberty. Occasionally Clyde popped his head through the open sunroof, shouted out into the night, giving a joyful double thumbs-up to dumbstruck passersby as the limo sped past. Dad tossed his arm around Clyde's shoulders as he flopped back down into the white-leather sanctum. "The boy's still a cutup, all right."

Me, on the other hand, he regarded with pensive sympathy. When we stopped in Chinatown for a midnight snack, he prodded me with questions about my divorce. Clyde vacuumed up pot stickers. "What was the real problem with Winnie and you?" he asked delicately. "Communication problems? Lack of sexual closeness? Of course, she was away a lot. Could be an avoidance tactic, could just be her job. Hard to say."

I squirmed in my seat. "Dad, really, it just wasn't meant to be."

"You don't have a problem with me, I hope—identity problem, anger?"

"No."

"It's just—your running out last night."

"I am . . . I'm under stress at work. A patient of mine has proven . . . problematic, and it's become"—I struggled to find the words—"a bit of an obsession. I want to handle the case correctly. Maybe I'm overwrought."

He nodded sagely and spat out the shell of a salt-and-pepper shrimp. "That's just how you tested at six years old, Son. Very strong superego. Extraordinarily conscientious. A stringent follower of the rules."

I smiled weakly. "Another accurate Lundquist result. Unmatched predictive accuracy."

"Unmatched," he said, nodding. He turned to Clyde. "And then there's this boy. I do worry." My brother raised a chopstick in acknowledgment. "That bakery job, how's it going, Son? You see a future there?"

I gestured surreptitiously to Clyde, trying to get him to tug his shirt cuffs down. In his degustatory frenzy, he'd pushed them up above his elbows, and his track marks were showing. He shrank back into the sleeves. "Oh, sure, pie is always in style, Dad."

Dad didn't appear to notice the pocked arms. "I suppose that's true, Clyde," he said softly. "Pie isn't going anywhere."

"And I know how to make all the flavors of the rainbow, Dad. All of them. And then some."

THE NEXT MORNING, DAD FLEW HOME AND CLYDE MELTED BACK TO
Jimmy's, his pockets stuffed with the gift vouchers I'd bought
him, supermarkets, chicken rotisserie chains. I hoped these
would serve him better than cash. I bought myself a brand-new
Hitachi, with the latest picture-in-picture and surround sound.
Back at the Counseling Center, just before lunch, Charlie Polkinghorne called me into his office. A large framed lithograph of
Arthur Ashe adorned one wall, and dusty hanging plants hovered behind his head. "Well, it's confirmed," he said, flipping
open a file on his desk. "Investigation shows that your client, the
suicide attempt, was indeed stockpiling her medication. Saving
her daily dosage up, hiding it in her private space somewhere."
He looked up at me, thinning eyebrows knit. "Like a little pack
rat, eh?" He shook his head. "Shows a great deal of premedita-
tion. You had no clue?"

"No," I said, rubbing my unshaven scruff nervously. "I
didn't see anything in her that—"

"Relax, my friend," Charlie said. "This is strictly procedural
here, I'm not pinning anything on you. You know I need to fill
out these confounded forms for Albany."

"Right. I know." I took a deep breath.

"How did you come to recommend a shift from Zoloft to
Elavil?" he said, glancing through the file.

"Well. I suppose I just—I thought she could benefit from
a tricyclic, the Zoloft didn't seem to be hitting the right buttons
for her . . ."

"Of course, of course." Charlie scratched a few notes. "Elavil
is one of my favorite items in the toolkit. Would have done the
same myself, in all likelihood." He closed the case folder and
turned a benevolent gaze upon me. "Put this behind you now,
Frank. Remember, you are a valued member of our counseling
community."

When I returned to my office, I shut the door behind me

and stood in the center of the room. Stared for a long time at lozenges of sunshine trembling on the floor, shadow and light shaken by the hot breeze that swept in from far away upstate, perhaps as far away as Oneanta County, then down along the Hudson and across the hills of Westchester to trouble the tired lilacs outside my basement window. I tried to think back. Back to M's face as she requested "something stronger." To all the sessions that followed, when she quickly studied her medication remand as she took it from me. Stockpiling. Of course. And I had been sure that I was helping her, that we had—for Christ's sake—reached some "therapeutic stride."

She'd had her own plan.

She'd played me.

Recognized me as a mark. Her mark.

How had I allowed this to happen?

And this fucked-up notion of "freeing her." Just what were my motives here? This woman was a killer, after all.

But.

But perhaps she wasn't. Perhaps it was self-defense, an accident, a miscarriage of justice. Perhaps M was just what I'd perceived—lost and lonely, bereft, catapulted into a terrible circumstance, plummeting in painful slow motion toward a fate so dire she'd grabbed her only chance to upend it. To end it. Willing to go to any lengths, to deceive whomever she needed to deceive, in order to ease her cares, to release herself at last.

SOMEHOW, I LANDED BACK IN MY APARTMENT THAT EVENING, I HAVE no clue how. I don't remember driving down the Saw Mill, parking my car. I changed, hoisted my basketball, and wandered out to Riverside Park in a daze. The Hudson off-gassed a steamy mist, like a steam table in an old Eighth Avenue saloon. The last dog walkers meandered along the promenade. Down at the bankside courts, I began to shoot listless free throws, observed only by a mangy squirrel foraging through the trash can for its dinner. I tried to figure it all out.

The squirrel found a burger bun. A jogger pounded by. A helicopter buzzed vaguely overhead. The moon surfaced through the haze, softened, wavering, an underwater light in a murky swimming pool. And of course, the answer came to me, because it had been buried within me, just waiting for a moment of honest self-reflection.

Core concept: We age, we grow, we struggle very diligently to evolve and progress, but by some inescapable law of nature, the teenage self remains the essential self. The unalterable core. You can run from it, but it will run with you. It will follow you down every byway and basement corridor. And sometimes it will catch up to you, throw its gangly arms around you, dampen your neck with its hot breath.

I was in the grip of that high school freshman. That boy. And I was still in her thrall, still clinging to the locker-room wall, unable to tear my gaze away.

If a passing dogwalker had handed me a sketchbook, I could have drawn her wrists from memory. Delicate and knobbed, traced with veins of lavender under the ivory skin. I could have traced the arc of her eyebrows and the curve of her jaw. The tone and sheen of her hair, like copper brushed with rain.

I'd been unable to tear my gaze away, and I'd been blinded by her.

I WALKED THROUGH SECURITY WITH A STONY HEART A FEW MORNings after I saw M in the Psych Sat. Only one way to proceed, this was clear as could be. I tried not to blame myself—we in the therapist's chair are no less human than anyone else. Sometimes a client is attractive to us—we share their secrets, after all, and laugh and cry together, and our hormones aren't left behind in a box at home. Emotions arise. The intimacy of therapeutic exchange is intense. And when stirred, the therapist needs to reach deep inside for strength. Self-restraint, self-control. Self-deprivation.

I realized that I had to stay the course, stick to the decision I'd made during our last session before her overdose. Ensure no further contact with M.

I picked up my daily schedule from our receptionist, Imelda, her hair whipped up into an elongated shape, her head an exclamation point. "Hey, how are you, Doc?" She smiled.

"TBD," I said.

Continuing down the hall to my office, I glanced at the sched. The name in my 9 A.M. slot.

I looked up. She perched there, the bench outside my office door, fidgeting nervously with the ponytail fallen over one shoulder. My lungs compacted, air became blockage. "Good morning," I managed.

She rose, stepped toward me. "I'm sorry."

The irises, variegated, the spray of pale freckles. Look away, I scolded myself. "You're out of Psych Sat already?"

"I'm not. They send me back to population next week. I made a special request to come here."

I opened my office door and gestured for her to enter. Muddled morning light smudged the room's shapes. I left the overheads off. "You look much improved."

She didn't sit in the client chair. She wandered about a little as I set my papers and briefcase down. Aware of every step she made, the angle of her chin and where she rested her fingers, the corner of the cabinet, the chrome chairback.

"I'm so sorry," she said again. "I hope my . . . what happened . . . didn't cause any trouble for you."

"Well," I said carefully. "I suppose I was overly focused on my own deceptions."

She glanced up at me. She didn't seem to register this. "I

came here to apologize. For seeing you under false pretenses." She leaned one hip against the desk, looked at me with solemn eyes. "I wasn't really interested in the therapy. Getting better. I just wanted to get out."

I nodded. "Understandable," I said. Moisture—where did it come from—popped up at my hairline. The small of my back.

I took a deep breath. "And you sensed I might help you."

She raised her brows, confused.

"Because of our connection," I said.

I attempted to compose my face, but it had gone soft and hot, like warm rubber, unable to keep its shape.

She slowly lowered herself into the client chair. "So you do remember me," she said finally.

"The first second I saw you. Instantly. I knew you."

She stared at me, then lowered her eyes. "It took me a while," she whispered.

"Your locker was outside the typing room." She nodded. "You always wore this white denim jacket. And a Pegasus earring. You sat next to that friend of yours in Showalter's trig class."

"Ellen Something." She lifted her eyes to me.

"You dated Brian Fuller. You did ceramics. Your car was sort of maroon brown. A Toyota hatchback?"

"Your powers of recall are much better than mine," she said.

"You won the fifty-meter dash against Westlake."

"Jesus." She shook her head, studied her hands in her lap. "I don't remember much of anything. But vaguely . . . just your name. It had a very slight echo."

"I was shy. A shy kid." I blushed when I said this. Ridiculous. "But now you see . . . we're deep into ethical violation territory here."

She sighed. "I didn't think you knew me, but . . . I sensed you . . . I don't know. Had a soft spot for me."

"And that I'd give you the Elavil," I added, quietly.

"But now I'm so grateful it didn't work," she said. "So grateful. I just wish I knew how I'm going to live my life." Palms up in her lap, she seemed to read them for a long minute.

"So you were in my trig class." She peered up at me again. "I just cannot remember."

"I was shy back then," I heard myself whisper again. I turned away from her. Out the window, up above the shrubbery, dark-breasted rain clouds hurried east, toward the oceans. I felt the most extraordinary burning in my chest. My heart was burgeoning, a bulb of pure adrenaline. My hand came back from my brow dripping.

"M?" I said, still staring up at the window. "How about we get you out?"

Silence. I could feel her eyes on my back. I turned to her. She regarded me as if I were a stranger on the bus.

"Do you know what I'm saying." My voice had gone very low.

"Not a clue," she said.

I sank into my chair again. "I really want to help you. And we have a kind of history. Don't we?"

She didn't say anything. I stumbled on. "You were . . . you are . . . a very key person to me."

Across her cheeks, a pinkening. Rising gradually, like water through sand, grain by grain. "I'm not sure what you're saying," she said slowly.

"Truthfully, neither am I." I rubbed my jaw, trying to summon some useful words. "See, I'm at a strange moment. In my life."

She stared at me.

"I lost my practice, I'm divorced."

"A lot of people are divorced," she said. "That's nothing. Jesus, that's nothing. Look at me, for instance."

I lowered my gaze to my desktop. "That's all I can do. Look at you. Think of you. Think how I can help you. I'm feeling like I want to help you."

The silence, for a long moment, settled in around us. It enrobed us. Her, me, desk, chair, cabinet, teakettle, the entire godforsaken room.

Then I vanquished it.

"It seems that counseling is not the solution, M."

"It seems not," she said. In her eyes, then. A distant flicker, as down a deep cavern. A remote flare of—I couldn't quite see what. Alarm, maybe, or hope.

"I should just say it straight," I said.

She nodded slightly. "Please."

I leaned forward, steadied my hands on my desk. Didn't stop the shaking.

"Escape," I said. "We get you out," I said. "You escape," I said. "Out."

CHOICE

10

The snow. Surely the snow played a role. Hurled down from blackness, coming from nowhere, so otherworldly, so abundant. So transforming. The prideful city fell mute and pale. New York submitted. The snow took the upper hand.

A birthday party in Morningside Heights. This was five years ago. The weatherpeople marveled on the TV all night, cooing like new parents boasting about a robust baby. Two feet, two inches. Two feet six. And get this—two feet ten just called in from west of the Pelham Parkway. Unreal.

Only five people showed at the party. Five people and a case of so-so red wine. One of the people was Miranda, who had ridden a skidding bus uptown, balancing a boxed almond-cream cake in her mittened hands. One was the birthday girl, a graphic artist named Gillian, Miranda's favorite on her floor at Jacobs-Hahn, with her laughing, skeptical eyes and streaked hair, spiked on top, twitching like insect feelers. One was the hostess, Ann, a pretty, cuticle-nibbling painter who knew Gillian from school, and one was Gillian's boyfriend, a dandified stockbroker from Spain.

The last was Duncan McCray.

Miranda had reached the plateau of twenty-six. The why-not years were over. Nicky Scorza had given her a scare, she had been wary and abstinent since the incident with him the previous fall. She had ventured an occasional date, but kept the men at arm's length. She avoided bars, she worked, she spent evenings reading.

"—and this is Duncan. Duncan, Miranda."

He nodded. He said her name.

In the slotlike galley kitchen, taking the cake out of the box. Gillian barreled in and just managed to bang the half-broken door closed behind her, muffling the music and the sound of Ann's high-pitched giggle. "Please, please get with him so you can tell me all about it," said Gillian. "And I want every sordid detail."

"I don't have a clue what you're talking about."

"He's checking you out, Miranda. And you are definitely checking him." She leaned against the counter and grinned at her. "I can tell."

Miranda eased the cake onto a platter. "He and Ann are sitting in that big chair together."

"He's her cousin, Miranda," she said. Gillian chuckled. "I've heard legends about him. I wouldn't recommend him for long-term investment, but in the short term, oh my."

Minimetallic crashes as Miranda opened and shut Ann's drawers, searching for a knife. "I've taken a vow of celibacy."

Gillian turned and plucked a carving knife from a rack on the wall. "I can't take my eyes off him," she said, handing the blade to Miranda. "If Raf weren't here, I'd be a lost cause," said Gillian. She dipped her finger into the frosting, then licked it clean. "Yum. I love my birthday cake." She looked up at Miranda. "So are you a lost cause?"

She bisected the cake, quartered it. It was far too large for this blizzard-thinned gathering. "Truly, I'm not."

"Save your breath, Miranda." Gillian held out a plate and smiled. "You and I always go for the same kind of men. You can't fool me."

Miranda left the party alone. She thought she did. But as she turned the corner for the elevator, there he was, shrugging on a black wool coat, winding a gray scarf around his neck.

"How're you getting home?" he said.

Was it his eyes? Deep-set, darkest blue, watchful, reluctant, suppressing something, a submerged intent. She couldn't look at them for more than an instant—not long enough to accurately read them.

"I'm not sure," she said. "Whatever's running." The doors lurched apart; the elevator offered up its crimson walls and brass handrails, then welcomed and enclosed them. "How about you?" she ventured, glancing in his direction. His hair flowed just over the back of his coat collar. Brown with whispers of red. Like hers, a bit, but nicer, actually.

"I live around the corner," he said. He turned to her, caught her glance. He smiled. "If you can't make it home." To her astonishment, she felt her pulse click into a new gear. The elevator's descent seemed to be making her queasy. She looked away from him, trying to steady her breathing.

She didn't sleep with him that night. She fled into the subway, which never came, so she ended up taking an intrepid radio cab home and paying thirty bucks. He called the next day, though, and after a cursory tramp through the snowbound Village, they ended up in her apartment. She was amazed by how practiced he was; before she even noticed it, while she was still going through the pretense of making coffee, he was coming up behind her, reaching around her, undoing a button on her shirt. She carefully finished feeding water into her kettle, the stream quavering. Set down the carafe and turned to him, feeling as if her breath, maybe her soul, was abandoning her, but not caring, particularly.

There was a moment when she realized: she'd never felt anything like this, she'd never wanted anyone so much in her life. At that exact moment he stopped and held her away from him for a minute. Her breathing was ragged. He regarded her with—what was it? Detachment? Affection? "Too fast?" he murmured. "Because we don't have to fuck, you know. I could just hold you."

MIRANDA STARED AT THE CEILING OF HER CELL ALL NIGHT, THE WATER stains that, in the light filtering in from security, seemed to form a trio of sad faces. Sad, splotchy faces. She tried closing her eyes, reading, running through old radio lyrics in her head.

If you leave me now, you take away the very heart of me.

Sleep wouldn't come.

This had gone on for a week. She dragged all day. At her new job in the literacy center, she'd been nodding off as the women beside her fumbled aloud through the stories about Bill and Jan that filled "The Adult Learner." "Bill and Jan Cook," "Bill and Jan Jog," "Bill and Jan Fly." One of her tutees caught her snoozing. "See? Books are fucking boring," she said, throwing the thing down.

She could thank Frank Lundquist. The vaguely remembered schoolmate. Yes, she had tried to play him a bit, after slowly, slowly, it dawned on her. She could just about recall his name, from a roll call or class roster. Couldn't bring his face into focus, he had left no impression, apparently. Still, a name, the faintest outline of a shared history, this was something she could work with. She thought she'd play it quietly and cleverly, but he had already pinned her, long before. Recognized her from the very first moment she darkened his door.

Clearly, she was no criminal genius. This much, if nothing else, was certain. Anyhow, she'd gotten what she'd wanted, the pills, and used them, and she was glad her plan hadn't panned out. She had only decided to see him one last time, simply to apologize. To come clean with him, as part of her new leaf.

And now his preposterous proposal.

If, by some miraculous turn, he did actually succeed in realizing this bizarre idea of a prison break, what then?

Preposterous. This is the word that came to mind.

He was, apparently, a good person. Apparently, he had some concern for her well-being. And yes, she had taken note of his forearms and his large, long-tendoned hands as he turned a silly little foam basketball while they talked. Yes, she considered his face to have a certain appeal, humble and ruddy. The ruffled blond locks often gone a bit too shaggy.

She kicked at her blanket, kicked it off her bed.

She just wished she could sleep.

BACK ON C UNIT, SHE DEVISED A PERSONAL PROJECT. GATHER TO-gether the ingredients to make risotto for April. It had been her best dish when she used to cook for Duncan McCray. Now she wanted to make it for her best friend ever. Her small savior, their bond so very deep, so foundational to this life. But lately April was off. Miranda had found her sobbing in her room twice in the past week. Maybe the new arrival, Nessa, had hurt her in some way? Miranda found the girl dull and cranky, but April had seemed charmed, beguiled; she'd been all smiles around her, and mascara-widened eyes. Now something had changed, but she wouldn't say what. All she did was curl herself up tightly on her bed, bury her head in her hands, and say, "I'm scared shitless, Mimi. If I die in here, my folks won't be coming to get me. They'll bury me with the homeless. I am so scared." She wouldn't say more. She lay in her bed and wouldn't get up.

Carmona came by, saying, "You ladies better get in line, you wanna get your outside time."

"I've got cramps," sniffed April.

"All right, then. Missy May, what's your story?"

"I'm coming." Miranda reluctantly left the cell. As she joined the other ladies lined up at the unit exit, she wondered what had shaken April.

"Mimi!" Lu appeared on line beside her. "Walk with me, I'm very happy."

A triangle of white cotton knotted over her yellow hair, Lu looked like a comely factory girl from a Stalinist mural. Her swooped cheekbones and vivid turquoise eyes.

The doors to the unit swung open and the column of women, jostling and nattering, moved down the hallway. "Yes, I am happy happy today," said Lu. "Visha and little Visha are coming for a trailer visit."

"My mother's coming. Not for a trailer."

"Your mother is a beautiful lady," said Lu. "Her earrings were very pretty the time I saw her."

A cluster of COs watched them fan into the yard. The September sky, smooth and bright as blue-tinted glass, the trees surrendering a leaf here and there to yellow.

Miranda turned to her. "April is so down. I don't know why."

"We all get sad here, Mimi." Lu leaned toward her as if confiding a secret. "It is not a fabulous place." She hugged herself, rubbing her hands over her bare arms. "Getting cool. Winter will be soon. I think maybe the weather makes April sad."

"She did grow up in the Sunshine State."

"Not like me. I am from the snow." Lu frowned and surveyed the yard. The usual clusters gathered by the usual picnic tables, others on the blacktop. "Visha did a hit last week, Mimi. They cut off the guy's tongue and also balls."

"Jesus," said Miranda.

"They killed him after, of course. He was talking, they think." She shook her head and clucked in dismay. "So bad to rat. He will go to hell."

They reached the fence line path. Miranda clutched the chain link with one hand, felt dizzy, as she often did when Lu talked about her husband's exploits. This was information she did not want to know. Lu trusted her with it completely. She seemed to think that Miranda had also been a gang moll of some kind, though Miranda had tried to explain that this was not the case.

"I am going to bathe myself in Chanel number 19 gelee de bain before my trailer, Mimi. For Visha. A hot bath."

"How are you going to manage that one?" asked Miranda. There was only one bathtub in their building, in the fourth-floor health-care station's bathroom.

"My Mr. Liverwell. He will take me upstairs during count." She grinned and winked at Miranda. "I maybe give him a peek."

Miranda shook her head in wonder. Nobody worked the angles better than Lu.

"Now I will shoot basketball with the B-Unit ladies," said Lu. "Bye bye, sweet little crow." She gave Miranda a peck on either cheek and strode away across the grass, swinging her long, elegant arms.

SHE DISCOVERED SHE COULD GET BUTTER, ONIONS, AND GARLIC from one of her literacy tutees, who worked in the Zoo pantry and would steal them in return for Miranda writing out her pleas to the parole board—ordinarily, Miranda would have done this gladly without any bartered payment, but Cristal was happier not having to feel indebted; she was in for credit fraud.

Mami, queen of the unit kitchen, promised her a few bouillon cubes.

"Arborio rice and—what does this say—saffron threads?"

Barb Greene stared, mystified, at the scrap of paper Miranda had given her at their next visit. Barb had never been much of a cook. "Can I buy these things at the Safeway?"

"It'll be an adventure for you." Behind them, a family of Nigerians—an inmate and her four sisters—were singing hymns in low tones. Everyone in the visiting room, even the COs, even the children, seemed soothed by the sound.

Barb tucked the note into the pocket of her blazer. "Risotto in prison. I never would've dreamed."

Something about her face. Something about her mother's face. "I don't believe it. You had your eyes done."

Her mother pursed her lips. "I changed my hair."

"Who decided you needed plastic surgery? Alan Bloom-field?"

"Not surgery," her mother scolded. "A tiny incision. Two. Local anesthesia, in the doctor's office. It was my idea. And Alan was nothing but supportive."

"I don't think you needed it. But if it makes you feel good." She did deserve it, of course. The ordeal Miranda had inflicted upon her.

Her mother smiled. "Do I look thirty-five?"

"Mother, *I'm* almost thirty-five."

"Good grief." Barb sighed and took Miranda's hand in her own, held it there, studied it. Blessed assurance Jesus is mine, sang the women, oh what a foretaste of glory divine. "I was thinking, the other day. In January it'll be twenty years since the accident. I can't fathom that. Can you?"

"Not really. No." She put her free hand over her mother's. "Time passes so slowly in here. But it seems like Amy . . . like she was alive ten minutes ago. And I was sitting in her room watching her get ready for some dance. Homecoming maybe. That blue dress with the long sleeves."

A slight smile. "You wore it to your senior prom. In her honor."

"I did?" Miranda didn't remember, she hadn't remembered that.

Yet some memories were so precisely focused, so Technicolor, she could remember them in sense-soaked detail. The rustling as her sister and mother unfolded magenta pleated-paper flowers to hang before a birthday party. The burnt-gravy smell of TV dinners in the oven, Salisbury steak and green beans. Jingles and theme songs, naturally. Velvety tickle on fingertips brushed over flocked wallpaper. A pencil cup, painted macaroni pasted to a frozen orange juice can, sitting on her father's Rayburn Office Building desk. The names of lifeguards Amy flirted with at the beach, her bathing suit printed in shooting stars.

But the post-Amy years, the few years after: those memories were sparse. Miranda had transferred to public school, instead of continuing at Potomac Day, where she would always be known as the little sister of the dead girl. She didn't want to be singled out that way. So, though her parents had misgivings—a small school is so supportive, they said, at a big school you'll just get lost—she started at sprawling Lincoln High. She could just about remember the day, a few weeks in, when it looked like she might be cut from the track team. Her mother called the coach and he singled her out during gym class and said she could join the JV squad if she still wanted to. Barb swore she hadn't told the man about Amy's death, but Miranda knew she was lying. She could see sympathy in his eyes every time he looked her way.

And beyond that? After Frank Lundquist's confession and his preposterous proposal, she had passed hours and days trying to reconstruct those high school years, those lost post-Amy years. The whole period of her father's ill-starred second campaign, his so-called comeback: this happened when she was a freshman at Lincoln, but she couldn't recall anything. Except that she'd refused to campaign. And so had her mother.

Otherwise, those months and days were missing pages. Swept away in the wake of her sister, flying.

She did remember graduation. Wobbling onstage in too-high heels, extending a hand toward her diploma, her eyes falling on a lone figure in a dark suit, standing at the rear of the crowded auditorium, an uninvited guest. Her father. And he saw her see him, and he waved at her. A tense little gesture, a slightly tentative smile. And the burning tears that sprang to her eyes at that moment, and the tremor she felt sweep up the back of her body, into her belly, her heart. She thought she might topple, but she didn't. By the time she marched out of the room—or stumbled, in those awful heels—with the rest of the grads, he had vanished.

That image had stuck. If ever a bar or two of "Pomp and Circumstance" played somewhere, that tremor swept back into her.

HE WAYLAID HER IN A HALLWAY OUTSIDE THE EDUCATION ROOM A few weeks later, as she rushed to her tutoring job. He'd been hoping to run into her, this she could see. His white button-down snowy, one side untucked.

"Miranda," he said.

"I don't think we should talk anymore," she said.

"Wait—"

"Please leave me alone," she urged. "I'm blooming where I'm planted." She turned and continued down the deserted hall.

She heard him call her name again but she didn't turn around.

11

PARAMOUNT CONSIDERATION SHOULD BE GIVEN TO THE CLIENT WHEN INTERRUPTING THERAPY

(Standard 10.09)

As a teenager, I devoured stories about men driven by a ruling passion, a quest that dictated the hero's every move. A Patton, a Jack London, a Joe Montana. Men of action, of motivation. Men who would've shared my notch high on the Lundquist curve. Tucked in bed at night, staring past the curtains into a night sky blanched of stars by the neighborhood streetlights, I prayed that my secret mission might be revealed to me. I tried to summon laserlike direction. But instead, morning would arrive with Top 40 on the clock radio, and the days would roll out, aimlessly pinballing from one thing to the next, chemistry quizzes and driver's ed movies and people who didn't really activate the imagination. Was this life, then?

One day in seventh grade my mother dragged me to buy a pair of dress shoes for my granddad's funeral. He had been an optometrist. "So he fitted people for glasses," I said as we sat waiting for the salesman to bring me a brown brogan. "That was his purpose in life."

"Well, yes." She adjusted the blankets over baby Clyde, sleeping in his carrier on the seat beside her. "And he married your grandmother and raised Aunt Laurie and Aunt Betsy and me."

I sighed and rested my chin in my hand and watched the traffic out the wide front window, tan, blue, red, brown, blue, silver, blue. Colors repeating, a mysterious code transmitting only to me, here in this shoe store on Rockville Pike. I didn't get the point.

"Are you upset about something, Frank? Is there a girl?"

I turned back to her. "Just admit it. Nothing means anything. That's the big secret everyone's trying to hide so their kids will keep doing their homework."

She shook her head at me with a smile. "You are a darling," she said. "Do you know how much your mother loves you?"

"Come on. I'm serious."

"Look, why not suspend judgment on this one," she said. "By the time it's all over, you'll have it figured out. Or you'll forget you ever asked."

I rolled my eyes. The salesman knelt at my feet with his shoehorn. As he winched my feet into stiff, shiny lace-ups, my mother reached over and brushed my hair back from my forehead. "You are a person of immense character," she said. "It may not seem like it now, but you're going to surprise a lot of people. Just like Granddad Dan."

I have never understood what she meant by that. Who did Granddad Dan ever surprise? He lived his entire life in Baltimore, sold eyewear. As far as I could tell, the only things he ever pursued with passion were gin rummy and crabbing the inlets with a chicken neck tied to a string. But I suppose she knew things about him that I never will.

And as for me being a person of immense character? Perhaps, depending on the variety of character one has in mind.

THE DAY AFTER I PROPOSED ESCAPE TO M, WINNIE CALLED MY OFFICE from an airplane over the Gulf of Mexico. She said we needed to talk, asked me to meet at a bar on Columbus that she'd always liked. I considered the pours stingy and overpriced. But fine, I said. At least we were on speaking terms again. I'd felt sorry about the way we'd parted.

Winding down the Saw Mill River Parkway on my evening commute, I soaked myself in sounds from the seventies. Little Willie, Willie won't go home, but you can't push Willie 'round, Willie won't go. Anything to occupy my brain. Anything to distract me from my realization that a drainhole had opened in the bottom of my existence and that my heart was being tugged by suctioning, centrifugal, inexorable forces down into it and away. I had plunged into something with M. I had cast my line into dark water, and there was no spooling it back in. And I didn't know where it would end, where the string would run out, on what claw-scuttled, bone-littered floor this venture would come to rest.

This escape. And M. Maybe she, at last, was the ruling passion I'd been longing for, that directedness.

But then, more likely: M was just one more avatar of randomness. Another lurching twist of fate. A minor player from my distant past, thrown again into my life by the dumb wheel of fortune, come back to spin me dizzy then push me forward into an unknown, unwise, and probably unpleasant future.

I couldn't decide.

I didn't dare ask myself: Did I love M. Was I in love with her. Did I even really understand the concept of love, for all my counseling, my training and certifications, my attempts to heal my clients' exhaustively broken hearts.

After all, I'd gotten a late start. I'd hardly even spoken to a girl until I was about fifteen—before that, the comics rack at the drugstore held much more appeal. Then came the unrequited crush on M. And that pretty much set the template for college—I dashed myself to bits on the berms of diffidence thrown up by various unattainable fellow students. By the time I was twenty-three and living in New York, wrestling with grad work at NYU, I had given up on beauties. Instead, I allied with a series of sensible women: professional, health-conscious, with wash-and-wear haircuts and reliable birth control.

And so there was Vie, the grimly driven science reporter for the New York Times. She phoned after meeting me at a conference, asked me out for sushi, ordered for us in Japanese, quizzed me on my father's work, gave me a pretty decent blow job, and moved me into her apartment the following week. At night, in bed, while I massaged her tense buttocks, she would spin office-politics strategies aloud, baroque and ruthless scenarios worthy of a coup plot at Wehrmacht headquarters. About once a week, a superior at the paper would sneer at her in a way that would make her sob all night long. She wore huge, pearly-framed spectacles perched high on her thin nose, which gave her eyes intense, insectoid magnetism, had a ringing, sweet laugh that I heard all too rarely. She was always trying to get me to cut down on saturated fats. But what can I say—I wasn't about to give up potato chips. When we had been together nearly two years and I still was reluctant to talk marriage, Vie kicked me out.

Then came Shelby, squat and jolly, an analyst for Goldman Sachs. We met at a wine tasting in December of 1991. With an expansive circle of friends, a love of adventure, and a truly generous spirit, Shelby kept me busy. We bicycled in France, walked shelter dogs, took culinary tours of Flushing. I cheered her on through hard-fought round-robin tournaments at her racquet club in Midtown. She never made an issue of the difference in our tax brackets; she never insisted on paying for me, she let me keep my pride. Shelby had bought a cottage in Quogue with her fat bonus money, sea breezes and shingles and squeaky floorboards, where we summered together for three fairly happy seasons. Fairly happy, I say. Days at the shore with Shelby meant having her trounce me at beach volleyball and badminton, her little legs churning up the sand, her eyes narrowed with competitive zeal. I wouldn't call it fun.

I loved Shelby as a friend, but I had never felt more, and finally I had to tell her. It hurt but didn't devastate her, I think. We parted ways for a while, and then became pals again. The last time I saw her, the market was soaring and she had become the single mother of twins.

I strolled over to Columbus on the early side, posted myself at the bar, and waited for Winnie. Winnie was my last sensible woman. Capable, genuine, no stars left in her eyes after nearly a decade of New York dating—and undeniably attractive, in her way, willowy, with a pile of corkscrew curls. She happened to be a few years older than me, but we were both a bit overripe, I guess; either we would fall off the tree and rot unattended, or be picked. We picked each other—if, for no other reason, I guess, than to prevent our own wastage.

Winnie strode through the door wheeling a roller bag behind her, wearing a bread-colored pantsuit. We had a quick embrace. An awkward moment. She seemed distracted and tired.

"You look wonderful," I said.

"You look kind of yellowish," she replied. "Have you been ill? Or maybe it's just what I'm used to seeing." She sat down next to me. "I've just come from three weeks of sickly kids." She told me about her trip to a town in Guyana where ptomaine poisoning had felled a schoolful of children. I ordered a dirty martini, and for her, the usual, a club soda with a splash of pineapple juice. She plucked the straw from the glass and gnawed on it.

"So?" I said. I could tell she was full of something portentous.

"I'm getting married next week." She blinked at me.

"That was fast." I gulped the martini, welcoming the shock of it, harsh and saline, on the roof of my mouth.

"Gary wants a baby," she said.

"Yes. Well." I felt as if my bar stool had begun tilting and bobbing, like a buoy. "Marriage would be a logical first step, then."

The straw was mangled now. She dropped it on the bar. "You should have made it to that surprise party, Frank." Her voice thickened.

The surprise birthday fiesta. My idea, but she discovered it, of course; you don't hide things from Winnie. She took charge. She ordered the cake, edited the menu, chose the tequila brand for the signature cocktail. Because, she said, "You don't have the feel for social things, Frank, you're awkward in that area. All you have to do is walk me in there." Then the Fehler thing happened. I mean, that day, the day of Winnie's birthday. I forgot all about the party. She ended up having to show up alone.

"You dropped the ball."

"I didn't intend to."

"It was like a marriage of convenience with you most of the time. Like something arranged for expedience. Remember my wedding toast?"

"Let's not rehash."

A microphone in her hand, her puffy skirts ballooning around her, the band behind her in sparkling sequined bow ties. My parents standing to one side, pretending to be happy, though they didn't approve of Winnie because she had said my mother's poor housekeeping triggered her allergies, and they thought she undermined me. Her parents, pretending to be happy though they made it clear they considered me a very poor catch. I couldn't remember her toast.

"I said that I felt our union was based on sound reasoning. And that because of that, it would probably last a long, long time. I was wrong, though."

"Yes."

"Love doesn't require sound reasoning."

"No." I thought about M.

As we were leaving, Winnie turned to me. "Should I invite you?"

"Nah." I helped her on with her coat. "Probably not."

Winnie and I had lived separate lives in close quarters, and that was about all you could say for our two years of marriage. I watched television in the living room, she read in bed. She fell asleep at ten, I drifted in around two. She didn't wake when I slid into my quadrant of our California king. She'd leave for the airport in the dark before dawn, and I woke up as a bachelor, padding around the apartment boxer-shorted and alone.

AND SO I WAS AGAIN, BACK IN OUR GLOOM-FOGGED APARTMENT. Seeing Winnie had reacquainted me with certain truths. I was drawn to M, in a mysterious, and perhaps even extraordinary, way. Something about her wrapped itself around my psyche from that first moment I glimpsed her in the clattering hallway outside the typing classroom, and had never really let go. But was that enough to lead me to put my entire life at risk? I didn't have much to lose, in terms of material goods, and I had no bright future ahead. But still. This apartment, my brother and father, even the cat. I had these things.

And I had that possibility, the possibility of making the good and right choice. You get to keep that, do you not, until you let loose your final lungful of oxygen? Until then, the possibility is yours.

The sofa beckoned. Truffle appeared and stretched himself along its back, behind my head, a neck pillow, a bit rank but warm. I found an old western playing, Ride Lonesome, and stayed with it late into the night. Randolph Scott's stoic resignation seemed instructional. A life of solitude is brutal but clean.

M was the woman I had hoped for my whole life. Not sensible, not convenient. The one. Plain and simple.

But this was folly. A prison break is a federal crime. I could end up in some place much worse than the wretched prison where I now worked. An orange jumpsuit in Attica or Auburn or even Leavenworth.

I vowed I would not see her again. I would not.

Bloom where you are planted, for once in your life.

12

November unnerved her. The waning of the year. The election days of her childhood, always so fraught. The cries of geese as they fled in the V formation that seemed to her an urgent symbol, a sign of warning. Get out while you can. Get out.

On her lap, a weighty book: Pathways to Adult Literacy. She aspired to be a better tutor. On the book, a sheet of paper, carefully, neatly, detached from a legal pad, yellow with red rules. At the top of the page: Dear Ms. Hance.

And then blankness.

Down the unit, she could hear someone singing: My name is Michael, I got a nickel.

The yellow page stayed yellow and blank, devoid of what she was unable to write down.

Ms. Hance, I have died and come back. Life won't leave me, and I must live it. I understand that now, Ms. Hance.

And if, Lenore Patterson Hance, after committing unbearable wrongs, I am to live a life of any worth at all, I must be redeemed. I must be redeemed. If possible. If at all possible. If remotely possible.

Is it possible, Lenore? Is it acceptable for me to call you that? I think not, I suspect you'd hate it.

I think of him hourly, Ms. Lenore. How many brook trout did he catch, on that Saturday morning? At around six, early light, he headed up to Otego Creek, just up by the state forest, he had a spot he liked there, below the falls. He would always bring a Coke and a bag of peanuts, and that would be his breakfast Saturdays.

I remember you saying that, Ms. Hance. Ms. Hance is better, is it not?

The day after, you also said, the day after the event, we all hiked up there, we were in shock you know, me, my son Wade. And my dad, even with his bad knee, he made it up there. Peanut shells all over the bank. We picked them up, brought them home.

It was a Jif peanut butter jar, Ms. Hance. The shells were dirty and the plastic jar was smudged and clouded. Your lawyer smacked it on the table, not three feet away from me. Jif, blue top.

For you, Ms. Lenore Hance, for you, maybe there is nothing I can offer. Only just my apology every moment of my existence, and this I intend to do. In here, in the blocks and units and workrooms of Milford Basin State Correctional Facility, I will be toiling for your brother, accomplishing whatever small good deeds I can.

Would it help to know that torments fill most of my waking moments? Would you rest better hearing about the daily tragedies?

The sentence—the punishment that is my life as it is lived now—is proving effective. Even in here, my losses keep mounting, my pain multiplies, and I will not run from them. Perhaps, Ms. Hance, this information might provide a measure of peace.

THE DAY BEFORE, THEY HAD SUMMONED MIRANDA TO APRIL'S ROOM.
"She is bugging, she is freaking," Cherie had yelled.

April was standing on her bed, her fists wrapped around the window bars. She seemed to be addressing herself in a very reasonable tone.

"Hey." Miranda came up and tugged at her pants leg. "Come on down."

April turned to her and slapped her. Miranda stumbled backward.

"You don't touch a fucking sergeant at arms," said April. Her eyes were not quite set right in their sockets. Too much whiteness.

Miranda tried to remember—did she ever mention a history of seizures, or epilepsy, or God knows what?

"You hear 'Taps,' you stop and salute, even if you're in the gym or the PX parking lot. This one lady didn't stop and I reamed her out, you know. She just kept walking, and I shouted, you respect your flag, bitch!"

"April." Miranda managed to turn her from the window.

She sank to the bed. Her eyes still untethered, bright and empty. "You ever been on the subway over there? It's so fucking clean."

April buried her face into her pillow. Miranda approached her cautiously, kneeling by the bed.

Then from behind the privacy curtain, a voice. "Nicholson, who've you got in there now? I have to charge you?"

Beryl Carmona pulled the curtain aside. The Velcro gave way with a nervy rip. "No guests in the cell when the curtain is closed. Now what part of that rule is so hard to understand? Greene, you oughta know better."

"April's having a hard day," Miranda said apologetically.

"Don't you think I'd love to write up two tickets this morning?" Carmona smiled. "But I'm in a good mood. Just placed my nut bars in a gift shop upstate. I'm an entrepreneur." She hooted. "I'll be quitting this job soon enough, right, Missy May?"

"Right!" Miranda smiled so hard at Carmona she thought her face might break.

"Leave the curtain open, ladies. I don't care if you're having the worst day in world history."

"Thank you, Officer." She smiled with all the force she could, trying to get the CO to leave the room. At last Carmona moved on.

Miranda crossed quickly to the place where the guard had stood, with her big sneakered foot, her enormous foot with insteps that rolled out over the sole, just touching the little item that lay exposed on the floor. Carmona had nearly kicked it. Thank God her feet didn't feel it. Thank God she couldn't see down over her midriff.

Miranda picked up the tinfoil crack pipe and stuffed it down her shirt.

"THOSE ARE GODDAMN GOOD CIGARS." EDWARD GREENE LOOKED past her, over her shoulder, toward the security desk at the door to the visiting room. "Montecristos. You think I'll get them back?"

"No telling," said Miranda.

He shrugged, loosened his striped tie. "I forgot I had them in my pocket, tell you the truth." He smiled at her. "The old lobbyist's credo. Always carry a couple of good cigars."

Miranda attempted to return his smile but found this very difficult.

"So I learned something on my trip last week." He seemed to be trying another conversational angle. "Bahrain is a shithole." He rubbed a hand over his bald head, gazing at her. "I'm sorry it's been so long, sweetheart," he said. "You have a right to be angry, of course. It's a lot harder for me to get here than

I would have expected. Busy season. November. The elections. New faces."

Miranda was determined not to cry. "So the firm's doing well."

"Well, the Bahraini thing is a good deal." He frowned. "You look dog-tired, Miranda. How are you managing, really? Do you need anything?"

"No," she said.

"About the appeal."

"I don't want to focus on that."

He leaned toward her, lowered his voice. "Sweetie, we are looking into further options. This thing is not over."

"I need to focus on what's right in front of me."

"That judge—bad luck, what can I say. Bloomfield may be a bastard but I know he's giving a hundred and fifty percent to us. And we'll keep pushing." He nodded determinedly. "We'll keep pushing this thing up the line."

She nodded. "But please. No shady maneuvers."

The CO with the strangely twisted lips strolled up to them. "You two need to go to the bathroom? I'm escorting folks to the bathroom."

"Thank you, Officer, no." Her dad flashed a broad smile. He waited for the woman to move away again.

Then he angled himself toward Miranda, scooped her hand into his larger one. How many years since she'd held his hand? "Nothing shady. Promise." He squeezed her fingers a bit as if testing their thickness. "But to circumvent obstacles, we always have options," he said. "We just have to determine what those options are. Take it from one who knows. Find a way around the obstacle, and the obstacle disappears."

Her father looked dog-tired, too, thought Miranda as she waited at the traffic checkpoint to be searched after his visit. His decade and a half as a lobbyist, years of halfhearted prom-

ises and humbling concessions and too many twelve-ounce rib-
eyes and thirty-year whiskeys and sixteen-hour flights. All this
showed on his face. After his failed congressional comeback,
he'd signed on with one of the big K Street firms. But there'd
been clashing styles, never a great fit, Edward Greene would be
the first to admit. Then the firm was investigated for influence
peddling, and his more established partners—a former majority
whip, a former secretary of commerce—tried to set him up as
the fall guy. At least, that's how Edward Greene painted it. The
charges didn't stick, in any case. Now he ran his own firm out of
an office suite above a pasta restaurant on Connecticut Avenue.
Miranda had never been there. Alan Bloomfield said the place
smelled like Ragu.

The funny thing is, said the attorney—this was during the
trial, when Alan and Miranda had spent a lot of time locked up
in antechambers waiting for things to happen and he'd make
idle chitchat to take her mind off the disaster at hand—is that
the place is right across from the Woodley Funeral Chapel. Well,
not funny, certainly. But odd, he said. Odd. The place used to be
white brick, though, didn't it? Now they've done it over in some
godawful kind of gleaming metal, and it looks like an industrial
refrigerator. Awful.

Yes, it had been white brick; Miranda remembered it precisely, glossy white brick with black shutters to disguise it as a
charming old house instead of a place for tending to dead girls.
It must have just been freshly painted because it blinded with its
whiteness that day, an unseasonably warm January day, snow melt-
ing, little rushing river along the curb out front. Miranda waited
by the glass doors, holding them open as people arrived. She was
glad, finally, after three days of sitting around the grief-drowned
house, to have something to do. In came Amy's girlfriends with
swollen eyes, clutching little travel packs of tissues, and boys in
awkward quiet bunches. Some teachers brought ungraded papers,

art projects, Amy's last schoolwork, to be pressed into the hand of her mother or father. Grandma Rosalie, in a wheelchair. Out front, the youngest cousins fooling with the power windows in the black cars lined up for the cemetery ride.

And then she saw Neil Potocki. He passed through the door without looking her way.

Next, the strangest sound. A low screeching. And out of who knows where, her mother appeared, charging across the carpeted lobby toward him. Was that screeching coming from her? "Get out of here," she wailed. "Out." She held her hands in front of her, as if she were going to push Potocki, or wallop him, but at the last moment, they fell limply to her sides. "You are not welcome here," she said, her voice shaky. "Go."

A quiet had fallen over the lobby full of mourners. "Barbara," he said, moving his hand toward her shoulder.

She jumped back at his touch. "Don't you . . ." she said. "Eddie!" She turned and frantically scanned the dumbstruck crowd. "Where's Edward?" she demanded of some nearby relatives.

"No, no," said Neil Potocki. "Please don't bother." He turned back to Barb. "I only wanted you and Ed to know that I was thinking of you, and of Amy, on this difficult, terrible day."

"Don't you dare say her name," said Miranda's mother, and then she broke into sobs. She began to buckle, someone gathered her up, led her into the sanctuary, where an organ version of "Greensleeves"—Miranda's idea, the only song Amy had ever learned to play on the piano that gathered dust in their living room—warbled.

Potocki turned to leave. Because it was her job, Miranda opened the door for him. "Thanks, cupcake," he said, and gave her a pat on the head as he walked by.

MIRANDA AND APRIL HAD BEEN RUNNING A SATURDAY NIGHT BINGO game in Building 4D, a min-max ward where tighter security measures meant residents didn't get out much. This had been part of Miranda's new leaf. She'd heard about a once-upon-a-time bingo game up there, highly popular, run by a wealthy murderess who had been released a decade ago. Miranda decided to revive it, talked April into helping her.

The local order of nuns donated money for the cigarettes, plastic combs, toothpaste, scented soap, Twizzlers, and Butterfinger bars they used for prizes. The ladies played mostly for the cigarettes, though. Miranda could only get rid of the soaps and combs when all the smokes and then all the candy were claimed.

But this Saturday night, there would be no bingo. April had used the cigarettes and candy and soap and even the plastic combs as barter for rocks of crack. Miranda found her out in the November-hardened yard, shivering and hugging herself on the bench.

"Who are you getting it from?" she demanded.

"You'll just rat." She looked at Miranda haughtily. The skin on her face looked ashen and dry. "And what did you do with my pipe?"

"I flushed it."

"I wish I could do the same thing to you." April pulled on her lip. "I have another one, anyway."

"I hope you aren't stashing in your room, April. You know we've been having all kinds of searches."

"I can take care of myself," she said with a scowl.

"Is it Nessa? Did she do something to upset you?"

This made her laugh. Her teeth were outlined in blood.

Then Lu came striding across the yard, her hands shoved in the pockets of her windbreaker. A hand-drawn smiley face embellished the O in the printed NYS DOCS across her chest.

"She's a mess," said Miranda, her voice breaking.

Lu shook her head, bobbed hair whipping around in the

bluster. Put her hand tenderly on April's face. April glared at her. "Sweet girl," Lu said. "This shit will kill you. You want to die?"

"Sure do." April's dimmed eyes instantly brimming.

"Come lift the weights with me," said Lu, tugging on April's arm. "Who else will spot me as good as you? Please?"

"Leave me alone." She sniffled. She clasped her knees to her chest and buried her face. A small human compressed into a bundle you could easily slip into a trash bag.

Lu took Miranda's arm then and pulled her out of April's earshot. "Mimi, I can find who is giving it to her. If I have to slice their throat, I will make them stop. I will fix this trouble. Please do not worry."

That night, enraged by the lack of bingo, two ladies on 4D set fire to a bed. A schizophrenic paraplegic almost died of smoke inhalation in her wheelchair. The min-max ladies were split up and sent off to Marcy, Beacon, and a modular unit on the grounds of Altona, seven hours to the north.

THEN MIRANDA ENCOUNTERED A HEADLESS BODY IN THE HYGIENE room.

Smelling of dank concrete and overchlorination, the row of shower compartments was the grimmest part of Building 2A&B. On this day, as all others, she had come into the room just before dinner, when it was ordinarily empty. Despite the grottiness, she appreciated the respite from the noise of the unit.

A metal folding chair had been dragged into the corner, where the ceiling plaster peeled away and dangled floorward in fronds like elephant ears, exposing a grid of steam pipes, bits of insulation, and dark intermural spaces that were notorious hiding spots for contraband. On the chair tottered a headless body, on tiptoes, a skinny twist of torso and legs in baggy state pants and a black shiny shirt. The long feet were bare, and one taut arm clawed at the ceiling in a desperate fashion. The other arm appeared to be shoved up into the same hole that had swallowed the head.

Miranda stopped stock-still. But it was too late. The body had heard her enter.

"Who is it?" a voice hissed from the hole.

"Greene," she replied reluctantly.

"Greene! Help me. I'm fucking stuck up here!"

It was Dorcas Watkins. Miranda put down her soap and shampoo with a grimace. She approached the chair warily.

"What do you want me to do?"

"Help me the fuck loose!" The free arm began scrabbling at the ceiling plaster again.

Miranda climbed up on the chair, holding Watkins around the waist to steady herself. "Don't you try anything on me," muttered the stuck woman.

Miranda let go of her waist and braced herself against the top of a stall. She began breaking off bits of plaster, ducking this way and that as they dropped past her to explode on the floor.

"It's hot up in here," complained Watkins. "My neck is twisted."

"Hang on," said Miranda.

As the hole grew larger, Watkins was able to move a bit. "Okay," she muttered, "we are getting out, getting free."

A wide slab of plaster collapsed as Miranda grabbed at it. She lost her footing.

A glimpse of the head above, freed, face glittered with sweat. Miranda landed, hard, on the concrete, and as she stared up, dumbfounded, she saw Dorcas slip a white plastic bag down the front of her pants.

Twinges ricocheted through her rump and back.

Dorcas jumped off the chair and looked down on Miranda, her gleaming face hanging over her like a moon. "Thank you,

Greene." She extended her hand and Miranda took it. Dorcas pulled her up to her feet. "You tell anybody about this, I will gut you."

Miranda just glared at her and turned away. She picked her way through the plaster debris.

"You are thinking of what's in that bag and your sweet April," said Dorcas. "You might be thinking about discussing with folks you shouldn't."

Miranda chose a farther stall. Turned the faucet, which let out an alarming squeal. She didn't take off her clothes, didn't step under the water. She stood aside, listening. Suddenly an arm reached around the stall wall, Dorcas grabbed her by the hair. Miranda swung her arms, but before she could strike, her face went first through the hot spray and then smashed into the rust-striped wall. Immediately, pain, a soaring thought-obliterating pain, overtook her nose and forehead. She crumpled to the floor, clutching her hands to her face.

"You need to be more careful. You slip in the shower, you will hurt yourself. Or rat on folks. That's a dangerous lifestyle, Greene."

Miranda just lay there, slowly curling in on herself like something crustacean amid the wetness. Her blood flowed over her hands, she heard the smacking of Dorcas's feet against the cement as she left the room. The shower's weak streams patted her back in ineffectual solace.

I seek redemption now, Ms. Hance. I hope to find a path back to a meaningful life. On the yellow paper with the red lines, she had finally written this one line only, looping and teetering. But think about it. Surely Ms. Lenore Patterson Hance would not, could not, care a jot about this line of thinking, about this particular individual's search for meaning. After all. To see a sibling die because of someone else's desultory attitude toward fate, toward morality, toward life itself. Miranda knew about this. Yes.

Ms. Hance, I won't trouble you any further. Rest assured. If you rest at all, that is. Rest assured that this meaningless scrap will not be sent to the U.S. Postal Service, but instead to the refuse collection on Tuesday morning, when the scowling Opal trundles along the block with her disposable rubber gloves and her rolling bin. In it will go, Ms. Hance. You need not bother with it. You need not know how I am this day burning with a desire for absolution, how determined I am to collect some portion of it. It's November, the holidays are looming, and I will not send you a scrawled ramble or a Christmas card or anything at all but only silent tidings from this concrete box. I send you only wishes. My sincerest silent wishes for comfort and for peace in this final season of the year.

13

DO NOT EXPLOIT THOSE OVER WHOM
ONE HAS EVALUATIVE AUTHORITY
(Standard 3.08)

I abhor the term "therapeutic incest." It assumes a level of sordidness that might not exist, depending on the circumstances. It is, in fact, the term one might use, in a textbook, to diagnose what happened on November fifteenth, 1999, and in the months that followed, between M and me. But that would be a mischaracterization. The implication is all wrong.

The term brings to mind perverted uncles. And something Clyde said when he visited me. I remember Riverside Park radiant with leaf color, just before wind swept the city and stripped it all away. I buzzed him up and he came in trailed by a scrawny girl with a ferret on her shoulder and a dog collar around her neck. Clyde encircled her with an arm and said proudly, "Francie, Frank. Frank, meet Francie." He smiled. "Frank and Francie."

She peered at me from under a fringe of greenish-blond hair that framed a small, bone-white face. "Hiya," she said, in a tiny childish voice. The ferret leapt off her shoulder and scampered down the hallway toward the living room.

"Hup—there goes Luigi!" said Clyde.

Its mangy tail disappeared around a corner. Francie grabbed my arm. "He won't poop unless it's shag. You have shag?"

"No, but I do have an antisocial cat. Tell you what, it's so nice out. Why don't we take him for a stroll in the park?"

Francie hurried to the living room, then reappeared with the ferret dangling over her wrist like an elongated fur purse. "Nice stuff you've got in there," she said.

"No, nothing of value in there," I said, ushering them out. "Secondhand junk, most of it."

In the park, Luigi gamboled through the leaves that splattered the walkways with yellow and orange and red, and Francie trotted along after him, her stick legs in their zebra-striped spandex catching the afternoon light. She kept trying to get the ferret to fetch a ball. Clyde and I strolled behind them, watching.

"We met at the TB vaccination van," he said. "I saw her and I said hey, that girl's cute." He grinned at me. He appeared to be cultivating muttonchops.

"Jesus, Clyde, she couldn't be a day over sixteen."

"She said she's twenty-two, Frank," he said, "and I don't think she'd lie to me." He gave me a reproachful glance. "I mean, I saved her."

"How?"

"This priest was giving her the whole free-Greyhound-ticket-back-to-Indiana, free-Burger-King-voucher bullshit. And I turned up at Port Authority just in time to talk her off that bus."

I watched her skipping after the ferret, who plucked an onion ring from a cardboard container tossed in the gutter and shook it in his mouth. "That girl should be in algebra class."

"And every day after school she should come home to her

drunk daddy? That's a great idea." He turned to me, dead serious. "She said they were planning to sell her to the Satanic underground. That's why she ran. She tells stories that would blow your mind out if its socket."

I sighed. Once again, I'd reached that point with Clyde. The edge of reason.

"Hey," he said, abruptly brightening. "Whatever happened with you and that girl from Lincoln High?"

"She terminated treatment. I haven't had a session with her in a couple of months."

"That's probably a good thing," he said. "I was worried you had a little crush."

I laughed hollowly. "Right." I heard the girl yelling: "No no no! Luigi, no!" Up ahead, she bounced from foot to foot at the base of a telephone pole, face toward the sky. The ferret shimmied above her, sliding nimbly out along the wire. It was two hours and four hot dogs before he was lured back into her arms.

NINE A.M. ON WEDNESDAY, NOVEMBER 15. A LOW PRESSURE SYSTEM squatted over Westchester, threatening icy rain or flurries. The usual collegial banter along the hallway of the Counseling Center, Corinne and Suze teasing me about my lack of weather-ready outerwear. In my office, I hung my too-thin jacket on the back of my chair. Absentmindedly glanced over the daily sched that had been left on my blotter.

Scribbled into my 1:30 slot, as if written in blinking neon, like a signal, like a sign, like a siren screaming past me toward my future.

M, it flashed. M, it flashed. M.

What follows is a key event in my narrative. An irreversible step that launched me down a difficult path. But that path ultimately led to, as we say, a more coherent self.

Before I begin, let me call to mind the words of the greatest mental-health worker of all time. Judge not, lest ye be judged, I believe that's what he said.

The morning sessions jumbled past in a blur, and though I could make an informed guess, I'm not really certain which of my clients haunted the chair opposite. I took my custom-ary place in the cafeteria at noon, but couldn't choke down my chef's salad. Charlie and Corinne seemed to be discussing a new book by some celebrity shrink. They might have been speaking Hungarian.

At a quarter to one I was back in my office, and I sat in my vinylette throne, my hands glued to its smooth cool arms as if nailed there, staring at the door, attempting to compose myself. At exactly one thirty: a knock on the door.

She entered tentatively. I stood. The bandaged nose stunned me, of course. I felt my face go hot, and my nose throbbed in reflexive solidarity.

"This is a true surprise."

"You painted the walls," she said, looking around. "Minty."

"Admin's choice, of course, not mine. Glad you like it, though. What's with the bandage?"

"Oh, stupid thing," she said. "It's not supposed to be easy here, right?" She perched on the edge of my desk.

Her thighs were level with my eyes. Avert your gaze.

"But my appeal is in the works, my family is pursuing every avenue. So who knows. Slim hopes are still hopes, I guess. In the meantime, I might as well get some free therapy, as long as I'm here. That's what I thought." She looked at me with a strange, sad smile. "I've tried so hard to remember more about you. From back then. Lincoln."

The radiator began to rattle and moan, as if agitated by her presence.

"M." I had to ask before another minute passed. "Did you do . . . what your file says?"

"Oh," she murmured. She stared up at the ceiling, then down at her hands. The radiator sputtered. "Yes. But not like it says." I saw a tear drip from under one thick crescent of eyelash.

She turned to face me. That gaze over the gauze, vertiginous. I was plummeting. "I believe you. I know about regrets," I said. Suddenly we were so close together, I could feel her warm breath brushing my cheeks. She slid into a blurry zone, out of focus. My breathing was haphazard.

She tasted like a warm pear.

"This is not happening." She backed away.

Torrents of blood and battering heart, a rushing sound in my ears, creating not quite enough white noise to counteract the alarms in my brain. "You're right." Recouped my breath. "I'm really very sorry. It's been this way since the ninth grade." I retreated behind my desk. "I mean, I've just wanted to reach out to you, to help you."

She lowered herself into the client chair. She contemplated me for a long moment. Her face looked veiled, with the gauze.

"But this is not what I need," she said at last. "An appeal is what I need. They say I have a real shot. You could help me last in here till that."

"So the plan I proposed. It's not in play?" The three feet between us seemed to open like a sheer canyon.

Then she reached out a hand over the void. "I'm pursuing the appeal. But your plan has potential." She laid her palm on my arm for just an instant, a connection, a benediction, one second of skin on skin that I still could feel a week later.

14

NOVEMBER 1999

A mimeographed sheet was taped to the wall by the unit door:

The commissary is out of the following:
Potato chips, Fritos, Cheezits, etc. Substitute Melba Toast, rye or
  cracked wheat.
Kleenex, pocket pack. Substitute: Dinner napkins, family-size
Cookies, Oreo, Chips Ahoy, fig sandwich type. Substitute: Melba
  toast, rye or cracked wheat
Cigarettes, all brands except Virginia Slims. Substitute: Cigarettes,
  Virginia Slims
Multivitamins, generic. Substitute: none

The ladies formed a crooked line by the sign. Waiting, shouting, shoving, their dollar bills and coins clutched in their hands.

"Jojo signed me in, she signed me in second," proclaimed Vera, who was trying to take her place at the head of the line.

Cassie pushed her away. "Hell no. You go to the back."

"Friends can't sign friends up," said Jerrold Liverwell, who'd been charged with taking the ladies down to the commissary. He leaned against the door, thumbs hooked in his belt loops.

"She did it last week. Last week it was allowed."

"This week ain't last week," said Liverwell. "That's what you call the march of time."

Cassie bumped Vera with an expertly wielded hip. "Now get to the back of the line, gutter cunt."

Vera turned to Liverwell, her eyes wide. "You hear what she called me?"

Liverwell grinned. "You're an adult. Don't come crying to me like I'm your daddy."

"You wish you was my daddy."

Liverwell narrowed his eyes. "You get to the back of the goddamn line or I'll ticket your ass so fast—"

Miranda watched all this through a kind of mist. All the time a voice murmured, worming through the spaces between every other thought: You could leave all this behind. You could.

Her fracture had healed. And she felt a good deal safer. She'd taken the razor blade Chica had given her those long months and months ago and tucked it beneath the sole of her sneaker.

Lu stepped into line behind her. "You look almost smiling, my crow. Something wrong?"

Miranda shook her head. "Just thinking."

"Oh, thinking." Lu winked at her. "Good to do." She tugged on her arm. "Look who's coming here. Your nose breaker." Miranda turned around to see Dorcas Watkins joining the end of the line. Lu gazed at her thoughtfully. "This is a good moment," she whispered to Miranda. "Watch now."

Liverwell called out, "Single file, ladies. IDs out to the left," then unlocked the big unit door and swung it open, disappearing behind it. The line began to move. Lu clutched Miranda's arm and let the others pass them by until Dorcas, carefully counting her handful of money, had moved up next to them.

Lu stuck out her long leg and tripped Dorcas in midstep.

Change scattered across the floor as she tumbled to the ground, "Motherfuck—" she cried out. Before she could finish the word, Lu sashayed like a dancer, found Dorcas's sizable shining forehead and, taking a tiny step back for momentum, kicked it, planting her foot like a soccer player making a penalty shot. Gave a little grunt as she did this. Dorcas's face crumpled in pain.

"No more selling crack to my crackhead friend, no more breaking noses," said Lu, as she bent down to Dorcas's face. She picked her head up by one round ear and whacked it against the floor.

Miranda gaped. Lu looked up at her, motioned for her to contribute a kick. Miranda shook her head. "Big baby," scolded Lu. Blood trickled from Dorcas's nose. Miranda was a baby. No way she could kick anyone in the head, not even Dorcas Watkins, or slash someone with a razor blade, for that matter. She started to kneel down to help, but Lu grabbed her arm, stopping her, and called out to Liverwell, who was checking IDs as the ladies filed out the door. "Officer," cried Lu. "Wait! Officer Liverwell, this girl is sick, she hit her head!"

Liverwell looked up. "Shit." He shouted down the hallway, toward the next locked door, where the ladies had pooled up, waiting for him. "Get back here," he called. "Commissary visit is canceled, no commissary today."

A roar of outrage could be heard down the hall. Lu looked at Miranda and whispered, "You see, I told you I would fix this problem."

THE PRISON WAS COLD AT NIGHT, SO MERCILESSLY COLD. MIRANDA hugged herself into a ball, teeth chattering. Pulled all her clothes out of her shelves and arrayed them over herself, atop the bedcovers, in a mound. Lay on her side, knees to chin, watching the yellow box of light that stretched from her window trace its slow, inevitable path across her room.

Since her last meeting with Frank Lundquist she couldn't sleep. During the day, she'd turn over in her mind this idea of escape, but at night it terrified. Had she really kissed this deluded man? God help her.

In the morning, she had felt coolheaded. She had sent cash in an envelope to a company that sold lingerie by catalog. Coral-colored set, lacy bra and matching bikini.

At night, she lay wrapped in her fears and recriminations. She was thirty-two years old. She should be married by now. She'd had a proposal, once, from that college boyfriend. But there had been only one man she'd ever wanted to marry. And he had never asked. Or at least not until it was way too late.

DUNCAN McCRAY WAS A TAD BIT OBSESSED WITH FUNDING. THE reality of it, but also the concept. Funding was his favorite word. He was always in need of funding. Because he owned nightspots, three of them, in an era when such establishments could be stormed by the club crowd then shunned by it in the space of a few months. Duncan's bars weathered this period well enough, though, patronized by artists and royals of business and media who shared a taste for illegal substances. A taste Duncan obliged. Certain well-vetted dealers were waved in even as leggy models dusted in glitter powder and men in fine suits were kept waiting, grudgingly acquiescent, beyond the ropes. He always made it a point to find space for a few high-finance types, overexcited boys of low overhead and rocketing salaries, guys hooked into funding.

But for his first club, he'd found funding in a more creative fashion. "Credit cards," he'd said, gazing at Miranda, running his fingers through her hair as they lay in bed. "Other people's. Don't ever tell anyone."

He had turned up in New York in 1986, age twenty-one, still smarting from his upbringing by a menacing widowed dad in a dying Ohio town, armed only with a hospitality degree from a community college and an overgenerous helping of star quality. His first job was working the desk at the city's trendiest hotel. The uniform was an inky blue Nehru jacket that set off his eyes. In America's airport VIP lounges, businesswomen traded stories about him. He had a large following in the gay community. He collected their credit card numbers—businesswomen, show biz types, traveling sales associates, whoever—writing them down in endless lists in small notebooks when he worked the overnight shift. He wasn't sure what he'd do with them, at first. He just collected credit card numbers.

At some point later, he romanced a girl who lived in San Francisco. She wanted him to visit over Fourth of July. He was flat broke, having spent all his money on coke and high-end audio gear. He thought of the numbers. He used one to order a first-class ticket on United. Through a classified ad in the Village Voice, he sold the ticket for half price. Took the cash, bought himself an economy seat, flew to SF, saw fireworks.

Using variations on this nifty little trick, Duncan amassed a healthy cache of funding. He was canny and cautious and hid his tracks well. He knew when bill statements went out and timed things accordingly. He paid careful attention to issuing banks, steering clear of those that were particularly vigilant. Made all calls from pay phones, kept no evidence at home.

The cardholders weren't even charged. "A victimless crime is a beautiful thing," he said, smiling. "I know, I'm so fucking bad, aren't I?" He laughed, his eyes faceted with dark energy. Miranda could drift forever in them, as in deep space.

She only learned all this after they'd been entwined for a while, when she was already entirely a goner, a lost cause. In any case, she found she could shift her gaze from his misguided moments, the discomfiting elements, by simply refocusing on his eyes, face, smile, hands, and how these things made her feel.

And of course, by the time they were entwined, the credit

card scam was long over. No need for it. The bars were raking it in. And the credit companies had cracked down. You couldn't pull a scam like that anymore. Measures were in place, and new technologies.

Duncan shrugged off other women for her. "When they come on to me now, I'm just . . . blank. Not interested," he marveled. "I really never thought it would happen. I never thought I would fall in love." He put his arms around her. "You conquered me," he said.

"You conquered me first," she reminded him.

One damp night in early spring, when they had been together about a year, narcotics police in riot gear shuttered the first bar—the one that really brought in the money and kept the other two afloat. Duncan was hauled in, but released without charges the next day. A friend at City Hall, perhaps, or a nightlife-loving prosecutor with an interest in tamping down the fuss. Miranda never knew. Still, the bar was sealed, police tape binding the handles on its graffitied doors. The mortgages kept coming due; a few shadow investors asked to be cashed out.

One night Duncan turned to Miranda. "I was just thinking about this guy who came into the bar a while back. He was from upstate somewhere. A fireman. Shit-faced, and he wouldn't shut up. And he said they run this monthly casino night, it's like the only thing going up there. Brings in ten grand a month."

"That's a pile," said Miranda.

"Drunken idiot. I didn't want to hear it. Then he said people think it's all going to charity, but he's been skimming for years. Already has something over two mil tucked away. Buried somewhere, believe it or not. And he told me that."

Duncan shook his head. Back-country dumbshit.

"Said he's waiting until he has three million, then he'll just disappear."

He laughed wearily.

"That kind of funding I could use," he said.

In the middle of the night, he sat up in bed, unable to sleep. "Weird, right?" he said. "Some shit-faced fireman? I remember the name of the town," he said. "Candora."

A WINDOW IN THE TV ROOM OVERLOOKED A YOUNG OAK TREE, WHICH refused to give up its last leathery leaves to the sunny gusty day. A soap opera blared. April and Miranda sat on the windowsill, watching gray squirrels clamber up and down the tree's trunk.

"I love those goddamn squirrels," said April. "Life has so many sweet things in it." She turned to Miranda. "I'm never touching that shit again, Mimi. Not in here, not when I get out. You hear me?"

"Of course I do." A squirrel as it sat on its haunches, turning an acorn over and over between its paws as if admiring its perfection.

"Aren't you glad your pills didn't take?" said April. "Aren't you glad you're still hanging around alive?"

"Sure." Miranda smiled.

"I know I am. I don't know what I'd do in here without you."

Miranda's smile faded. She glanced at April's face, honeyed in the afternoon sun, from the side. She had the longest eyelashes. "Your parole hearing's coming up."

"Fifteenth of next month." She turned away from the window, toying with the golden bracelet around her wrist, the dangling heart. "Trying not to get all nervous."

"I think you'll get approval, though—don't you?"

"I hear the board can be tough." She looked at Miranda. "Thank the lord Carmona didn't find that pipe. You saved me, girl."

"You're going to get parole. I'm sure of it."

"I just wish you were getting out, too."

Miranda turned back to the window. Lines of dead leaves

swept across the browning grass, like ripples on a windblown water. "April," she said, "you really believe in life after death?"

"I do."

"Well, I don't. I'm pretty sure this is the only one I've got. I can't let it go to waste in here. Even if I deserve to—and I probably do—I can't let it play out that way."

"Maybe you'll get clemency or something. You never know. The appeal might take."

April wrapped Miranda then in a fierce hug, her chin resting on her shoulder, a gentle weight on a pressure point, a node of reassurance.

She longed to confide in April. Wished she could ask her what to do about Frank Lundquist. But knew she was doomed to be utterly alone with this. Once again, she was contemplating placing her fate in the hands of an extremely flawed man.

"You'll write to me about your new life," she said into April's ear. "I want to know every last detail."

FRANK LUNDQUIST SMELLED LIKE A MUSKY LIME. HE WAS WEARING aftershave for her. They hadn't touched again. She knew he wanted to. She could see that. But he seemed overwhelmed by the transgression of it. Occasionally he would wander over to her side of the desk and sort of hover near her. This made her uncomfortable. She would ask him for a cup of tea.

But this time he stayed put behind the desk, light from the basement window framing his head like a bright square halo. And he seemed pleased. "So I think I've got it," he said as she took her place in the client's chair. "I was thinking about what our obstacles are. And of course, the biggest is security." He leaned forward. "Where is security most lax?"

"Here in Counseling?" she guessed. Miranda noted that his hair was neater than usual. Grooved with comb marks like the grain on light wood.

"Wrong. I have seen you guarded by a single guard. Asleep. One single, snoring guard away from freedom."

"If that had ever happened, I probably would have made a run for it myself."

"You didn't because you weren't really there at the time."

Now he stood, glided around to her, hovered in front of her chair, leaning back against the desk. "While you were in the hospital, still drugged, I visited you. And there was one lonely CO there. And he was asleep, Miranda. And there wasn't another soul around. I could have done it. I could have done it then." His eyes searched her face. "I wish I had."

"So what's your plan, then?"

"Don't you see?" He smiled down at her. The glow from his gaze. "We'll get you another dose of Elavil. You'll kill yourself again."

Miranda shook her head. "Oh, no."

"You'll try to, I mean. And you'll time it so they find you. And when they bring you to the hospital—I'll come and get you and take you away in the dead of night."

"I promised my mother I'd never do that again." She said this with a crack in her voice. She could already see the intelligence of the plan. She hated the idea. She despised it.

"Miranda. I've thought this through and through. I think it's the best way. But if you can think of something better, I'll listen."

She looked up at him. "And then what will happen?" These words sounded tinny in her ears.

"Then we'll disappear. You and I. We'll disappear together." He crouched down in front of her, gathered up her hands in his. His eyes scanned her face. She could see how possessed he'd already become by his visions of this future.

Disappear together.

She couldn't picture it. Disappear with this person?

And yet. The lure of another life. Wipe away her whole mangled story in one night. A clean stretch of years opening ahead.

She looked at her hands resting in his. Those smaller, paler ones. Those were her hands, correct? They transmitted no sensations to her brain.

LU HAD SEEN HER, WALKING DOWN THE UNIT. DOLLED UP FOR HER meeting with Frank. Lu had stopped her, lifted a lock of her carefully arranged hair, and smelled it. "Like a plum blossom." She winked. "He will like this."

Miranda had smiled and shook her head. "You're all wrong."

Lu laughed, and in one swift move, tugged Miranda's shirt up to reveal the lacy peachy-coral bra. Miranda batted her hands away. Someone catcalled down the hallway.

Lu pulled her close and kissed her on both cheeks. Gripped her arms tightly. "This is our power, Mimi," she whispered. "We must use it. Always." Then she released her with a little shove, propelling her toward the exit doors.

15

STRIVE FOR ACCURACY, TRUTHFULNESS, AND HONESTY
(Principle C)

Risk assessment is a funny business. It comprised a large part of my work at Milford Basin. Admin needed to know: If Emilia is housed in a dormitory setting, how likely is she to pummel some-one's skull with a blunt object, as she did back in that crumbling row house in Troy? How likely is Brittni to beat her children again, if she regains custody while on parole? Should sad-eyed Minh be allowed to work in the kitchen, with its access to sharp implements, or would that simply lead her to self-laceration?

And "risk" doesn't have to be understood as a negative. The five-stage process of risk assessment (from Stage One: Specify Target Behavior to Stage Five: Specify Appropriate Monitor-ing) could be used to determine, let's say, the chances that one's spouse will show up for one's surprise birthday party, or the likelihood that one's junkie little brother will kick his demon habit.

Towl and Crighton cooked up a neat little definition in

their latest book: risk assessment is simply "the estimate of the probability of a target behavior occurring, combined with a consideration of the consequences of such occurrences."

So I'm wondering—how would the risk assessment have been calculated in my case?

If Towl and Crighton themselves had cranked my psyche through the five stages, could they have foreseen that I'd become so entangled with a client of mine? Could they have predicted that I would plan her escape? Would they have known that I would break a dozen principles of professional ethics and a few very major laws to come to her aid, to fulfill my desire for a life of true impact?

I doubt it.

Not even the Lundquist test, long considered unmatched in its accuracy, could have predicted this outcome for me, its own Baby Zero.

POOR SAD CHARLIE POLKINGHORNE. I HAD TO PLUCK HIS STRINGS, because he was my instrument. I asked him out for a drink after work. The holidays approached, the evenings came early and dark and cold. I chose a little dive by the river. He ordered rye, I ordered a beer. Mournful country music and garlands of feeble yule lights helped the mood along. We were sitting by the window, and a pulsating Santa perched above it made Charlie's face go red, then dark, red, then dark.

"Well, my ex-wife called me," I began. "She's pregnant. You know when we were together, she was all about childless by choice." This happened to be true. Winnie had phoned to wish me a happy holiday. And she had announced this news.

Charlie shook his head, glowing red. "Try not to take it personally, Frank. Some things aren't meant to be."

Pool balls were racked somewhere behind me, laughter

erupted. "I never knew what made her tick, I guess." I smiled into my beer. "And you'd think I'd be able to analyze female behavior."

"Hell," said Charlie, now darkened. "The contours of a therapist's own life are often a mystery to him, you know that."

I swigged my beer. "I do."

Charlie raised his gaze toward the bleary window. "In fact," he said, "I'm just running through a mental list of shrinks. And you know, I think I'm one of a very few that hasn't been divorced at least once."

"Takes a toll, I guess."

"I could tell you our success secret, Sheila's and mine." He took another slug of rye. "Hobbies."

"Oh?" I said. "I didn't know you had a hobby."

Washed in red light again, he nodded. "I draw from life. I hire models to come to my apartment, and I sketch them."

"Nude models?"

"Sure, nude models, Frank. It's about art, anatomy, et cetera." He shrugged. "It's good fun. It's an outlet."

"And what does Sheila do?"

"She collects rocks and minerals."

"Huh. Never knew that."

"Oh, yeah. She's got a whole pebblehound set she pals around with. She gets a charge out of it."

I finished off my beer and motioned to the waitress for another round. Fiddled with the damp paper-pulp coaster. "Charlie, I can't sleep. I lie awake and think about how I'm going to die alone."

He sighed. "Yes, well. Those sorts of fears are to be expected. It's a rough time, a transition. A stressful life event. You need something, then."

"Well, I hate to take pills. I feel like I should be able to talk myself down."

"Don't be ridiculous. Let me give you something. What do you want, Halcion? Valium?"

I hesitated for a moment. Poor old Polkinghorne. His face glowed crimson then sunk into darkness once more. He looked haggard, a crumpled, distressed version of the Cornell boy he'd once been, his colorless hair and creased cheeks. Could this cost him his job, his pension? When the whole thing busted open, could they find a way to pin some of the blame on him? But he's close to retiring, I reasoned, and I knew Sheila came from money. I decided Charlie would come through it all pretty unscathed.

The waitress set fresh drinks down on the sticky table. I picked up my beer and took a casual swig. "Actually, I was thinking Elavil. Say a few months' worth?"

I held my breath. I knew this was a major ask. But this would be enough to do the job for M, plus extra—a back-up dosage for me, just in case. Because the whole venture could go awry.

"Any way I can help, Frank," he said. "Any way I can help."

In my office two days later, M tucked pills, one at a time, beneath the bottom band of her brassiere, a pinkish-orange one, the color of a spring evening cloud. I cut my eyes away from her torso of cream, her waist, navel, the white-flag undulations.

HOW COULD I HAVE GIVEN A STORE OF PILLS TO A CLIENT WHO HAD tried to kill herself once, with the very same drug? Risk assessment. I had never seen such a strong will to live, as I saw in her eyes when we talked of her escape. I had felt it coursing through her, so powerfully, that moment I'd held her in my arms, kissed her.

It gave me the courage to overturn my life.

From that moment, I began to pass my days in a state of heightened reality. My bafflement about my function here on Earth: gone. The sense of my unfulfilled potential as the quintessential child: vanished. Now that M and I had come together, the world seemed topped by secret sauce, every moment crackled with extra sensation. Everything I saw seemed shaded with portents.

I began to plot and plan and take control as never before. That sense of mission, of success, that had been predicted by my father's test—apparently, it was manifesting. But in a way that not even the most acute scientific mind would have proposed. Born of a force that M understood down to her marrow: the thrall of dangerous love.

ON THE EVE OF THANKSGIVING DAY, I HUNTED BY CAR FOR CLYDE. Well past midnight, Stevie Wonder on the airwaves, I spotted my brother hopping from one foot to the other, looking gray with cold, on the corner of Fourteenth Street and Seventh Avenue. Socks bundled into two tattered shopping bags, cardboard-box-cum-display-table neatly collapsed and propped against a lamppost.

When he saw my car roll up at the curb, his face lit up. I leaned across and opened the passenger door. The radio spilled Wonder into the frigid thin air: I was born in Li'l Rock, had a childhood sweetheart.

"Come on, I'll spot you a burger."

"Naw, thanks, but I'm waiting for Jimmy. If I'm not here for the pickup, he gets a little pissed off." He craned his head to peer down Fourteenth. "He's running late."

"Well, at least climb in and wait. You're half frozen. And where's your hair."

He slid in and ran his hand over his newly shorn head. The top was bristly; he'd kept the truncated muttonchops on the sides. "Francie's idea. She said the long stuff was dragging my whole look down."

"So she's still around?"

"Oh, sure. We're in love."

"What about Flor?"

"She dumped me. For Jimmy." He rubbed his hands together in front of the heater vents.

"I see," I said.

"Jimmy's wife, Agata, she's a big lady with arms like George Foreman's. I wouldn't mess with her. She stays out in Forest Hills with the kids, though. Six-car garage out there. So I hear."

"I want to take you out for Thanksgiving dinner tomorrow." I hesitated. "Francie could come, too."

"Aw, that's nice, Frank, but we have plans."

"Plans? What plans could you possibly have?"

"St. Joseph's Shelter puts on a spread—turkey, stuffing, a shitload of sides. And guess who's baking twenty-five pumpkin pies?" He turned to face me and beamed proudly. "Yours truly. Francie is helping roll out the crusts."

"Oh." I must have looked really crestfallen, because he tilted his head sympathetically and said, "Maybe next year?"

"Look, Clyde. I have news." Heat exhaling around us in the car, familiar old pop tunes lending profundity and encouragement, I laid out the whole outlandish scenario. My bold plan for the next chapter of my life. I told him I wanted his help, his and Jimmy's. I said I needed to meet with his boss, that he should tell Jimmy I would pay for his help. I didn't want to trust the man, but I couldn't pull it off alone. I just hoped Clyde was lucid enough to understand the stakes.

Then the boss himself pulled up alongside us in a grimy, muffler-deprived white van, chubby faced and beetle browed, looking angry. Behind him, a bobbing cargo of wild-haired people and Mylar balloons. Clyde jumped from my car, leaned down to the open door. "I'll talk to him, Frank. I don't know if he'll go for it, he's got headaches out in Brooklyn, you know.

The Russians. That's been making him super touchy. But I'll talk to him. For you."

A hitch in his voice then startled me. I realized that his eyes had gone sad. "Happy Thanksgiving, Frank," he said, and quickly turned away. He picked up his box and his bags of socks and dashed around to the waiting van.

I watched it go, threw the car into gear, headed downtown. Before I knew it, I was driving south through Jersey on the turn-pike, my seventies station ebbing into static, my gas needle hovering just above empty. I pulled into a rest stop, filled up, then found a pay phone.

"Dad," I said. "Will you tell Irma to set a place for me?"

I followed the brilliant vein of the interstate through the night, down through the slumbering mid-Atlantic muddle, toll booths, oil tanks, random brackish rivers. Over the Delaware bridge, the moon made a guest appearance, a narrow crescent far, far above, a dimple in a face of stars.

I thought mostly of M, of course, as I drove. I pictured us living away somewhere, hidden, under assumed names, assumed identities. A room with a view of a strange city. A table, a pair of chairs. Morning sunlight, a bed. M lies asleep in the bed. I'm at the table, drinking coffee from a small cup and saucer, read-ing a book, glancing at her now and then when she stirs in her dreams.

She wakes and smiles at me. I replay it again: she wakes and smiles at me. She says my name. She says it and smiles.

It could happen. It was a possible outcome. She could utter my name with love. Even with desire.

A possible outcome indeed, but by no means guaranteed. And Towl and Crighton were no help to me here. My emotions overwhelmed any attempt at a rational assessment of probability.

It was too late for probability, anyhow. My life was becoming determinate, laserlike, directed toward M. All I could do for the others was say good-bye.

YOU NEVER SEE PICTURES OF WASHINGTON IN NOVEMBER. NO, ON the postcards it's always a hypersaturated spring, the trees all a-popping with cherry blossoms and chorus lines of red tulips ranked around the white monuments. And a blank blue American sky. I always hated this Washington. The tourist version. Jason DeMarea and Anthony Li and I used to go downtown and make fun of sightseers. We'd give them the wrong directions, and yell things like "Go home, hillbillies!" as they trundled by in those little open-air trollies that carried them up and down the mall. Anyone wearing socks with sandals got squirted by Jason's purple water pistol.

No, the Washington we lived in was not the Kodak version, especially when it was bleak November and the lawns were browned and hardened. The alabaster blended into the overcast, no one went up the lonely Washington Monument, and the workaday world of government was what counted. We had kids in our school whose dads were being held hostage in Iran. We knew moms who shopped for missile hardware and teens who spent their summers answering phones at the IRS. We didn't know the fat cats, the billionaire senators, the country-club cabinet members. We had the midlevel bureaucrats and the two-bit congressmen, or two-bit former congressmen.

My dad still lived in the split-level ranch in which I'd grown up, and in which Clyde had grown up, too, tacked to a slope just behind the high school. Tiny pink clouds like the footprints of some celestial toddler dawdled across the blanched sky as I drove into the street at dawn. The low-slung Eisenhower, Kennedy, and Johnson vintage homes were mostly dark, just a few yellow windows here and there where some early-rising cook might be rolling out dough for dinner rolls or poking fretfully at a half-defrosted turkey. I turned into the driveway. The shrubs needed pruning. They obscured the front windows. Colleen would have seen to that. Three years she'd been gone. Long enough for the yews to grow unkempt.

We called my mother by her first name. Clyde started doing this when he was about four, and it tickled her. So I started doing it, too—I was eighteen and thought it sounded urbane. It made her smile. She had that open, magnetic smile, fine-boned face framed with soft tendrils the color of milk chocolate, tender blue eyes. Tall like me, like Clyde. A looker, Erskine liked to say, she had to beat 'em off with a stick. She played the piano and sang Dylan tunes at parties, but actually, like me, she was quite shy.

She left us so suddenly. She was buried on a brutally hot July day. The service was held in the parking lot of the cemetery, despite the heat, to make it handicapped accessible. For years, she had volunteered at a home for the disabled; thirty-eight men and women in wheelchairs came to bid her farewell. Fanning out across the sun-stroked parking lot, they made a profound statement: this was a human who did good. Who had a life of true impact.

I sat in the car for a while, conjuring her. Since she died things had gone a bit haywire. Clyde, me.

It was 6:43 A.M. when I entered the house. The kitchen was lit brightly, the pink dish towels Irma crocheted glowing like fallen scraps of sunrise. My father poured me coffee. Frail, he looked, in his terry-cloth bathrobe and his peeling leather scuff slippers. He told me he'd been up all night.

"I just got so excited when you called. No way to get back to sleep. Sat up playing Solitaire and I saw a fine documentary on snakes. And Irma was up till two making that cheesy rice ring."

"She didn't have to do that."

"Well, you boys always did love that cheesy rice ring. And Irma's just so glad she's got somebody else to do for, you know."

After we'd finished the coffee, Dad said he might catch a few winks. I wandered into the living room. Nothing had changed there—same brown-and-orange carpet, same Quasar TV, same pilled plaid sofa from my school days. Propped on a bookshelf was a curling, yellowed snapshot of me, braces on my teeth and hair in my eyes, holding baby Clyde, giving him his bottle, Colleen smiling down at us from over my shoulder.

Behind that photo, in the bookshelf, a row of yearbooks. The dull foil-edged pages stuck together slightly as I leafed through the one from my freshman year. The girl's JV track team page. A team photo, and down in the corner, a solo shot of a girl running across a finish line. I tore out the page and folded it into a small square and slipped it into my shirt pocket. Then I pocketed the snapshot of Colleen and her boys, too.

I must have fallen asleep on the sofa after that. When I awoke, I heard a distant thumping. My heart? I stared at the dust-fuzzed brass hanging lamp. The window buzzed to the beat, vibrating just a bit to the rhythm. Bomp. Bomp. Bump-bump Bomp.

Go. Bears. Go Blue Bears. The annual Thanksgiving Day football face-off, Lincoln Blue Bears versus their eternal rivals, the Bulldogs of Winston Churchill, under way just down the hill. The marching band, their drums booming up through the fir trees.

Of course, we had to go, Dad and I, for old time's sake. Irma, who had cooked and cleaned for us for decades, packed us off with her native Finnish breakfast rolls in our pockets, Dad in his tweed hat and parka, me in my too-thin jacket.

We bushwhacked down across the overgrown backyard, through a thicket of saplings and bittersweet vines, just as I had every morning of my high school life. Cut across the parking lot, and I realized: here is the place where M first entered my life. And there in my mind is her little maroon-brownish Toyota, it's the start of the school day, and here she is climbing out of this begrimed compact car, her hair freshly brushed and arrayed luxuriantly across the shoulders of her white denim jacket, her just-glossed lips gleaming with sticky, watery brilliance in the morning sun, her jeans patched adorably with scraps of calico. A fringed suede shoulder bag dancing as she walks. The soft planes of her face, the expression carefully aloof but so alive to everything around. So intelligent, so deep. And the double-pierced ear, daring, just a bit on the edge. And there I am, gawking, unable to muster up even a "nice day, huh?" Just watching her walk on by.

She always just walked on by, that girl. And now? We had climbed into a barrel together, and we were about to go over the falls.

Dad and I climbed the bleachers, rising through the throb of the marching band playing from their seats in the lower ranks, up through the mist of popcorn and hot-dog vapors. And this funny thing happened: I felt a great sore lump growing in my throat.

This kind of all-American normalcy, this scene from our hometown, would be forever out of reach for us, for M and me. These whooping pom-pom girls, these pimpled boys and backslapping dads, were drowned deep in the moment. Truly concerned about the game, truly swept up in the pageantry. They abided by the laws of this nation. They loved this nation.

But so do I. So did I.

I just loved M more, that's all.

And that meant good-bye to all this. Good-bye.

It was already nearly halftime, and the Bears were ahead,

thirteen to seven. "This QB this year is supposed to be cracker-jack," my dad said. "Maybe as good as that kid your year. Bush-miller. You know he retired from the pros?"

Cheerleaders flipped, flashing round, stockinged thighs.

"Dad," I said. "I wish I could have made you more proud."

He turned to me. His hat shaded his eyes under their un-ruly white brows. "You've made me plenty proud. Even as a child, look how well you did, the test. And since then, of course. I've always been proud of you."

"I wish I could have been a better therapist. The Fehler case—"

"Could've happened to anybody, Frank."

"It never happened to you." An emphatic buzz ended the half. The hotshot quarterback tossed the ball to a ref.

"I never got out of the lab. That's why. I just stayed in the lab." My dad tapped his knuckles on my knee. "You're out in the world."

The marching band surged into center field, tuba swinging this way and that, a high-hatted boy plucking an electric bass, trailed by a kid pushing the amp in a wheelbarrow. All of them to-gether made an astonishing noise, a blurting and blaring so loud it might've been heard clear across the Potomac, like a Civil War bombardment. We sat side by side, pummeled by it.

The lab did consume him, those long years before Clyde was born. I'd been an only child back then, and the truth is, most of my memories of my father from that time revolve around departures. Him leaving in the morning, tousling my hair. Buy-ing me gum at the airport when we'd go to see him off. Dad driving the station wagon, dropping me and my friends at the Rockville Pike roller rink while he headed back to the lab on a Sunday afternoon. Of course, we spent hours together when he tested me and perfected the Lundquist, but sadly, I was so tiny, I don't recall those hours at all.

A pickup truck from Harry's Donuts drove onto the field, as two boys, chosen for their donut-hurling prowess, whizzed cinnamon pastries into the stands. "Hey, look," said my father. "They're still doing the bear claw toss!"

A donut flew toward us. "Grab it!" someone shouted.

"I don't know when I'm going to see you again," I said.

He glanced at me quickly. "What? Why?" Then he lunged for another bear claw, coming his way. He stretched to make the catch, then lost his balance. He started to tip, stumbling over the steep stairs of the aisle.

Too late, I reached for him. A few folks had already clustered around him. I could hear a low wheezing moan.

"He's my father," I yelped. "Let me see him."

Dad's face was twisted with pain. "Where are you going?" he whispered to me. "Are you going away?" Far off, down on the field, the band began to play "Luck Be a Lady Tonight." A teenage girl tapped me on the shoulder and pressed something into my hand. "Here's my Startac," she said. "Call 911."

16

NOVEMBER 1999

April Toni Nicholson was the dearest friend Miranda had ever had. A connection stronger, deeper, closer than hers with Gillian in New York, or with any of the girls she'd met in school. To be a friend in the poisoned realm of corrections—to be a true friend there—called for a profound level of fellowship, a mighty flexing of love and grace. And April gave that to Miranda, and Miranda gathered it up gratefully.

They shared more, backgroundwise, than one would have thought. As they talked away their days, when Miranda first appeared on the unit and April first befriended her, they discovered that they both came of age in worlds that demanded a household's public image be as groomed as its front lawn: April's father an enlisted man striving to climb the rungs of rank in the navy, Miranda's a politician shouldering his way into office. Both women's downfalls had been public-relations disasters for their families, but with a crucial distinction: April's father had not forgiven his daughter; Miranda's had, because he understood a thing or two about transgression.

In time, April grew to love Miranda like a sibling. "I only ever had three brothers, so you are my one-and-only sister," she'd say in her plush Pensacola lilt. Miranda loved April like that, too. As a second sister. At least as much as she dared.

Holidays, April and Miranda tended to cling together; they saved up new magazines and a few nice things to eat, to make the day pass easier. For Thanksgiving, along with the risotto Miranda had at last managed to pull together, April secured a can of cranberry sauce and a box of Lorna Doone cookies. Neither of them cared for turkey. They agreed it was all about the cranberries.

Which made it even stranger that April didn't live to see the day. Strange that she would succumb on the eve of the feast. Strange that she would ingest so much crystallized cocaine so fast that the drug convulsed her heart. Wrenched that small vital pouch inside out.

Thanksgiving dawn, she was cold and hardening in her cell. The prison went into lockdown. The COs' turkey buffet was canceled.

Miranda saw them roll April away in a black rubber body bag, NY STATE DOCS stenciled on the side, a fat silver zipper slithered up its center like a rivulet of mercury.

She lay huddled in bed for the better part of the next three days, thinking of the Elavil hidden in a hollow plastic hanger. That last overdose had scrambled her soul, and though she'd accepted the pills from Frank Lundquist, she'd not yet accepted his plan. She hadn't yet been able to swallow this idea, the second suicide. But now she felt herself wavering. To gulp them down, to sleep. Forget the unhinged talk of escape. In the end, perhaps, wouldn't it be so much simpler to dream this place away. Forever.

BUT INSTEAD, SHE HEARD HER NAME BEING BARKED OVER THE PA system. "Greene to unit exit 3."

She sat up, stepped into her sneakers, heard Carmona's shuffling footsteps, then her blocky form damming up the light. "We're locked down, but they say to let you out. Are you pulling strings on me, Missy, or what?" The dead bolts thunked and Carmona swung the door open. "Don't you think I've got enough to do with the dead girls around here?"

Miranda flinched, Carmona saw this. She lowered her voice. "I know she was your friend. We'll find out who's bringing that shit in. Get down to visiting. It must be someone, hauling you out of lock."

For a hallucinatory moment, Miranda thought it might be the governor, maybe even the president, come to pardon her. She hurried down the unit, clutching her ID in a damp hand. Carmona buzzed her out.

She burst through the doors to visiting traffic. There was an inmate already waiting to be processed there, and the station was deserted. As she hurried closer, Miranda was astonished to recognize Lu. "Aren't you in lockdown?" she said, coming up behind her.

Lu spun around. "Mimi!" She blinked, stunned. "I am waiting for a CO. One called me out. Don't know which. You didn't tell them about what I did to that Dorcas, you didn't say something, you didn't, did you?"

"Of course not," said Miranda, a little put out that Lu would even suggest such a thing.

"I know you didn't, baby. I'm crazy because why does some CO want to see me? Oh, Mimi, this about April, I am so sad and I am so sorry." Lu shook her head and seemed to be having a hard time catching her breath.

Miranda lowered her eyes and shook her head. "Can't talk about it, Lu. Please, let's not."

"I understand, sweet little one. I do." Lu squeezed her arm. "We will talk later. Now why are you out of lock?"

"I was called to visiting."

"And for this they let you out of lock? Must be some big deal."

Miranda shrugged, looking over Lu's shoulder as Jerrold Liverwell came out of the men's room on the far side of the gate and ambled toward them, clutching his keys. "I don't have a clue," she said. "And here comes your CO."

HOW COMPLETELY OUT OF CONTEXT HE WAS. PERCHED ON A STOOL far too small for him at a long table, in the empty visiting room ablaze with too much light, in a gray suit that fit so perfectly he looked vacuum packed. If she hadn't seen him there next to Edward Greene, if she hadn't seen him in the company of her father, she likely would not have recognized him. When was the last time she'd seen him? The funeral.

Of course, she easily recalled the first time. Nineteen seventy-six, a room in the Pittsburgh Hilton, Edward Greene's very first election night. The returns were coming in. Greene up by thirty-five points in Homestead, Greene sweeping West Mifflin. Miranda and Amy bounced from bed to bed, rebounding high enough for fingertips to graze the ceiling, while the grown-ups milled around hugging and splashing their fizzy cocktails on the rug. Barb sat at the desk near the TV, peering into a compact mirror, touching up her makeup for the victory rally. Blusher, mascara, powder, lipstick. Miranda loved to watch her. And then she had to go pee, and she rounded the corner to the bathroom.

And there she saw her father open the door to the hotel hallway, and out of that glittering, gold-carpeted realm glided this man, a chubby man in a tight brown suit, the skin on his face shiny and smooth in spots, slightly nicked in others, a face like an unfrosted cake. In his arms, he held a big box. Her father thumped him on the shoulder—"Hey, great to see you"—and helped him set the box on the floor.

"Asti Spumante. Short notice, best I could get, in this shit-hole city of ours," said the brown suit. He glanced up and saw Miranda then. He winked at her. "Excuse my French, cupcake."

Her father turned. "What do you want, honey? You need to go?" He nudged her toward the bathroom. "Come in and have a drink, Neil," he said, turning back to the brown man. "I know we've got talking to do."

"Time for that later," the man said. "Lots to come." Just before she shut the bathroom door, she saw the man reach out and straighten her dad's tie. "Told you you'd be pulling down some numbers, right?" he said. When she came out, the man had gone, her dad parading around with an open bottle in each hand, Asti for everyone. Amy and Miranda got to share a glass, filled with little frightened bubbles that tasted like pinpricks, and they finished the whole thing.

Months later, on the TV in the house on Holloway Drive, they glimpsed the man with the Asti Spumante and the ice-blue car. He had bid on the Steelers, said the woman reading the news. She called him a "mogul."

"What's a mogul?" asked Miranda.

"It means a businessman," said Amy. "He owns most of Pennsylvania."

"Including a few of its most prominent representatives," said her mother.

Nineteen seventy-eight. The campaigning in the cold again. Miranda didn't mind it so much, but for Amy it was agony. The humiliation of standing up there, midpuberty, in front of gawking crowds, wearing clothes she hated, they were either too little-girly, she said, or else too grown-up. Wave and smile and flash her braces. It had been awful for Amy, but Miranda had been even more worried about her father. She could see sweat on him, and she noticed that sometimes the crowds were smaller than the last go-around and so she understood that things weren't going so well this time. Between these speeches, they'd camp out in the chilly, half-empty Pittsburgh house—"three years on the market and not a nibble," her mom said every time they pulled up into the driveway. In the musty paneled rec room, over plodding games of Sorry, Miranda and Amy could hear everything. Terrible sentences leaked down the stairs and through the vents. Her mother and father in the kitchen with Mr. Bloomfield who was always around. "What's happening to him, Alan? Look at those numbers."

"No ads, no numbers," said Mr. Bloomfield, calmer.

"Why in Christ's name won't he cough up something?" said Edward Greene. "What did I do wrong? I thought he was happy."

"I've tried to explain it to you. It's not that you've done anything wrong. It's just that Denny Hilyard has done more things right."

"What did he do?" Her father was yelling now. "Blow him? Christ," he said, his voice climbing. "I'll get on my knees and blow him, if that's what it takes."

"Edward. Even if Potocki rolled out fifty grand tonight, I don't see a road map. You need to start getting your head straight about other scenarios."

"Get him on the phone."

"Won't take your calls, Ed. I've tried, believe me."

What was that noise then? Was it her father sobbing?

"I'm not moving back to Pittsburgh, Eddie." How furious her mom sounded.

"He'll find ample opportunities in D.C.," said Mr. Bloomfield. "Ample."

AT SOME POINT AFTER HIS LOSS, HER FATHER APPARENTLY PATCHED things up with Neil Potocki. Two years and two months later, in January 1981, they were all eating little cups of beef stew at his Super Bowl party in the Virginia hunt country. And nearly nineteen years after that, Miranda sat down across from the two men in the Milford Basin visiting room.

"You're looking well," Potocki offered with a faint smile.

"Mr. Potocki's in a hurry," said Edward Greene. "We have some wonderful news for you."

"Really?"

Potocki folded his arms across his chest, exposing a dull gold timepiece strapped to one wrist. "I have close ties with your governor here in New York, dear. Your father came to me, and as an old friend, I feel it's only right to do what I can."

Miranda stared at him.

"Isn't that terrific? What Mr. Potocki here's proposing."

"I'm not promising anything, you understand." The deepness under his eyes, the many folds laden with dark information. "It may take some time, even years. But he does owe me a favor or two, the governor."

Miranda shifted uneasily in her chair. "I don't know what to say."

"No thanks necessary." Potocki rose. With a casual air, he laid a hand high on her father's shoulder, almost on his neck. "I know your dad would do the same for me. We're dropping you at the airport, Edward?" He removed his hand then, straightened his suit, and gently checked his airy puff of gray-brown hair. "I'll let you two have some time alone."

They both watched him stride through the visiting room, past the curious glances of two COs who, in their admiration, neglected to sign him out. Her father turned to her.

"Well?"

"No."

He shifted back in his chair and frowned at the floor for a long moment. "Listen, Miranda," he said finally. "Your sister died a long time ago. This is about now. Don't you see what this is about?" He leaned forward. "You're wasting away."

At this, burning drops careened down the slopes of her cheeks. She swiped at them with the back of her hand. "You thought I'd agree to this."

"You're hardly in a position to stand on principle, it would seem." Edward Greene's gaze took in the grim room, the grim point on Earth that they'd ended up occupying together. "Listen to reason, Miranda. Be practical."

"Like you?"

"Yes." He sat back, away from her, face hazy with weariness. "Like me."

Just then a CO called out to him. "Sir, the driver's out there, says your ride's leaving."

"Go," she said, wiping at her tears, so sticky and thick they clung to her hands like sap.

MIRANDA STOOD ONCE AGAIN AT THE WINDOW IN THE TV ROOM, April's squirrels once again flinging themselves around the slender young oak. She didn't see the squirrels.

Instead, her father in 1978. Before the concession speech, pacing by the hotel-room window, spewing curses out over the disorderly vista of Pittsburgh, his shirt untucked in back, while her mother struggled to get the wrinkles out of his jacket, phoning for room service to bring up an iron.

Instead, April. Looking up every time the mail cart came, weeping through old hymns during Sunday morning worship. When Miranda had returned from visiting, someone on the unit told her that they'd heard April's family had refused to accept her body. The ladies whispered that she was being cremated and stored in a government locker.

Instead, Frank Lundquist. And Neil Potocki.

A sparrow perched on the sill outside sensed her presence through the glass, startled off the ledge, and shot out of sight.

And then she saw the Oshandaga River. A bridge, a little

rickety old two-lane bridge three miles outside of Candora. Lit by a single weak moth-bothered streetlight. Slowly, the car rolled to a stop there. She couldn't grasp what she'd just witnessed, what she'd just done. Then she looked down at the seat next to her. Gun. She picked it up, so heavy against her hand, metal just slightly raw, rough. A low-end, bargain-priced gun, she presumed. She slid out of the car. There wasn't a sound but the whine of crickets. She crossed to the railing of the bridge and leaned over. She didn't see the thing after it left her hand, but then in a heartbeat she heard it—plunk—and she glimpsed a small white break, like a tiny flower blooming briefly in the darkness below her feet.

She walked to her car and leaned back against the hood, cool and hard in the night air. She could feel the day's heat, stored in the pavement, seep up through the soles of her shoes. She rested there, both cooled and warmed, and waited for the next thing to happen.

17

DO NOT ENGAGE IN SEXUAL INTIMACIES
WITH CURRENT CLIENTS
(Standard 10.05)

Turns out Dad was bruised and abraded, but the EMTs fixed him up right there on the sidelines and then gave us a lift home. None of his bones were broken. In the ambulance, he was silent, brooding, embarrassed by his undignified trip down the bleacher stairs in front of the crowd. And we never did get to see that whiz kid quarterback complete a pass.

Irma fussed over him when we returned to the house, the house that was heady with cooking smells. She laid out a spread that would have fed a dozen. The three of us sat around the kitchen table, its yellow plaid Formica faded but still cheery, overhead the familiar pendant of white glass bells, half its bulbs always burned out. There must have been eight or nine dishes to go with the big steaming bird, and two pies besides.

"God, thank you for not letting me kill myself while grabbing for a donut," said my dad, bowing his head over his full plate of food. "It would have just spoiled my appetite, anyhow."

"Amen," I said.

"I made you that cheesy rice ring," said Irma to me. "Whipped it up last minute."

"And I love you for it." I mounded my plate with all the trimmings.

"You don't." She blushed.

After dinner Dad and I washed up while Irma packed leftovers into a cooler that she insisted I take back to New York. "I don't care if you eat it, give it to the bums. I just can't take seeing it go fuzzy in this fridge here." Then she waddled down to the basement where she liked to needlepoint and listen to Peggy Lee.

My father and I retired to his study. Dad rummaged around for his pipe and tobacco. "Never smoke anymore but on national holidays," he said as he sat at his desk opening drawers and riffling through them. I lowered myself into a recliner, groaning. When did I get so old that I groaned when I sat down, groaned like middle-aged men all over America do as they succumb to gravitational forces over soft seating after Thanksgiving dinner? Above my head, the shelves were crammed with the testing toys that had confounded and entranced me as a child, the wooden stacks of rings and cubes to be assembled according to size and color, the plastic spatial-relations doodads with their nontoxic colored knobs, piles of flashcards with pictures of bland-faced humans engaged in ambiguous pastimes. They were all relics now; testing was done on computers these days.

His old Pentax camera, complete with its big boxy flash, sat on a lower shelf. He'd used it to document my successful completion of the puzzles. He captured me for posterity, thought I was a genius. Thought the photos might have some value someday, scientifically. I picked it up—there was film in it. As my father fished his walnut pipe from a bottom drawer, along with a pouch of Black Watch tobacco, I positioned the camera on a shelf across from the desk, set the timer. Pressed the self-timer button and hurried around the desk, crouching beside him.

"What the heck are you doing, Frank?"

"To remember me by. Smile."

Click. The flash went off. Dad turned to me. Our faces were inches away. "You going to tell me where you're going, Son?"

Whether to tell him. What to tell him. I could smell the pumpkin pie on his breath, the coffee. His blue eyes a bit milky, the eyelids slack. Across his forehead, tissue-paper skin molded itself around several prominent veins. Why did I feel so certain that I would never see him alive again after this day. The thought jarred me. I straightened up, away from him.

"Dad. I wish I could have been . . . better."

"So do we all, goddamn it." He shook his head at me, mystified. "You worry me, Frank. Someone listening to you might think you were going to do away with yourself."

"Kill myself?"

"Yes, you're talking like a nutcase, in my professional opinion."

I smiled, rested my hand on his head. The sparse hair, soft and white as a dandelion puff. "Don't worry, Dad. In some ways I've never felt better about my future."

He scowled up at me. "Now what the hell is that supposed to mean."

"I'm going back to New York tonight. I have to get back."

"You came all this way."

"I just needed to see you. Because I love you, Dad."

"Just needed to see me," he grumbled. He lit his pipe, sucking on its stem, his cheeks hollowing, his face veiled momentarily in haze. "Good-bye, then, Frank. I don't like mysteries. Good-bye."

I INCHED THROUGH TRAFFIC UP THE GREAT FRONT SLOPE OF THE VERrazano and hit its high point just in time to see the smoke over

Brooklyn glitter silver in the waning wintry light. I was bound for Sunset Park to finally meet Jimmy.

The evening cold bullied the neighborhood where my brother bunked in the junkie house, the little brick and aluminum-sided buildings crouching together in the shadow of the roadway overhead. Vagabond trash cans tumbled along the curbs, torn from their homes by the wind off the bay. At the corner by Clyde's place, a pay phone spilled its guts down to the sidewalk, its receiver dangling like a hanged criminal.

The door opened immediately after my ring this time, an attenuated toast-colored man smiling at me with a mouth lacking teeth. "Good night, friend," he said.

"I have to see Clyde Lundquist, please. I'm his brother."

"Clyde's brother! Come in, Clyde's brother." He ushered me through a dark hallway smelling of burnt soup, and into a spacious room that had once been the parlor of the row house. The last bits of elaborate molding clung to the pitted ceiling, scraps of lace trim on a tattered nightie.

Big boxes belched their contents all over the room, and a crew of peddlers stood picking through the mess, loading up for the next day: impassive men and women pawed through piles of blue and pink stuffed dinosaurs, filled trash bags with velvet headbands. In one corner, I saw Jackson sorting through stacks of uninflated balloons in the unlicensed shapes of characters from the latest Disney hit. Looking up from his work, he spotted me. "God bless the fucking Lion King, know what I'm saying, Doc?" He laughed. So did I. I hadn't slept in two days. The world was starting to go a bit wobbly around the edges.

My toothless escort piped up from behind me. "Where's that Clyde?"

"He's upstairs, I expect," said Jackson. "See you around, brother of Clyde. Keep trouble far from your mind."

I took deep comfort in his words. "Best of luck with the

balloons," I said, then followed the skeletal man up a flight of stairs, stepping high over a few missing planks. Paper printed with purple roses curled off the wall in scrolls. We entered a back room where a circular bed served as a sorting table for plastic-wrapped socks and T-shirts. Bent over the bed were about a half-dozen people, among them Clyde and Francie.

She saw me first. "Hey, look, it's Frank," she cried.

Clyde straightened and grinned at me, a bundle of socks in one hand and a shopping bag in the other. He was six feet of sharp angles, ribs, collarbones, assembled under a threadbare T-shirt. "Your Turkey Day good? How's Erskine?"

"Great, great," I said. I looked over their shoulders to see the pluglike Jimmy pop out from an adjoining room, scowling.

"Who is this joker?" he demanded. In an obliging tone, Clyde reminded him that they'd talked about this brother, this brother with a situation. The man was a foot and a half shorter than me, I think. Still, intimidating enough. The shape of his head, like a cudgel.

"The kids, they are working," he said coolly, nodding Clyde back to the textile mountain. My brother flashed me an en-couraging, slightly worried smile. Jimmy led me into the next room, a dormitory crammed with stale, unmade bunk beds that towered four high toward a black-painted ceiling. The windows were painted black, too, and the only light came from a dangling lampshade painted with rocking horses.

Jimmy sunk into a lower bunk, motioned me to do the same on a bed opposite. "You want to take the kid, I ain't going to stop you," he said. "I say he will be back to me here in a week."

"This isn't about Clyde. I mean, I think you are right. Clyde has to want to clean up."

"You are smarter than some," he said, nodding. He sighed. "Also, you know I love that kid. Clyde. He is what they call a good boy." He smiled down at the floor. "He is nice-looking, too. My wife and I have only girls. Agata, she loves Clyde. We say a lot, too bad he is a fucking junkie. Because he could be somebody's son."

"Yes," I said, nodding.

"So you are Clyde's brother. What do you want?"

"What I want is, uh, a gun, just as a loaner, possibly."

"Loan you a gun?" He grinned at me, resting his fat cheek in his hand. "Jesus Christ. What you gonna do, mister, rob a bank? What, you need money?"

I tried to steady my breathing, banish a manic sleep-deprived twitch in one eye. I needed this gangster to believe in me. "Actually, I'm going to break someone out of prison. Also, I need identification, passports. Maybe you know someone."

He glanced up at me then, eyebrows raised. Leaned back, elbows on the bed. From the darkness between the bunks, over the small arc of his belly, he gazed at me appraisingly.

"I didn't get your name," he said at last.

"Frank Lundquist."

"Frank Lundquist, you tell me why you want to do that."

"It's a long story," I said.

"Homer was a fucking Macedonian, Frank. A long story is no problem for a Macedonian."

I ended up staying through dinner—fried rice from the bulletproofed Chinese on the corner—as Jimmy critiqued and honed my plan. I left profoundly impressed with his ingenuity. Back home, I crept into bed next to the cat. He mewled and stretched to show me his ugly tummy. I scratched it for a bit, then slept like a shipwrecked man washed ashore.

JIMMY'S WHITE VAN TRUNDLED FURTIVELY DOWN MY BLOCK AT 7 A.M. on Sunday. He had me ride shotgun. We sprinkled his minions and their wares across a desolate Manhattan, then, after dropping the last, a fragile-looking girl with a yoke of plush toys, in

Washington Heights, he steered to a shabby little house near the Whitestone Bridge, a shop of sorts, specializing in impossible-to-trace weaponry smuggled from the former Yugoslavia. There he advised me on the purchase of a small Russian-made service revolver. And some ammunition.

"You won't load it," said Jimmy. "You won't even need it, if you listen to me, no need, Frank."

Then a crawl through midday traffic past LaGuardia to a white stucco bunker in East Elmhurst, a restaurant called Nove Skopje, if one were to believe the vinyl banner strung crookedly across its front. Inside, globes of bumpy amber glass dangled above deserted ranks of tables and chairs. Along one wall, a mural showed huge-bosomed peasant girls milking goats. I think they were goats, anyhow; they could have been dogs.

A young mustachioed man emerged from the kitchen, wiping his fingers on an apron that seemed to be smeared with engine grease. Jimmy spoke with him in their tongue-mangling language. The young man nodded. "Five thousand five hundred," he said to me, with a heavy accent. "Two Canadian passports."

"He is the best, this guy," Jimmy said. "Rolex all the way. Last week he turned a very big-league Russian into a Mexican."

The young man shrugged. "With big-league Russki you don't fuck."

Jimmy chuckled. "If you like your hands."

His colleague turned to me. "We will take photos when you and the lady get here, I will give them to you the next hour. I see no problem."

When I bid good-bye to Jimmy back at my building, he hugged me as if we were comrades. "You and your brother," he said. "Two fine boys."

By the way, I later checked: Homer was not Macedonian.

THE FOLLOWING MONDAY I CROSSED YET ANOTHER LINE WITH M. THE professional code I had lived by, had even prided myself on, felt abstract and distant now. A set of laws for a dead civilization.

But first we simply talked, as per normal. About her friend April, which scraped my heart. About the visit with her father, and an associate who might leverage the governor. For me, this fired a complex sequence of emotions: clemency would be a solution for her, but clemency would spirit her away.

Then she whispered, "I can't." She bowed her head. "I can't accept a favor from that man," she said. "I'd rather choose another way."

I admit it. It's problematic, of course. But the truth. My mental engine flooded at this, flooded with a rush of gladness. So. She saw it, too: at bottom, my proposal was an act of idealism.

"I am so afraid, though," said M.

"The plan is all worked out now, and it's simple and I know it will go well."

"But do you know why you are doing this?" She raised her gaze, studying me. "I mean, are you entirely sure about it? Because I don't have anything to lose, you know. You do."

"Not as much as you think."

A long minute of scrutiny. "What if it works and then I ditch you? You must have thought of that."

"I'm acting on faith."

The corners of her mouth turned down. Rueful, maybe. "What if I take the pills and they don't find me? What if they're late on count? I'm dead."

"You have to time it right, M. Set it up like we planned. The pills won't kill you for five, six hours. You've got a fine window." I smiled reassuringly.

She bit her nail, gazed at me. "I don't know," she said, speaking slower, softer. "Maybe I need to bloom where I'm planted."

I nodded.

"I could do some good here. Find some meaning for myself. And then, maybe that pardon . . ."

I made some noncommittal noise. Restless, up out of my chair. Pacing, just a bit. I rounded the desk and stopped in front of her. "I can take care of you."

"I can take care of myself."

"Of course!" I grabbed both her hands, half kneeling. "Of course you can, and you will." I tugged on her then, powered by a surge of tenderness and urgency, tugged her straight into my arms. At first she was everywhere tensed but then she started to melt into me; I felt the softness travel right down between the blades of her shoulders and along her spine and I imagine my heart sounded thunderous, rebounding all over the cage of my chest.

Everything had become momentous.

"Freeing you will make things better," I murmured into her warm hair.

"I am at a loss," she said.

The silky solidity of her. "In a week, you could be living far away from here." I felt her nodding against my shirt front. I lifted her face to mine. Kissed her. Then she pulled away from me, hair mussed, face faintly pinkened

"Whatever you decide, I'll respect your choice," I said. "Shrinks have a saying: choice is power."

"Choice is power," she whispered. Then moved toward the door.

I followed her. Before she turned the knob, I put a hand on her wrist. "It's all set, M. From now on, I'm just waiting for the call. You'll set things in motion."

She regarded me. "Your name definitely rings a bell," she said. "I do wish I remembered more."

"You will," I said.

18

Orion's Belt looked more like a tiara, crowning the ancient willow tree at the far end of the gravel lot. How clear the night was, and how dark in the place where she sat waiting. The stars meant business that night behind the firehouse in Candora, New York. They shone as if they meant to burn themselves out by morning.

Miranda sat in the car telling herself to relax, trying to comfort herself with a careful stocktaking of her surroundings. In the parking lot, long black puddles shivered with starlight. A single frog croaked from the weedy fringe of the gravel; she guessed there might be a little stream running back there, a little gully. Dumpster, stack of three tires. Weak June breezes tickling the old royal willow.

How did she come to be here. How could she have allowed him to bring her to this moment.

The frog fell silent. Best explanation she could summon: some serious malfunction. Something had gone wrong in the workings of her soul.

And it had gone wrong far in time and space from any whispering star-crowned willow tree.

Some place freezing cold under a pale sky.

Don't you cry. Don't you dare cry now. Way too late.

The engine hummed obediently, the car nestled close to the cinder-block wall, the rear wall of the one-story firehouse. Light fell across the car's hood from a small window cut into the blank metal door through which Duncan would come. Yellow light, cheerful light. It made a parallelogram on the hood of the white rental car.

Then she heard a thud. Another thud. Two dead sounds, full of finality. She sat for a long time, her heart pounding so hard it threatened to break free of her body and go bouncing down the length of the lot and into the weeds and the trees, to live down there among the frogs. Nothing happened. No one came bursting out of the door. Duncan.

She stepped out of the car. She peered into the square of yellow light, the window cut in the metal. She saw a gray steel desk, shelves spilling papers, stacks of orange traffic cones, a set of mops, a row of hooks hung with Day-Glo yellow helmets. She saw a leg, in denim, and a foot in a scuffed brown boot. The foot was twitching.

She hauled open the heavy door and rushed in. Then she saw the gun. Resting on the corner of the desk, like a paperweight, like a souvenir, the black pistol she had seen back in the motel room for the first time—was it just twenty minutes ago? Twenty minutes, twenty years, whenever, whatever.

She picked it up. She held the gun instinctively. She'd seen this her whole life; everyone has. Finger on the trigger. Point the gun.

The gun started to shake in her hand.

THREE DAYS AFTER HER LAST-EVER SESSION WITH FRANK LUNDQUIST, winter rain poured from the sky, shreds of silver hanging from the eaves of Building 2A&B. At rec time, everyone was herded to the gym. Miranda retreated to the bleachers by the wall, beneath the giant painted rainbow and a shiny American flag.

Lu plopped down on the bench in front of her, panting a bit from a handball match. "Hi, Mimischka," she said. "Where are you all the time these days? I never see you."

"I'm around," said Miranda. "I'm just not feeling so sociable."

"What's social, you can't talk to your friend?" Lu bent over, brushing an invisible smudge from her pristine white tennis shoes. A gold bracelet slid from beneath the sleeve of her sweater, heart charm dangling from a chain. Miranda stared at it.

Lu noticed her gaze and smiled wide-eyed. "Yes. She gave it to me before she died, sweet April."

Miranda blinked at the thing, disbelieving. "So she knew she was going to die, you think?" She couldn't help being hurt that April would make such a gesture toward Lu rather than her.

"Who knows? She was a funny person sometimes." Lu twisted the bracelet farther down on her wrist, regarded it thoughtfully. "Not bad," she said, turning the charm this way and that. "Eighteen carat, I think, but very nice."

The heart lay with its back side faceup in Lu's palm. The inscription had been sanded away. Miranda felt her insides go icy.

"I will order a necklace from QVC to match. You heard they now have cable on D Unit?" Lu stood and looked down on Miranda with her most beguiling grin. "We need to hang around like girlfriends, Mimi. You come visit me tomorrow, okay? I will do your nails, your polish is all chipped."

She laid a light hand on Miranda's head. "You are a wonderful thing, you know how I love you, right?"

Miranda forced herself to smile. "Right."

Lu jogged to the far corner of the gymnasium. To Dorcas Watkins, bouncing a blue handball, watching her approach with an expectant look on her face. They talked intently, sending the little ball between them in halfhearted bounce passes. With the usual ferocious combat being waged beneath the hoops and the hip-hop babbling on the boom box at the COs station, no one could hear what they might be saying. Miranda observed them for a long while.

Finally, flipping the ball to Dorcas with a nod, Lu walked to the exit of the gym. A tall CO unlocked the door and ushered her out. When he turned to lock it behind him, Miranda saw his face, framed for an elastic moment in the door's oblong window. Jerrold Liverwell.

VERWIRRT. THE WORD CAME BACK TO HER FROM HIGH SCHOOL GER-man. She'd forgotten most of her lessons, but she remembered this. Verwirrt: completely confused, baffled, but with a touch of panic, a whiff of menace in the air. Alarmed, afraid, but not knowing exactly why.

She took her place in line as the ladies were herded out of the gym and back to their units. There was the usual pushing and elbowing and cackles and complaints, but Miranda was more or less oblivious. Trying to process what she had just seen.

"You ladies gonna act like children or you gonna act like ladies?" bellowed Beryl Carmona as her group flowed through the unit door. "You decide, you decide." Miranda drifted down the long passageway to her room. The polished floor reflecting stripes of fluorescent lights, the walls punched with precisely spaced doorways, the cinder blocks: everything converged on a single vanishing point.

She entered her cell, sat on her bed, tried to think things through. Verwirrt.

She turned and gazed up at the rectangle of sky, seeking comfort there as she had so many times. But the sleet continued, the window showed only a gray frizz like a broken TV.

Looking around her cell then, seeing everything as if for the first time: the peeling metal, the concrete, the smudged plastic curtain. All down the block, the stink of drugstore perfumes and powerful hair products, the mildew-infused steam from the hygiene room, the smell of onions from the kitchen. And the voices, scolding, murmuring, screeching, humming, coming from everywhere, filling all the empty space and time with their dissatisfaction and boredom and grief.

She stayed for a long while like this and her thoughts passed, many of them. She tracked them, as if watching planes winging from horizon to horizon.

Frank Lundquist, who was waiting on the call. His embrace, which had awakened more in her than she might have imagined. He waited even this very second for the phone to ring in his apartment. She could picture the place, the hand-me-down sofas and chairs, the bumpy old Upper West Side walls encrusted with decades of paint.

But no. These were the memories of Gillian's apartment. The snow-silenced night of that birthday party.

Miranda. You need to be a different person now. Different, not the same. Not the same as you were, that snow-smothered night. Not the same as you were, through that black tunnel of love, lust, whatever in the days and months that followed. The corridor that led to Candora.

Candora was the last time you followed a plan not your own. A plan by a man.

Be different, not the same.

Miranda eased the privacy curtain down across the front of her cell. She took her yellow robe off its white plastic hanger, folded the robe, and placed it on the floor. Lowering herself to her bed, she held the hanger in her lap and peeled the little piece of tape away that held it together where it had once been split. The tape came away.

The pills had to be destroyed. She would smash them, then flush the dust.

She shook the hanger. No pills came.

She peered into the tubular space inside the plastic. Empty. Gone.

THE 6 P.M. COUNT BEGAN. SHE COULD HEAR CARMONA COMING UP THE passageway, calling the ladies to stand at the front of their cells, joking and haranguing as she counted. Miranda did as required, staring out into the passageway.

She bid farewell to Frank Lundquist, still waiting on her call. His unassuming manner, his troubled-sea eyes. Willing to risk everything to save her, to empty his life of everything in hopes of refilling it with her.

She never actually bought in to his preposterous plan. Not really. She knew it would break down, one way or another along the line.

And, even more sadly, she bid farewell to the Frank-Lundquist-manufactured version of Miranda Greene. His was not inmate 0068-N-97, not a debased nonentity in state-issued yellows. Instead: Miranda. Worthy of love, worth risking every-thing for, a valuable woman aged thirty-two years, grown from a good-hearted, well-raised girl of cherry lip gloss and calico patches. She had grown more than a little fond of Frank Lund-quist's Miranda. A bit addicted, perhaps.

But now she would manufacture her version. Or remanu-facture, because of course, she'd already made and lived her own Miranda once.

Though maybe she never really had.

In any case. Work on that appeal. Stop transgressing. Map your own route, then drive it. Alone.

"Moore, count. Get up." Carmona was in front of the cell opposite now. As usual, Weavy was lain out in her bed. She invariably conked after dinner; the woman slept quiet and solid, an old eroded landform on the thin cot, collapsing into sleep as the sun went down like some preindustrial being. Miranda had often marveled at it: Weavy must have racked up eighteen hours a day for the whole time she'd been inside. "Moore," bellowed Carmona. "Up! Now!"

No sign of movement. A poisonous thought seeped into Miranda's mind through some needle-thin brain chasm.

Carmona hoisted the ring of keys from the chain at her hip and stuck one into the lock on Weavy's gate. She swung it wide and strode into the cell, kicking aside sheets of sandpaper. Weavy lay facing the wall, Carmona took hold of her shoulder and shook it. "Dammit, woman, you deaf?"

Miranda turned away. Afraid to see.

"Aw shit." Miranda heard the guard say this, she heard her sigh, a strange and heartbroken sound, then a snap of a radio being pulled from its belt holster. "Get the med team up here, Unit 3, Number 45," she heard Carmona say. "I'm guessing OD."

WOMEN CALLED IN THE MIDDLE OF THE NIGHT, WOMEN WITH NAMES he didn't recognize, good girls who remade themselves as vixens and barflies, flashing smiles. Hoping to lure him. But how could they be blamed. Duncan McCray possessed quantities of masculine charm that were truly a surplus. Almost freakish.

And every night he came home to Miranda, apparently faithful, and she couldn't believe her luck. Indeed, she was enslaved by this luck. She'd landed an elusive specimen, a creature of pure magnetism and seemingly endless sexual fascination, and this unlikely fact now ruled her. When they moved in together a month after they first met, she realized how dangerous this relationship might be, because she knew without doubt that she could die for him if he so requested.

She had never wanted a passion like this, never asked for

it. What do you ask for in life, though? There are so many pos-sibilities.

So she found herself enslaved. When they drove up to Can-dora, June flaunted itself up and down the thruway, sweet green leaves everywhere, and daisies and other such nonsensical things twinkling at them as they drove into the dusk. This escapade was all wrong, she knew, but there were reasons to take comfort, as he reminded:

"I'll only be pretending to have a gun, I won't actually have a gun, remember that."

"And the casino nights, the bingo and the roulette, they think the money's going to help sick children and this guy should not be skimming, you know? He's a fire captain, for fuck's sake. So remember that, too."

"And it won't really hurt him to lose it. He's got a govern-ment job, he's a big shot in a small town. But for us it will mean everything, Miranda; we need the funding for the rest of our lives together. Right, our lives together?"

Duncan turned to her then, his hands on the steering wheel, and those famous eyes, navy blue, pure gold—what color were they, anyway, and why did God create such eyes, she won-dered. Or biology, whatever. Eyes that could enslave. Too much power for a person not to use. Use it he did.

The Candora Community Motel, ceiling light stippled with dead gnats, a slick polyester bedspread. She sat down and hid her face in her hands. "I can't believe I'm about to commit a felony."

"I'm committing it, not you," he said. "And it'll be over and done with and we'll move on. We'll get married, if you'll have me," he said. He put his arms around her then and they fucked and for a few seconds at the peak it seemed he'd disassembled her body and yanked her soul out to examine it. Then they dressed again and watched the late news until he unzipped his bag and out came this vile little gun. "But you said," she protested—"Don't worry it won't be loaded"—"I don't care, you said"—"Look, Miranda." He knelt and took her hands. "I never wanted to fall in love, you know that, I was determined to be on my own but I wanted you that much. Are you going to give up on me now? It won't be loaded, it's only for show and I promise you, promise that we'll throw it into the river together when we get out of there, you saw that river we crossed as we pulled into town."

"The sign said Oshandaga."

"Right. The Oshandaga. Looks good and deep."

THEY WERE FORCED TO DRAG WEAVY'S BODY BAG ALONG THE DIRTY floor because someone had stolen the wheels of the last working gurney in Milford Basin. For once, the ladies on the unit had fallen silent, and in the dead thick air, the bag made a fervent swishing noise as it slid down the passage, like the hissing of infernal reptiles. Carmona and two other COs poked around Weavy's cell, looking for evidence of foul play but all they found was a note.

I watched her and saw it all. Please don't burn me, bury me in the ground.

Watched it all? They turned to look at Miranda.

Carmona unlocked the door and Miranda met her there. "Be a good gal and put in a good word for me at Admin. There's been one too many flyers on my unit lately," she said and gave her a shove down the hall.

THE SECURITY OFFICE HAD PICTURE WINDOWS LOOKING OUT OVER the entire physical plant and on this night the sleet sparkled like tinsel in the white arcs of light sent up around the perimeter fence. Shining in the wet night, Milford Basin looked like a cozy settlement, a prairie town, a logging outpost in some northern wilderness. Miranda stared out it.

The chief warden swept in and sat across the table from Miranda, blocking out the view.

"So where did Moore get this medication?" She was a majestically built woman not much older than Miranda. Her white blouse was darkened with a large wet spot. Clearly she had вeen awakened in the night. She picked up a scrawled note. "This Elavil."

"I don't know what you're talking about," said Miranda. "I'm sorry."

The woman pursed her lips. The linebacker-sized CO who had entered with her loomed like a dark cloud.

"I would guess that Weavy got her drugs from the same place everyone else here gets them," offered Miranda.

The chief narrowed her eyes. "You want to elaborate?"

Miranda held her voice steady. "I don't want to, but I will if I can see my counselor. Frank Lundquist."

"You're talking about telling some truth here?" She cocked an eyebrow.

Miranda nodded. "If I can talk to my counselor."

"I will arrange that," said the chief. "Share what you have to share."

"Ludmilla Chermayev runs the contraband. Dorcas Watkins sells it for Lu." Miranda was aware of how they both edged themselves toward her. "A CO named Liverwell smuggles it in, I think. But maybe others do, too. That's all I know."

The burly CO let out a low whistle, causing the chief to glare at him. "There's a state trooper on his way up here, tell him we'll need a DOCS investigator, too." The linebacker rushed off. She turned to Miranda.

"I need to see my counselor tonight."

"It's awfully late for that."

"And, ma'am," said Miranda. "I hope you won't mind me saying this, but there's a spot on your shirt."

"Goodness," said the woman. The dark wetness had now spread across the left side of her blouse. She looked up at Miranda, mortified. "I just had my third six weeks ago," she said with a taut embarrassed smile. "Nursing, you know." She stood. "Excuse me." Arms folded tightly across her chest, she slipped out the door. Miranda heard her instructing the guard to find her the number of that shrink, Lundquist.

HIS VOICE QUAVERED. "YOU'RE JUST SCARED, WHICH IS UNDERSTAND-able."

She couldn't meet his gaze. She watched his hand at the edge of his desk. Trembling? Raindrops spattered the black window, the only sound in the night-abandoned offices of Counseling. A single guard sitting in a pool of light down the dark hall. Grumpy and drowsing, having been interrupted on his coffee break to escort Miranda down.

"No, I'm not scared," she whispered. "I'm done. I'm done with doing every wrong thing."

He crossed to stand in front of her for a long moment. She kept her eyes on his scuffed leather tennis shoes. One was untied.

"This is a chance to begin," he said. "Something good will come of it."

"I don't think you understand. I said I'm done. I stood up tonight and did the right and good thing. And that's what I'm going to keep doing."

"In here. For five decades."

"I'll consider Potocki's offer to help." She hesitated then, frowned. "Or maybe I won't. Maybe I will just serve the term."

"Fifty-two years? You—won't be you anymore."

She saw, in his anguished face, how much he wanted to save her. But she intended to save herself. "I'm sorry," she whispered.

He rose then and turned away from her. Walked to the little tea station atop the file cabinet, stood with his back to her until the electric kettle began to hiss.

She saw his shoulders shaking. She thought he might be crying.

He prepared the cups and poured the water as if in slow motion. It flooded her heart, a bit.

"I'm grateful for everything, for what you've tried to do," she said to his back. "But I need this to be truly over and done."

At this, he turned toward her, the two cups steaming. His face was blotched, eyes down.

"I understand," he said softly, not raising his gaze, just giving a little nod. He handed her the cup, wisps of vapor and milky beige. "So one more for the road."

FLIGHT

19

INFORM CLIENTS OF THE DEVELOPING NATURE OF THE TREATMENT, THE POTENTIAL RISKS, AND THE VOLUNTARY NATURE OF THEIR PARTICIPATION

(Standard 10.01.b)

Some things I never thought I would see up close:

> three kilos of heroin, wrapped in cellophane, sealed
> in Ziploc bags
> the julienned sweetmeat of a baby goat
> a heartbreakingly beautiful woman crying out for me
> in the night
> a singing serf dusting my dead mother's face
> an albino snail

But I have seen them all, in the era that began the night M died her second death.

The albino snail I am seeing right now, in fact. It has been climbing up the far side of the window, the flat smear of its underside like a bleached tongue pressed against the glass. The snail's body ruffles prettily around the edges as it uses its tiny muscles to advance its course.

It has moved clear across the window in the space of an afternoon. And as it has inched along, I have recorded these notes. The snail is white and pink and looks like a little Easter treat or a mangled plastic flower. It certainly doesn't look real. But when I look farther, past the snail, at the view from this window, the black hills, the strange huddled tin-roofed houses, that hardly looks real, either—when taken in the context of the life you might have expected a man like me to have, when compared with what you might reasonably expect to see from the window of the dwelling place inhabited by one Franklin H. H. Lundquist, Ph.D.

And I guess that's why I find myself setting the whole course of events down on paper. I record these notes by hand, in a lined composition book, meant for schoolkids and the only writing paper available here, purchased by our housekeeper in the little village shop.

Yes, unorthodox, as documentation goes.

But after all, I had to leave the official records behind. All my files, all my clinical case notes for all my clients, including a slim manila folder, obligingly placed in my Milford Basin cabinet under "G." I know this particular folder was carefully reviewed by Polkinghorne, by the chief warden, by various attorneys and detectives. What they read were the ordinary jottings of an institutional psychologist: the client's basic demographics and family history, the results of that MMPI questionnaire I administered in our first session, her two chief complaints ("occasional despondency, insomnia due to noise on unit"), and my interventions ("discussed positive coping skills, agreed pharma could be advisable"). A partial record of medication remands.

Those notes hardly told the whole story.

And so here, on this day, in this strange place, in this cheap notebook bound in gray cardboard, I have been setting the whole story down. It's confidential, as all such notes must be, and since I'm without the standard measures for securing private records, I've omitted the client's name. I simply call her M.

I write this to complete the clinical record, yes. To gain some insight, of course. But mostly to convince myself of something: that this albino snail is real. If the snail is real, this life is real.

FINALLY, THERE WAS THAT NIGHT. THE SLEET. THE SLEET, THE HOPPED-up, blowing sleet, forcing me to drive slowly, ranked battalions of raindrops hurling themselves against the windshield, crazing the pavement in the beams of the headlights. The weather seemed to have swallowed the suburbs whole; a three-car accident clogged the parkway; my wipers sang a tragic monotonous tune, and my hands were sweaty and shaky.

What I had done: set off an avalanche. Now, ride it down.

"Come on," I muttered, pounding the steering wheel.

"Easy, easy," said Clyde. He switched on the radio, munched fried chicken packed in a grease-spotted box. If you can't be with the one you love, honey, love the one you're with.

I just wanted to see her face again. To remind myself about the payoff for this wholesale demolition of my life.

What I had done. Why I had done it.

The extra pills I'd kept tucked in a box of Earl Grey. I'd meant those for backup—or maybe, for me. In case the worst happened. If she'd somehow died from her hidden-away dose, I would have ended my days as well.

Top of the hour news on the radio. The president had vetoed a budget. Albanian militants attacked a South Serbian base. Someone had been selling dog meat to tony restaurants, disguised as Australian-farmed lamb filets.

Clyde shook his head. "What kind of a person," he said. "Poor little doggies."

"You've got the first aid kit," I said.

"For the fourteenth time, yes."

"The hat?"

He held up a floppy-brimmed ladies' rain hat. "On loan from Agata."

"And the bags? In the back?"

"In the back."

Over the previous week, I'd been dispensing with my few possessions—I'd delivered the aged Truffle and our never-used crystal wedding-registry candlesticks to Winnie, and, as compensation for dumping a cat on his household, I'd given Gary my brand-new picture-in-picture TV. I filled a pair of small duffels with a week's wardrobe for myself and M. Yes, I took down her sizes and went shopping at Bloomingdales—a few sweaters, some T-shirts and jeans, underwear, and one splurge on cashmere socks. All of this, I folded solemnly into the bags. In mine, I tucked in a few family photos along with the clothes. And on top, the fisherman's jacket—seven cargo pockets and an internal waterproof stash zone—that I'd found in a dusty old angler's supply shop near Grand Central. I zipped the Russian service revolver, menacing and incredibly weighty for its size, into the jacket's largest pocket.

All this according to the plan Jimmy and I had fine-tuned during our meeting a week earlier at Nove Skopje. Agata, wearing an enormous pearl and coral brooch in the shape of an octopus, hurried from the kitchen and welcomed me with a crushing hug. She gushed in her mystifying language about Clyde. She showed me to a cluttered office behind the bar. Empty rifle racks on the walls, a window thickly curtained. She motioned me to sit and wait.

When she left, I saw the three plump plastic-wrapped

bricks of heroin, stacked in a corner next to a pair of child-size galoshes. I crouched down and studied the honey-hued bundles with mixed emotions: here was the stuff that was strip-mining my baby brother's soul. Yet I was strangely flattered that the Macedonians trusted me enough to house me with their stash. I poked one of the malevolent pillows of junk, taut and dense as a clenched muscle. Some kind of power locked in there. I wished it would relinquish its grip on my brother. I could only pray that it wouldn't conquer him.

Jimmy entered with a bottle of Balkan hooch, and Agata behind him, wielding platters of something fragrant and saucy. She served us while Jimmy and I ate and drank and worked out the last details. Routes to and from the hospital, weapon disposal. Monitoring Clyde's fix on the day so he'd be up to the task and not on the nod.

And at the center of it: M. She'd set it all in motion. Ring the pay phone at Nove Skopje, ask for me, hang up. Take the dose of Elavil she'd hidden in her cell. Done.

A not-very-complicated plan. A clear set of intentions.

But then, that frigid, sleet-spitting night.

The phone did indeed ring, but not at Nove Skopje. Instead, it rang at my apartment.

The woman's voice did indeed ask for me, but the voice did not belong to M. Instead, the chief warden.

So the plan got a bit more complicated. The intentions a bit muddled.

THE RAIN HAT. THE FIRST AID KIT. THE DUCT TAPE. THE CHANGE OF clothes.

"Check, check, check," said Clyde.

Once I'd dosed M with the med-laced tea—made that adjustment to the plan—I watched as she was escorted back to her unit, unaware of her fate, still awake but guaranteed to be down and out when the COs came around for the 10 P.M. count. Then I jolted into a previously unknown high gear—racing back to the city to scoop up Clyde and my readied supplies, figuring that I could still carry out the rest of the operation as Jimmy and I had charted it. And in under an hour my brother and I were swooping down the freeway exit to the brilliantly lit Hudson Valley Med Center, gliding to a stop in the drenched parking lot.

"I think we're ready then," I said. In the pocket of the fishing jacket, the gun's rubber grip gave slightly under the pressure of my hand. The revolver was unloaded, a scare tactic, but not a felony. Not a felony in case—oh my Christ—something went awry. My heart was pounding in deep reverb. The blinking clock on the dash read 11:20. Almost two hours since M had swallowed her Earl Grey.

Pelted by the miserable night, we lifted Jackson's wheelchair out of the trunk and unfolded it. Clyde, especially scarecrow-like in a pair of baggy pants and a denim workshirt chosen for the occasion, plopped the big rain hat onto his head. As I propelled him toward the main entrance. I read the sticker on the backrest: "Have you been saved?"

Into the cheery bustle of the hospital's lobby and onto the elevator. Clyde smiling up at people dopily from beneath the dripping brim of the hat. He really played his part extremely well. At the fourth-floor reception desk, a compact East Indian woman greeted us. I extracted my ID badge from my shirt pocket. "Dr. Lundquist, Milford Basin. Here about one of my clients. This is my brother, Clyde; I didn't want to leave him, of course."

Clyde gave her an inane grin.

"Of course." She gazed at him with sympathy in her eyes. Then she looked back at me and knit her brows. "But we haven't had anyone from Milford Basin tonight."

I gawked at her. Forgetting how to operate my tongue or jaw.

"Shall I call downstairs?" said the nurse. "She may still be there."

I could just about bob my head. Every thought extinguished except: she's dead.

I watched the nurse dial the phone, talking into it, as if I'd never seen such a thing before. She's dead she's dead. The mouth was moving as the hand hung up the phone.

"—up shortly, it took a while to pump her and she's in the recovery unit now."

She seemed to be smiling again.

"Wait in the TV lounge down the hall?" she said. "I can let you know when—"

I followed her arm as it pointed. "Yes, thanks," I garbled.

In the deserted lounge, we tried to behave normally. We stared at the TV. It was the last time I'd see American television for a long while, but I didn't think about that then. I could only think about M.

I HAVE NO DATA ON THIS, BUT I WILL ASSUME THAT THE AVERAGE MAN spends little time reflecting upon redemption. In this respect, then, I am not an average man. In this respect, I occupy a spot on the higher end of the bell curve.

I smacked Zach Fehler hard, and that was a bitter betrayal. I'd asked him to trust, then sent him reeling. His little face turned scarlet, his little legs splayed on the floor.

But Zachary wasn't the first small being I misused.

Because before Zach, I'll have to count Baby Zero. The quintessential child. A tyke I'd betrayed from day one, more or less. Since the day he was birthed in my dad's testing lab, amid gaily colored wooden puzzles and knobbed building toys.

I'd been in charge of that bright baby's fate. And I'd forsaken him. I let him wander in the wilderness for thirty years, give or take, then descend to an underworld, the basement of a prison.

So, yes, redemption had been a growing concern of mine for some time.

When M first entered that basement office and reentered my life—this person, this womanish incarnation of my teenage dream, fallen to the wolves, gone to the devil—I understood. M was my remedy. Through her, I would set it all right. Here, at last, I could rise up and do true good. Change a human life for the better, in the most unmistakable terms.

A MAN WAS INFORMATIONALLY SETTING CAR WAX ALIGHT WHEN THE reception nurse came to fetch us. I folded my fingertips into my palms so she couldn't see my nails, bloody from nervous picking. "Your client is resting in 403. She's groggy, in and out. Took a whopping dose, guess she really wanted to get the job done."

I attempted a little grin. As soon as the sound of her footsteps trailed off, I stood and wheeled Clyde around. "No bright ideas," I whispered.

"Aye-aye," he muttered.

No bright ideas were needed, I have to say. The plan flowed like a dream, as if God himself had written the screenplay. The CO on duty turned out to be a wan-faced rookie, name tag Jenni O'Dell, a slip of a girl who had pulled the night shift because (as she told us, whimpering at the point of my unloaded gun) it was only her second week on the job. I wheeled Clyde into the room and flashed my prison ID. "The superintendent notified me. She's been under my care for a while."

O'Dell nodded. "Gotcha, sir."

"And this is Clyde, my brother." Clyde lolled his head.

"Gotcha." She eyed him. "Well, I hear she'll make it. Don't know why anybody'd do such a thing. Guess you do, though,

Doc, guess that's your job." She flashed a smile, pleased at her own wit. She locked the door behind us, then returned to the chair by the window and her word-search puzzle book.

M. Her arms looked limp and translucent as raw shrimp, resting atop the snowy bedding, locked at either wrist to the bed rails. Her eyes slit, a lock of her hair plastered near her lips with spittle.

I called her name. Her eyes moved toward me, but didn't seem to see me.

Unzipped my jacket pocket, gripped the gun. I think I uttered a small prayer. My palms were exuding a kind of grease, and chilly sweat tickled the nape of my neck. "Jenni," I said, tugging the gun loose from its hiding place. "Please don't move. I have to take this woman now."

The guard looked up from her puzzle, confused. She stared at my gun, and this didn't seem to faze her, but when Clyde leapt up from the wheelchair beside her, she let out a little yelp. She dropped the book. "I've got a toddler," she said.

"No fear, Jenni," said Clyde. "We're nice guys. We'll need your belt, though." He began to remove his pants. Jenni O'Dell began to whimper, but undid her duty belt with scrabbling hands and laid it on the bed, her eyes on me and my gun. Clyde removed the belt's metal cuffs and ratcheted them around the guard's wrists.

"Really," I said soothingly. "Now sit." She did as she was told. "This is going to be harmless."

Clyde was finished taking off his clothes, revealing the second pair of pants and T-shirt he'd worn beneath (LIFE IS GOOD, a dancing stick figure assured us). The baggy pants and denim shirt hung over the end of the bed. He stuffed Jenni's duty pistol and radio into my roomy cargo pockets. I took her ring of keys, handed him the Russian gun. This made Jenni cry. Clyde smiled at her. "It's really okay," he insisted.

"Which key is it, Jenni," I said.

"The ovalish one," she said in a quavering voice.

I leaned over M, brushed that spit-stiffened lock of hair from her expressionless lips, unlocked the restraints from her arms. "You're alive and you're almost free," I whispered. Then I pulled down the blanket. White hospital gown sprinkled with dark blue dots, pale skinny legs. I slid Clyde's cast-off pants onto her legs, tucked the gown in around the waistband, but when I tried to slide her arms into the sleeves of the overshirt, she seemed to moan. I kept at it, whispering to her. I pushed the wheelchair over to the bedside; Clyde and I lifted her into it, her limp warmth reminding me of when I'd ease poor Truffle out of my favorite spot on the couch.

I pulled the rain hat low over her face. "Beautiful," murmured Clyde. "Now her," he said, motioning to Jenni, "and we're out."

"Oh, God," whispered the guard.

"Shhh," I took her elbow and urged her into the bathroom, sat her down on the closed toilet seat. I taped her legs to the base of the toilet. I comforted her as I began sealing her mouth with the duct tape. "Now the worst part of this whole thing will probably be when they take this off. But it'll only last a second." She regarded me with untrammeled panic. I felt a pang of deep, scouring guilt. "You're supposed to sit here and count to one hundred." I turned to shut the door. Her eyes pleaded. "I told you this wouldn't be so bad. Thanks for your cooperative attitude." I wedged a chair under the knob.

"Are we ready?" I said to Clyde.

"Yup yup," he nodded.

Peeked into the hallway, which stretched empty in both directions, faraway laughter from the TV in the lounge, trilling telephone around the corner at reception. I gestured to Clyde to get going. "See you down there, buddy," he said.

"Don't run," I whispered.

He headed left out the door and walked down about fifty feet to the hall's dead end, where a stairwell led down to the first floor. From there, he was just a quick trot through the lobby to the parking lot. I gripped M's chariot, pulled the rain hat a bit lower over her face, and wheeled her out toward reception and the elevators.

The nurse was bent over some paperwork as we rounded the corner, her long dark braid swinging over one shoulder. I pressed the button, angled M's chair to face the lift doors, and as we waited for the elevator, the nurse looked up.

"Have a good night, Doctor," she said, and focused again on her work.

The lobby, with its clusters of relatives lounging around and the hum of a floor polisher pushed by an aged janitor, seemed a wider expanse than before but in a moment the glass doors were sliding open like the gates to someplace miraculous and I was pushing across the glistening parking lot, through cones of orange light. Clyde had the car's motor already running. "You're doing great, you are superb," I said to M as we lifted her into the back seat.

Elation, the elation one feels when one is suddenly aware of being in the midst of a very pleasant dream, overcame me as I folded the wheelchair in the trunk. I was grinning like a fool when I heard a voice behind me just as the latch closed.

"Frank, they called you already about this?"

I turned. Charlie Polkinghorne, his face half shadow, half tangerine glow. Trench coat held closed with one hand and an umbrella aloft in the other. I remembered the rain was still coming down, that I was getting soaked again. I stared at him.

"She did it again. Terrible."

"Yes, yes." I thought about the gun—the loaded one, Jenni's gun—in my pocket.

He looked at me and up at the sky. "You don't believe in rain gear?"

"Just—rushing, you know—" I glanced over my shoulder, I could see Clyde craning his neck back at us.

"Come out of the rain," said Charlie, pulling me under his umbrella, close enough so I could count the individual hairs of his scanty brows. "Look, don't be too upset about this client of yours. You're too hard on yourself. She's clearly determined to leave us behind, you can't stop someone when they're that determined, right?"

"Right. Thanks, Charlie." I fumbled for his hand, pumped it a few times. "Now I've really got to run."

He clutched my hand, a surprisingly powerful grip. "Sheila's kicked me out."

"Oh, God, I'm sorry," I said.

"Could I bunk with you for a few days, do you think, Frank?"

"Sure, can we talk tomorrow? I'll come by your office." I wriggled my hand away, backing toward the car. I turned and dashed, climbed in behind the wheel. I backed out of the space, Polkinghorne still standing there, a gray specter in the rain. We slid off into the waterlogged darkness. The black, soaked, delicious night.

20

DECEMBER 1999

Curled up in the back seat of the car. Noting every little divot in the road, cradled in the aroma of new leatherette upholstery. Lights above the highway swooping past, telephone poles, leafy boughs slithery with drops.

"Nothing means anything anymore, you're saying?"

"Come on."

"You're worse than he is. He's evil. You're spineless. I'd rather have evil."

"Evil? Jesus Christ, Barb. A tad melodramatic, don't you think? When're you going to stop busting my balls."

"You must be mistaken, Edward. You bartered those off to the Nigerians in that oil lobby deal." Imitating him now. "Oh, no, they're not dictators, honey. They were duly elected!"

The jolt of the brakes. "I'm getting out. Go torment Karsten Brunner."

"Murdered your daughter, then lied about it. But so what? You can't live without him. His goddamn lunches at the White House. Upstairs in the private quarters. The private quarters!

How could you be so shallow. You weren't like that when I met you."

"I was nineteen and stupid when I met you, dear. And you were exactly the same. Which is why it was a beautiful match."

The ignition off. The door opening.

"You're not getting out here. What are you doing?"

"Tell your daughter I said good-bye. Hope she's still asleep. Nobody should have to listen to this bullshit."

The door slamming. The rain clicking like a diligent typist on the rear windscreen. The hiss of cars speeding past.

MIRANDA BOLTED UP. THE PAIN CAME A MOMENT LATER, MADE HER gasp. "Where's he going?" she cried.

"No, no, you're not up." Frank Lundquist's voice, many miles away. "That's my brother, Clyde. Don't worry, you're asleep."

Miranda watched the long-legged man springing up a flight of stairs. A suburban rail station, an empty parking lot. The car began to move again.

Oh. She was dreaming. The night-saturated world flowed outside the window, Frank Lundquist turned a steering wheel this way and that, she was slumping in a roomy back seat. She felt that dream-drowned sensation wrap her, the dark curtain, the leaden limbs. She oozed back down to feel cool vinyl against her cheek.

A few minutes later: *My face is wet, I'm crying.*

She marveled at these sleep-conjured tears.

Later, the dream car ceased its mumbling and she rose up again to see the man who seemed to be Frank Lundquist gathering up a gun, a handheld walkie-talkie, a circle of keys—of course, so familiar, the tools of the CO's trade, that's what had stirred her drowsing attention, the chiming sound of the keys. Milford Basin, that sound. April. Lu.

He opened the car door and stepped out, then flung the

gun then the radio then the keys then somehow a second gun into a stretch of black water bounded by fencing and concrete barriers. Must be as many guns as stones in the waters of this country, she thought, and then she felt all the world crumbling away from her again, abandoning her, consigning her once again to nothingness. As she slumped, slid rapidly into the hole, pulled by whatever hole-dwelling force so coveted her, she got one final glimpse: the white flower on the black water, then waiting on the cool car bumper, the car stopped on the bridge across the Oshandaga. The police cars scattered blue light across the river as they approached.

"FOR A JUNKIE, HE DID GOOD, YOUR BROTHER."
"And this is the lady."
"Yes, this is the lady."
"Look, her eyes, is she out or not?" This voice was deeper, words jammed up with strange accents. Through thick screening—eyelashes—brooms and pails and shelves of boxes. In the corner, a heavyset woman looking up from her knitting.
A hand on her face. Frank Lundquist's voice: "No, yes, I have more to give her."
"Don't," she whispered. Her throat was paper cut.
He shushed her. Don't you dare shush me, she thought.
"Leave it," the deeper voice. "We will do the photo, we need eyes open anyhow. Ani hhhow"—he said it a bit like Lu, she thought.
"Miranda, you're safe now." His hand on her face, his face in her vision.
You did this, she thought. What did he do, though? She could not pinpoint it.
He turned his Frank Lundquist face away. Music making a winding circuit of her ears. Standing on a corner in Winslow, Arizona, such a fine sight to see.

A pale young man made a little bow before her. "Don't worry now," he said. "We make the picture, we make the passport, no problem. Look here," he said, pointing to a little picture of a white-washed village nailed in the center of a wall stud. Flash stabbed her barely there eyes.

He drugged me. He stole me. He stole me! She tried to say this out loud. Did anyone hear?

"I'm giving you some water," he murmured. "Don't try to talk, your throat, gastric lavage, the pump, is hard on it. Shhh."

Don't you dare shush me, she thought. But she did drink, because her throat burned and her thirst suddenly controlled her.

Another face came close, with dark stubble, lush jowls, a gray tooth front and center in the mouth as it spoke.

"Miss, you are out of the joint, so be happy. Be quiet. Me included, some people have put out necks and nuts for you."

The eyes in this face, remarkable. Darkest she'd ever seen.

"You will be happy and quiet. What this Frank Lundquist has done for you, you will thank him every day you have left on this Earth."

"Jimmy," she heard Frank say.

"She needs to know. Lady, this is a done deal. No smart thinking from you, just be happy and glad, because he has fixed it so you can live free." The face started to fade but still it was her death in his eyes so she looked. "You start thinking too smart, it's over for you, because I don't give shits for you. You get this."

"Okay, Jimmy, okay. She's got it." Frank Lundquist swam into her view; she closed her eyes tightly, only felt his warmth now, head on his toasty bone-and-meat shoulder. The world was going down again. But before it collapsed entirely, she saw the girl, flying. Straight across the center of sight, just behind her shut-tight eyes. She saw and she understood.

21

IF ETHICAL RESPONSIBILITIES CONFLICT WITH LAW OR GOVERNING LEGAL AUTHORITY, TAKE REASONABLE STEPS TO RESOLVE THE CONFLICT

(Standard 1.02)

If you study the history of the Macedonians—as I am doing now, via bug-gnawed books, helped along by my rapidly disintegrating translation dictionary—you'll soon learn that, above all, they are deeply antiauthoritarian. Thousands of years of overlords— Byzantine, Bulgarian, Ottoman Turks, Serbs, Soviets—have given them a boundless appetite for rebellion. They like to form underground armies with long, fierce names—Macedonian Youth Secret Revolutionary Organization—for carrying out acts of guerrilla warfare, sabotage, and just generally as a way to organize around their shared disdain for whatever authorities happen to be in charge.

Given this tendency, it's not at all surprising that the citizens of the Republic of Macedonia scorn the NATO nations— who, not even nine months ago, rained Tomahawk missiles on their cousins in Kosovo—as well as Interpol, a nonstop meddler in the locals' most lucrative import-export ventures. Out in the stony-walled, bleached, and hunkered hamlets piled in the valleys of the farthest, highest hinterlands, they are not particularly impressed by the federal polizi from the urban centers of Skopje and Bitola, either. They fend for themselves, fight their own battles, and follow their own code.

In other words, Jimmy's ancestral village turned out to be the ideal spot to hide a pair of American fugitives. A disorderly huddle of perhaps two dozen homes, it clung to the lower slopes of Mount Ulsec like a burr in the folds of an old woman's skirts. It was populated almost entirely by Jimmy's relatives. Village life revolved around sheep, potash, a thirteenth-century church, and small-arms smuggling. In most of the homes, a photo of Jimmy, wearing aviator shades and gold chains, hung right next to a reproduction of the Mother of God of Sorrows from Saint Sophia at Ohrid.

With this hamlet in my mind as our ultimate destination— but very mistily, vaguely in mind, since how could I possibly have an inkling of such a place?—I leaned my head against the window and watched Greenland and Iceland sliding darkly under my feet. M lay across three seats just on the other side of the aisle. In the front rows of the cabin, low chatter and snores and a lone baby crying, large families and elderly gents from the Bulgarian enclave in the Bronx, headed home for the feast days of December. The tourist season had ended, and Jimmy's friends at Air Bulgar, a cut-rate charter line with a single U.S. node in a lonely hangar at Newark, had seated us in the plane's empty aft. Plenty of space to stretch out, and a peaceful spot to reflect.

MY DEED WAS RASH. PERHAPS UNWISE. I TOOK A STEP AND IT SENT me tripping and catapulting over the curb of reasonable behavior. But I won't say it was irrational. I understood the risks—I'd already thought it through at length, after all, the idea of fleeing with her.

Even at that crucial juncture, as I stirred my emergency stash of Elavil into warm milky tea, adding extra sweetener to disguise any undertastes—I understood that the move might bring deliverance but not love. I saw it that night for the self-ish thing it was. I told myself: there might not be any heartfelt declarations, sticky breathless passion, long years of sweet union and shared, still-charged memories of our reckless escape.

That may not pan out.

But she would be in a better place, and I would be the one who set her free.

Let the fates decide. Just take this unknowable ride with her. Get her safely launched into her future, away from institu-tionalized justice and half-hearted therapeutic interventions. Out of the basement and into the world. Grant her the remainder of her life, and play out the rest of mine, whatever shape it might take.

Redemption may require strange detours. But the end re-sult is what matters.

Also on my mind, an undeniably good turn: as we jetted over the icy zones, Clyde was being delivered by the very repu-table Balkan All Boro radio-car service to a fancy, discreet clinic, within visiting distance of Dad. One day, perhaps, we'll be in touch. I've left enough cash behind to pay Clyde's bills. I've got plenty of cash now, and Jimmy is well versed in Swiss banking.

22

DECEMBER 1999

Can you remember what you dreamed for yourself, once, when you were younger? Life blurs the dream, blears it, the endless wash of days, the constant tumbling of minutes, wearing that vision away, mote by mote, detail by detail. The daily worries, tiny grains that etch and abrade. And of course, a dream is sketched onto the softest of substances anyhow, isn't it? Not engraved in granite or marble, not even sculpted in sand. The dreams of your youth are merely ripples on your brain, subtle wavelets in soft tissue, malleable, pliable. Very impermanent.

For example: At twelve, she had dreamed she'd be the president. She saw, driving through Washington, the shattered neighborhoods and she thought, I want to help the world. I could help the world. If not president, then senator. Or congressperson, like Dad. She ran for the seventh-grade seat on the student council, and won.

But then, Amy. And that November. The second losing campaign, witnessed at a remove, because she and her mom shunned the dais, no waving and smiling at his side. Her father alone up there, exposed, his compromises, his failings, every day more achingly clear. At first too young to understand, really, but somehow, gradually she began to understand. And every moment of understanding that came after, an endless tidal wash of such moments, until that notion that she could help the world, that she should help it, was faint, then fainter, then gone.

By twenty-six, another dream. The dream was Duncan, the life stretched out in her love-drunk visions, when she allowed herself to indulge in those visions. He'd move beyond those druggy nightspots. Together, they would own restaurants. He'd be up front, she'd do the PR and the numbers. Artists and performers would gather around them, they'd fill private parties and become their close friends. Together, Duncan and Miranda, they'd buy a house out somewhere in the hills, their talented guests on the veranda, their children rollicking on the lawn.

Children. The thought made her open her eyes.

The car window cool against her head. Flat fields, low cream-colored houses with brown roof tiles, a power plant at the horizon, its three smokestacks chiseled in the bright sky. Hard cool glass against her head, and the smell of cigarettes. Snatches of static-edged pop beats on the radio. Then a soothing woman's voice, cooing random syllables.

How long had she been asleep? "How long have I been asleep?" she whispered, her tongue sticking to her mouth's insides, gummy, tasting like a licked envelope.

"You're awake," he said.

Cyrillic letters on a truck streaming by. Two men in the front seat, both with close-cropped hair. Sun razoring through the windshield. On the side of the driver's neck, a Mickey Mouse face tattooed. A crude Mickey, a deranged Mickey.

Frank Lundquist put his hand on her shoulder. "We're stopping. Food? Bathroom, maybe?"

His hair needed a shampoo, his beard was growing out, wheat stubble.

Look what he's done, she thought. You need to look at it.

INSIDE: A PASTRY TOPPED WITH CUBED MEAT AND A FRIED EGG. Tomatoes and cucumbers in sour white sauce. She devoured it.

"It's good, right?" Frank had finished his plate, now watched her eat. "It's pretty warm for that sweater," he whispered. "The clothes are in the trunk. You could change."

Whispering, she realized, because of their foreignness. The place was just a box of smoke-darkened glass, a cement floor, crowded with men, truck drivers, judging from the jammed parking lot and the rigs lined up at the pumps. Through a tobacco smog, she could see a television suspended behind the bar. And then a hairy belly blocked her view.

"America." The man loomed over them. His teeth were alarmingly sharp. A tight jersey rose over his fuzzy, round stomach. He hoisted up the belly to show them a Texas-shaped belt buckle. He grinned, the teeth stained.

The man called something out to the next table, five men slouched over fuming cigarettes and shots poured from an old water bottle. They stared at Miranda and laughed. The big-bellied man grabbed the bottle and two of the men's glasses and raised them in their direction. "Rakija. Bulgar." He poured and handed them the drinks. "America," he said, toasting with the bottle, swigging deeply. He nodded at them, watched until they followed his lead. She didn't meet Frank's eye. She drank it down and let it burn.

Mr. Belly grabbed her arm, squeezed, shouted something to his compadres with a laugh. His grip actually hurt quite a bit. Frank tried to shove the man away. The grip on her arm tightened. Chairs scraping, scuffling, and suddenly Mickey Mouse up close, inches from her face. The driver said three sharp words, her arm was free, and Frank's was around her shoulders, steering her outside.

"THE HOUSE HAS A VIEW OF A LAKE," HE SAID. "APPARENTLY THE lake is full of fish."

Still they drove, and with every minute, she was feeling more awake. And Frank Lundquist was speaking to her softly, as if soothing a cranky child. She moved her head to see the wide view out the windshield. More flatlands slipped by—slashes of irrigation ditches, a tractor here or there, a cinder-block silo. They were close to the border, Frank said, taking small roads now, all dirt and gravel.

They fell silent again.

From the front of the car, from the driver's neck, Mickey laughed in her face.

"How many times have you found yourself in the back seat?" he chortled.

How many?

Edward Greene up front at the wheel, bickering with her mom about money, Miranda stretched out across leatherette upholstery in back, pretending to sleep. Pretending to sleep! Mickey chuckled.

Taxi driver up front at the wheel: some why-not guy reeling off his address and breathing boozily into her hair.

Limo driver up front at the wheel: Duncan slipping his hand up her skirt.

Candora County sheriff up front at the wheel: no handles on the doors.

State corrections officer up front at the wheel: the van stinking of fear and vomit.

Frank Lundquist up front at the wheel: someone else's

damp clothes on her body, the streetlights wheeling by in a panic in the rain.

Now this. Whose car was this, even?

Thousands of miles from any place like home.

The Mouse leered at her. So when, girl?

When are you going to get up front, take the wheel?

She looked away from that mocking face. She glimpsed, way in the distance, far across the fields, a ruffle of blue mountains. At the sight of them, a notion arrived.

I'm free. I'm out. I'm gone.

And then the line of the azure mountains opened her mind to another thought.

I'm the new driver.

23

TERMINATE THERAPY WHEN THREATENED
OR OTHERWISE ENDANGERED BY
THE CLIENT/PATIENT
(Standard 10.10.b)

What joy compares to a risk that pays off?

Viscott delineates the many kinds of risks one can take: risks of emotion, risks of growth, risks of change. Despite the fears many of us have about risks, he reminds us that the very act of living entails risks.

In fact, believe me, you are risking everything at this very moment. Just by sitting there, taking a breath, you accept the risk that this breath could be your last.

SOMETIMES I LIE HERE STARING UP AT THE CRACKS IN THE CEILING, cracks that form a river delta in the old, smoke-smudged plaster, and the faces of my former patients flash by me. Quillaba, shoplifter of fine chocolates and expensive wines, because why should an Arby's paycheck stand in her way? Harriett, who couldn't sleep without waking up screaming. A dentist named

Hazen, who couldn't be faithful to his wife, though he yearned to be. Zachary Fehler.

And finally, M. And I turn to her and there she is, lying in her bed, sleeping, maybe dreaming, her newly short hair like a soft copper crown.

We share a room, but we sleep in separate beds. Why? I think I understand.

Jimmy found us a good place. There is indeed a lake, it does indeed teem with fish. The locals don't eat them; they say the potash spoiled the waters. Jimmy's oldest sister once lived in this house—never married, the village teacher, traveled each year to Frankfurt to buy schoolbooks. Her well-made German clothes are still hanging dusty in the closet. She died last year, we heard. The sister's funny little dog, white with brown and black patches, has adopted us.

All day, the men of the village are off at the potash mine up over the hills. At about noon, a local woman named Olla comes to cook. She does a little cleaning, singing strangely heart-wrenching songs taught to her by her Romany mother. I sweep the floors, when she allows it; I like to sweep the floors. M studies a French dictionary she found. She learned in prison, I guess, how to make the most of downtime. I'm still learning, myself. Of course, basketball is big in these parts, so I do play a bit, at the hoop behind the village shop. I'm thinking of taking up target shooting. There are a lot of weapons around here.

One day, I found a list she'd scribbled on the back of an empty sugar sack:

francophone
ivory coast
senegal
congo

algeria
burkina faso
haiti
guadelupe
martinique
st. martin
polynesia—Iles du Vent, Iles Sous-le-Vent

APPARENTLY, SHE'S NOT QUITE SETTLED YET, TO OUR LIFE HERE. SHE
spends long afternoons walking the shores of the lake. I see her
standing there, gazing across at Mount Ulsec. Sometimes she
stops at Olla's hut, which sits at the far end of the shore, and I
just make them out, M and the old woman, sitting on plastic
chairs on the dirt yard. I understand: female companionship. It's
all she has known for these last years.

She's so very much better off now than she was on that
spring morning she first walked into my office. She is free, so
to speak. Safe. Saved. I believe that she is beginning to appreciate this.

Though my professional peers would frown on my method,
this knowledge fills me with a sense of satisfaction, a feeling of
completeness. It's a new sensation for me.

M may not have turned the corner to contentment, not yet.
But she hasn't once talked of leaving here, of leaving me.

And we've had our good moments. One evening a week after we arrived, we walked down to the lake and we watched the
lights of distant airplanes passing over the mountain, drifting
away like stray thoughts.

CANDORA, NEW YORK, IS A BEAUTIFUL PLACE, IF ROUGH AROUND THE
edges. Dairy farms and trailer parks and deep woods. And that

river is just how you'd want a river to be. It looks clean, rushing along its sloped banks, trees dipping their limbs in here and
there, swimmers testing the current.

I sat parked alongside the Oshandaga three days before
M's escape. Staring down at the brown-green water. I'd just
driven past the firehouse. Where her boyfriend and the fire captain had been killed. Where M's life had ended, too, in a way.
Her old life.

People get mixed up into things. People sometimes want
something so much that they do things they never dreamed
they'd do. This I now know. This I understand.

After a while, I pulled back onto the road and headed north
out of town. Turning right at a narrow unpaved road, I drove
several rutted miles through state forest, then past fallen down
wire fencing and bullet-pierced NO TRESPASSING signs. The road
petered out, and I climbed from the car. Opened the trunk,
hauled out a shovel. Following a scant trail, I swatted at ragweed
and thorny shrubs. The old hunting camp sat a quarter mile
down the path. I didn't really have a clear idea of what a hunting camp might be. Turned out, just a tumbledown shack of
plywood and tin, and a rock-ringed campfire. Inside the shack, a
mattress spilling its rusted guts. A single blackened boot. Some
beer bottles strewn around, looking pretty new.

Safe to say that, by this point, looking around at the mattress, the bottles, the boot, the hair was bristling on the back
of my neck. The place was deadly quiet. No birds were calling.
Not even wind in the trees. I stepped out of the hut and hurried
around it to the woodpile, the shovel held up at the ready, my
hand gripping its neck.

As I pulled down that pile and dug into the ground beneath it, I saw sightless worms and enormous maggoty things
that I wasn't happy to see, not at all. But I dug without stopping.
Breathing hard.

"Are you sure it's still there? They didn't dig it up after you were arrested?" I had asked her.

"I tried to tell my lawyer about it. And he stopped me. He said, Don't breathe another word, don't ever breathe another word about it. To anyone. He said that, as far as the jury was concerned, the less I knew, the more innocent I was. And look, he said, no one alive knows that you know. So let's just say you don't know. Eventually you will forget that you know, he said, and at that moment it's the same as if you never did."

"Jesus."

"The guy moonlights as a campaign consultant," she said.

About two feet down, I hit it. Shovel sinking into something softer than the clay-thickened dirt, something that had give. I uncovered more of it. A sturdy bag of red rubberized cloth. CANDORA FIRE DEPT. printed on the side.

An hour later, I was driving carefully, extra carefully since I was shaking all over, veering up the on-ramp to I-90 East. Two point three million in the trunk.

THAT MONEY WAS HANDED OVER BY SMALL-TOWN CITIZENS, GAM-bling for a good time, taking a little risk, believing it would all be flowing toward a good cause. And, after some delay, it did. What better cause is there than the saving of souls?

The albino snail crawling up the window now, its red eyes rotating on their tiny stalks: it has crawled into my world, just millimeters in front of my face, to tell me that the unlikeliest outcomes are absolutely possible.

Yes, choice is power, and I made my choice. I urge everyone who reads this to do the same.

24

MARCH 2000

Frank Lundquist slept soundly, and he didn't wake as she pulled on a shirt and shorts, laced up her shoes, and, with the little dog following, slipped out of the house. The sun already fell hot on her shoulders as she began to descend, the dog skipping ahead of her, over small boulders and under the low evergreens and scrawny clumps of wild tarragon.

Reaching the lake shore, she turned to look up at the little cluster of buildings, the roofs shining. All was inutterably still. Nothing much ever stirred that place. The locals understood about silence.

Olla had seen her approaching along the rocks and had a small cup of her bitter coffee waiting. Miranda sipped it in the dark cottage, contemplating the ancient phone.

She and the dog were both panting a bit by the time they scrambled again up the last bit of the steep path that led back to the house. Under the shade of a gnarled yew tree was an old pump, and she sent water streaming into the trough. The dog lapped it happily. Miranda put her mouth beneath the spout and drank, too, though the water was warm and smelled slightly of sulfur.

ENTERING THE HOUSE, SHE HEARD FRANK LUNDQUIST SPLASHING IN the bathroom. She quickly pulled the two small duffels from under her bed and began to pack some things for herself, and for him: underwear, fresh shirts. As she stuffed the clothes into the bags, other items presented themselves. The curling old photograph, his mother and her sons, that he'd set on the mantel. A drawing she'd made of the little dog. A tiger-striped stone they had found one time when they'd sat together by the lake.

Finally she pushed aside the bed, lifted the loose wallboard, gathered the Canadian passports, fat envelopes of German marks, and Swiss bank documents. She held them in her hands and gazed at them, as if at an arrangement of tarot cards. She forced herself to read the message there.

Then something tucked under his bed caught her eye. A gray composition book, cheap cardboard binding. She didn't recall seeing it before. Flicked it open, the first page was covered with Frank's lopsided handwriting. She read the line at the top: What happened to me is universal. And I can prove it.

Then a grinding sound, a car crossing the gravel in front of the cottage. She tossed the notebook into Frank's bag, and as she did a folded piece of paper, thick and shiny, flew from its pages.

She could hear voices outside now, two or three men. She picked up the paper and stuffed it into her pocket, zipped both bags closed, and shoved them into a corner.

Frank emerged from the bathroom, stooping as always to miss bumping on the low door. Bare chested in jeans, rubbing his ruffled wet hair with a thin towel.

Olla burst into the cottage. "Russkata," she yelped at him and pointed toward the door. He turned to Miranda then, looked at her with a wrenching expression, a mix of rue and reassurance. "Stay inside."

Then he disappeared out the door. Olla frowned at her.

He put up more of a fight than anticipated, and when it was over, Miranda peered out to see two men, one just a T-shirted teenager, the other sturdy and weathered with a leather vest and a plaid shirt and blond buzz cut, standing over Frank. Both of them were haloed in white gravel powder, Frank was rolled in the dust like a floured loaf of bread, and there he lay, eyes closed, arms flung to either side, with dark red blood flowing from his nose and mouth and oozing across his dusty chest.

The older man entered the house as if he owned the place and looked her over carefully. "He may do okay in prison, he is not so much of a pushover." He brushed himself off, white puffs rising from his jeans. He extended one hand to her. "I am Visha."

She could hear Lu saying it, in her low, laughing way. "Visha, he is the best husband you could want."

She walked past Visha, out to where Frank lay, open as if to embrace the air, as if offering his blood to the sky. The teenage boy stood over him, gun tucked jauntily in his waistband—the son had his mother's yellow hair and pretty face.

She bent close to Frank.

"You're going to be okay," she said.

His eyes moved, but didn't open. "You're free," he said. "Because of me." She laid her hand against his bloodied cheek.

BLOOD, IN QUANTITIES, HAS AN ODOR. DENSE, SORT OF OPIATE.

The back office of the Candora municipal firehouse. Point the gun and walk, she told herself, point the gun and walk. The revolver, compact and heavy, wobbled crazily. It seemed to float ahead of her, magically, as she passed the cash boxes stacked up on the metal desk. Bills and coins. That night's proceeds. They didn't seem worth her notice. The gun at the end of her shivering arm luring her on, she rounded the corner of the desk. And there, on the floor, a folding chair toppled by his side, was the dead man. Later she would learn his name. Lewis Patterson. At the trial she would hear it a million times, each mention making her flinch. Lewis Patterson, bachelor, firefighter, catcher of brook trout, local-history buff, skilled mimic of songbirds, pillar of his community. Lewis Patterson sprawled on the floor before her with blood draining from his ear and a surprisingly large and neat hole in one cheek, slivers of teeth and shredded muscle visible through the hole. His eyes open, locked on the ceiling. One hand resting on his still chest, a splatter of blood already caking across one shoulder of his Pittsburgh Steelers sweatshirt.

The gun dropped to her side. She stood over him, staring, for what seemed like hours, at this city name spelled out across his broad dead body.

And then she heard a sound behind her. She turned. From around the corner, from the garage where the red laddered rig stood ready for service, appeared Duncan McCray. Dragged a bulging black trash bag, then snapped it open.

"Why aren't you in the car?" he said, barely glancing at her. Grabbing the piled cash from the desk, thrusting it into the bag.

"I heard shots."

"Look, don't worry about it now." He spoke excitedly as he worked. "He told me where he stashes the cash. Under the woodpile in a hunting camp. Six miles out on the state forest road. Did we bring that flashlight?"

"I don't know."

"That's what you can do, look around here, find a flashlight. I'm going to put this in the car." But he'd piled so much money in the bag that when he lifted it, it began to tear.

"Shit," he whispered.

"If he told you all that, why'd you shoot him?"

"He recognized me," he said, kneeling, gathering up some

fallen bills. "At least I think he did. From the bar. He was plastered, I didn't think he'd remember me." He cradled the torn trash bag from underneath, hugged it to his chest. "I think I saw flashlights hanging in the garage."

And then the little gun drifted into view again. She had almost forgotten about it, its cold weight in her hand.

"Duncan," she said.

He glanced back at her. At the gun. "Christ," he said, nodding his head toward the door, still moving toward it. "We're wasting time here."

"You said it wouldn't be loaded," she said.

"I meant it when I said it." He stopped, clutching the bag to his chest. "Then I changed my mind. To be safe."

"You said it wouldn't be loaded." She took a few steps toward him now.

"He was a witness." His face had gone so pale, it was almost blue. "I did it for you."

Her vision went blurry as the tears came, spilling down. "I can't believe you killed a fireman," she heard herself saying.

"No," he said. He released the bag and started for her. "I love you." Bills all over the floor.

"I can't believe you did that," she said.

Duncan's famous eyes were wide now and close to hers. They had never looked more vivid than when his hands closed around her wrist. "Miranda," he gasped.

The gun jumped when she pulled the trigger. She remembered blood bubbling out of the little hole beneath his chin like wine from the neck of a bottle, before she squeezed her lids tight and he dropped away.

OLLA BROUGHT HER THE TWO DUFFELS, SCOLDING HER IN THE tongue she didn't understand.

"He's bleeding badly, he should see a doctor first," Miranda said to Visha. He and the teenager were loading Frank Lund-quist into the backseat of the rusted black Lada, the blood and dust spackling into a paste on his bare chest. "They report to police at the clinic," said Visha. "It would be bad for you. He will be fine. Get in, we need to go." He tossed the duffels into the back seat.

"Let me dust him off, at least." She climbed in and un-zipped Frank's bag, wrestled out a shirt. She wiped at Frank's wounds with a corner of the fabric. The door slammed behind her, the engine kicked to life.

And so the village slipped away, Olla standing in the road waving, an envelope of Deutschmarks flashing happily in one hand. Visha drove fast while his son fiddled with the radio.

"Lu, she says hello, she is getting out in October, thanks to Frank here." Visha laughed softly, shaking his bristled head. "And the Macedonian, well, he sends apologies to Frank. We re-minded him of certain realities. He said to tell Frank sorry." He chuckled again. "Next time, don't go with balkanskiy, Frank. Go straight to Russians if you have a need. The Macedonians, they are small peanuts. The Russian is czar, the Macedonian, he is serf."

Frank didn't hear this advice. He was out cold, slumped against the door with his head bowed as in prayer.

The radio played them down the rough roads of the moun-tains, empty but for rocks, stunted evergreens, and for the oc-casional clutch of sheep nibbling dry grass. Miranda noticed the gray notebook in his open bag, thought about delving into it, decided against this. She didn't need to know his secrets. She balled up the bloodied shirt she'd used to tend his wounds, tucked it into the duffel, and zipped it closed.

Then she remembered the folded sheet and pulled it from her back pocket, undid the creases, and smoothed it over her leg.

One edge was ragged, the page had been torn from a

magazine—or a book? Her eyes scanned quickly—"Junior Varsity Girls Track." A team photo. Below it, a larger shot of a girl running, paper number pinned to the shirt. The runner's ponytail caught swinging up. Foot hovering just above the white finish line.

Did she win that day? The caption seemed to imply it. Miranda Greene, grade 9, flying toward first place. She remembered nothing from that day. From that year.

Except. The thick-aired passageway outside the locker rooms. The passageway led past the phys ed office. Inside the office, a little black-and-white television set, on a bookcase next to a yellowing spider plant. Sometimes the coaches would catch an Orioles inning, sitting around with soft drinks and snacks from the vending machines. Why was it switched on that Tuesday afternoon? Who knows—the World Series had ended a couple of weeks before, there certainly wasn't any football to be seen. But the TV was playing. As she walked past the office door, all suited up and ready to pick up her race number, Showalter, the football coach who taught her trig class, barked her name. "Greene! Get in here!"

What now? thought Miranda. More about her missing homework?

"Your old man's on TV!" he said, pointing to the little screen.

And yes. There was her father. It was election day 1982. He'd been predicted to lose.

". . . Greene, who is hoping to make a comeback, lost this same Pennsylvania seat four years ago after serving a single term. Watching early election returns with supporters, Greene paid special tribute to cable-television magnate Neil Potocki, whom he called his close friend and invaluable . . ."

And there he was, wrapping his arms around the man. A great big bear hug. An exchange of wide hearty smiles and shoulder thumps. A bear hug for the man with the blue car.

She stared at the yearbook photo. Something tumbling down inside, as if the car seat beneath might suddenly shift, break, give way. Like thin-crusted deep snow. And now she recalled more. The taste of tears in her mouth as she ran. The shouts of the onlookers. The waning sun, the chill clear November air, the world blurring before her hot eyes.

And afterward, alone in the locker room. Changing in the cold. Crying and remembering and ripping that sticker from her locker door. Greene for Congress. She could hear her father calling Amy's name, shrugging off Potocki's consoling hand on his arm as the officers stood in the grand entry hall under its blazing chandelier. Turning on the man, grabbing him by the throat. Potocki swearing she'd stolen the keys. "She didn't," cried Miranda. "Don't you ever show your lying face to me again," said her father to the man.

One year later, bear hugs on the television.

She quit the track team the next day. She started fucking a random varsity football player the next night. She couldn't think of any reason why not. Why not?

And now she looked at the photo in her hands one more time. She looked past the running girl. People in the background arrayed in a row alongside the track.

Tall enough to stand out in the row. His face: thin, beneath the forelock of blond. The face of a boy, but unmistakably him. And his eyes, bright, wide, fixed on the girl flying by. His expression—surprised? enthralled? hopeful, perhaps? His arms are half raised, as if he were readying to throw them up in the event of a win.

His mouth half open, frozen forever in its cry.

"HALLO," CALLED VISHA, STARTLING HER. "THIS IS THE SPOT." HE swerved the car into the lot of a forlorn-looking gas station and stopped next to a dented white Volkswagen. He handed her a car key. "The airport is ten kilometers south, the border is thirty to the east."

Frank seemed to be asleep. His face looked so young. Unlined. Like a boy's.

She remembered how bottomlessly alone she'd felt that race day, no parents there. No sister.

But she had new information now. She hadn't been alone.

She checked her bag one more time, passport, Swiss documents for the money, the funding from Candora. All there. She tucked the papers back into her duffel, along with the yearbook page. Zipped it tight.

She rubbed her fingers over his, trying to summon him to wake.

She thought she could hear his voice. Could she hear it, a boy's voice sailing above the others, urging her on? Could she hear him shouting her name?

And staring at his battered profile, could she see him? Yes. She glimpsed him there on the sidelines as she crossed the finish line, could see him clear and sharp. A tall, thin blond boy, surprised, enthralled, hopeful.

She rubbed his fingers harder, thought she felt him stir. She bent to his ear.

"I remember you."

In a minute she was seated behind the wheel of the white car, watching the black Lada recede in the rearview. Watching it disappear far down the road behind. She flung the car into forward gear.

Now drive.

Postscript

NOVEMBER 9, 2016

Maybe you reject the idea. The notion that what happened to me is universal. You think it could never happen to you.

Have you ever experienced impossible love? Have you ever wrestled with the demons and the devils? Have you skirted the fringes, flirted with poor choices, aimed for goodness, aspired to greatness?

If you have, then you've veered as close to my fate as to any other.

I'm not sure what prompted me on this particular day to pull the thick manila envelope down from its shelf. It has gone a bit stale, a bit musty with time, but still bears the typewritten label with my name and my number. 0281-J-00, because I was the 281st inmate to enter NYS DOCS Facility J, a.k.a. Auburn Correctional Facility, in the year 2000. The top left of the envelope is printed with my lawyer's address: Burwick & Spivak LLP, 42 Catharine Street, Poughkeepsie, NY 12601.

The envelope arrived at mail call back in December 2009, when they were closing down those law offices after old Arthur

Burwick retired. Sent by a legal assistant, containing a note-book that had been misfiled with some other case. A flimsy gray-cardboard composition book, filled with my scrawl. Arthur had discovered it in a bag of my few belongings—a barely used fly-fishing jacket, a yellowed old snapshot, an unusual striped pebble—and tried to enter my scribblings as evidence. The judge rejected it. When the notebook arrived here, I had no inclination to open it. I put it back in the envelope, stuck the envelope on the shelf with my books and papers, and tried to forget it was there.

And I did, for almost seven years. So what was it today? The turning of the season, the late-autumn sunshine? The flick-ering of that light in the last auburn leaves, refusing to let go of the trees, beyond the fence near the handball courts? The noise of another election season, so loud, so tumultuous this year that it has penetrated even these fortress walls?

IT DIDN'T MAKE FOR PLEASANT READING. GOES WITHOUT SAYING. Painful, even after the passage of so much time.

But still, maybe, I can claim some small measure of re-demption. Some positive achievement.

It didn't end well for me, that's safe to say. But I try to do good where I can. I run a peer counseling group in the lounge, every other Wednesday at 11 A.M., before TV hours begin, when the room is quiet. And though most of the guys just show up for the cookies and tea, I occasionally feel as if I might be having some impact. Bumping a life, here or there, onto a slightly better track. Admin has signaled its approval of the endeavor, finally granting me extra yard time and regular visits—Clyde brings his daughters, now and then—after all those years under tight restraint.

I served very hard time, when I first arrived, convicted, as I was, of recruiting CO Jerrold Liverwell to smuggle crack cocaine and Elavil into Milford Basin's C Unit, and of coercing the case's informant, Ludmilla Chermayev, to distribute those substances, thereby being party to the deaths by overdose of inmates April Toni Nicholson and Weavy Moore. And of course, for aiding the escape of my alleged coconspirator, Miranda Greene.

Yes, I can come out and say her name now. She is dead and gone, after all.

According to the official record, that is.

Per my testimony—and my testimony was upheld by New York state, federal, and Interpol courts—Miranda Greene died that day back in March 2000. The men—still at large—who dropped me by the curb in front of that flea-bitten backwater outpost of the Macedonian police, unconscious, encrusted with my own blood—they stole her, they killed her. I told the court: I saw what they did. I told the court: they burned her body to ashes and threw the ashes in the lake.

As far as they know, a few of her molecules drift there still, in the potash-poisoned waters under the slopes of Mount Ulsec.

As far as they know.

And here's what I know: she remembers me.

Acknowledgments

This story has a complicated story of its own. It could have so easily never escaped from my virtual desk drawer. That it did has been an incredibly happy twist of fate, and it would have been impossible without the kindness and bolstering faith of some very key people and organizations.

I offer my profound gratitude to: Virginia Paget, Bob Gangi, Susan Rosenberg, Robin Aronson, and Tara McNamara, for aiding my explorations of the lives of incarcerated women and men. The MacDowell Colony and the Corporation of Yaddo, for solitude and fellowship. The Immergut and Marks families, Deborah Lewis Legge, Kahane Corn Cooperman, and Doug Wright, for their steadfast love. Ann Lewis and Edie Meidav, for their illuminating feedback and spiritual uplift. James Hynes, Barrie Gillies, Miliann Kang, Anthony Schneider, Scott Moyers, James Yu, and John Townsend, for unexpected, generous, and utterly essential doses of encouragement as I walked a long path.

I also owe a towering debt of gratitude to my agent, Soumeya Bendimerad Roberts, for spotting me in her crowded inbox, for her revision genius, for her whip-smart advocacy. I consider it a great stroke of luck and a privilege to work with Megan Lynch, an editor of deep integrity and insight, plus Emma Dries, Laurie McGee, and the entire team at Ecco/HarperCollins.

And at last, for everything that underlies every word of this story and every moment of each day, I thank John, my rock and my redeemer, and Joe, my joy.